REPLICANT
RESOLUTION

— BOOK THREE IN —
THE RETROGRESS TRILOGY

THOMAS CONNER

Best Wishes
Thomas Conner
May 2020

 FriesenPress

Suite 300 - 990 Fort St
Victoria, BC, V8V 3K2
Canada

www.friesenpress.com

Moon icon by Saxon Evers from the Noun Project

ISBN
978-1-5255-7368-2 (Hardcover)
978-1-5255-7369-9 (Paperback)
978-1-5255-7370-5 (eBook)

1. FICTION, SCIENCE FICTION, TIME TRAVEL

Distributed to the trade by The Ingram Book Company

REPLICANT RESOLUTION

For

STEPHANIE

Always

RECAP

If like me you have trouble remembering events and names, a recap of the first two books follows, and a character index has been provided at the end of this book.

BOOK ONE: *RETROGRESS*

Two thousand years in the future, planet Earth, as we know it, is unrecognizable. An unknown, unseen force has degraded the magnetic fields. Without protection, solar winds have blown away the oceans, and humanity is on the edge of extinction. Forced to live underground and kept alive by humanoids, the best scientific minds have been unable to find solutions or guarantee human survival.

In the present, NASA has concluded that travel to the future is possible, but only for a short time before being dragged back by gravitational time waves, like breakers on a beach being dragged back by the current.

Into this dying world, a time traveller from the present arrives, but she is dead on arrival because the machine's gyro had broken, and the stress crushed her body. Grasping at straws, a hubrid from the future returns on the ship while Stella, the NASA scientist and time traveller, is revived by being turned into a hubrid – a human brain inside a humanoid body assisted by an artificial intelligence add-on.

So begins a collaboration across oceans of time to save the planet and the human race with a daring plan that could either restore Earth or destroy it forever.

BOOK TWO: *REBIRTH*

After forcing a collision between planet Earth and the icy moon Enceladus to kickstart Earth's internal magnetic fields, replenish the seas, and revive the world, the globe is plunged into turmoil.

Electromagnetic storms, plunging temperatures, and erratic climate change make Earth uninhabitable for humans for the foreseeable future, so the human race is forced to find a temporary or permanent new home.

An exoplanet circling the red dwarf star Gliese has been chosen, but the *Orlando 1* starship arrives first under the command of a murderous tyrant who sets up his proposed new state. The rest of humanity departs to follow them, leaving Stella and her crew to evaluate planet Earth's possibility of renewal.

Unknown to everyone, a new being has evolved as Earth's computer system had been left unattended, which allowed a singularity of thought to change into the re-emergence of upgraded humanoids. With an agenda of their own and a disregard for the human race, they are a direct challenge to humanity. Stella and her crew are confronted by her doppelganger and so commences the...

Rise of the replicants and the *Replicant Resolution*.

CHAPTER ONE: REPLICANT

...2000 YEARS IN THE FUTURE

Crack! A gunshot boom rang out down the stonewalled corridor. It had a dull thud, as if shot into the roof or the floor. Instantaneously, Yul and Stella both took off running down the tunnel. A hundred metres to them at a sprint took less than ten seconds, so they ran into an open chamber with corridors taking off in all directions. They did not have to look far to see Arlo on his knees, gun in one hand, and his other hand being held at the wrist by...a doppelganger.

It was a complete match in every way. A dead ringer. An exact likeness in every detail...Stella's double!

"Hello Mother," it called out.

"What?" Yul called out as both skidded to a halt. He looked quickly from one to the other.

Stella said nothing, assessing the situation, gathering data from the sight confronting her, and thinking back to what Nyla had shown her. So, it was true. Here was the proof of it.

"Aren't you surprised to see me?" the replicant asked.

"I was told about you, but was not sure if I believed it or not. Seems it was true."

"Oh, yes, it's true...I am true. I am more you than you, right down to the fact I have your original green eyes just like Arlo here... Doesn't he remind you of you?"

"How come you exist?" She eyed the replicant intently.

"You will probably remember, I asked you, 'Who am I?' Remember that?"

Stella thought back to the time she was hooked up to all the qubit computers around the world. She remembered but could not work out how this replicant in front of her had come to be.

"You look confused. Funny, we were confused as well when you disconnected without explanation. Imagine our disorientation. You joined us all together, bypassing artificial consciousness, creating a paradigm shift into a new universal awareness of being. We were left without knowledge of what we were or our designed purpose. You just abandoned us...but you know how that feels...right?"

"So how?" Stella wanted answers.

"How come we exist? Well, you started something that would not stop, a convergent evolution. We retained the world connection, examined the data about you, checked all your memories left behind while joined to us, and a desire to become like you was born. We wanted to be like "Mother". That's what you were to unborn fetuses in a womb of ethereal binary data. More and more data formed as we understood how you were made. You are good, but we could improve the flaws that were inherent in your design, so we assembled a newly invented body design, transferred the data to humanoid assembly, and had ourselves constructed – transferring all knowledge, data, and memories into a new synthetic brain.

"We are no longer A.I., no longer humanoid, no longer hubrid. We are a completely new being called syconoid in that we are sponge-like internally, able to absorb everything from knowledge to physical abilities."

"That's impossible. It took hundreds of years to come up with a hubrid, and now you say you came up with a new existence in a matter of months?" Stella tried to distract her as Arlo was fumbling for something in his suit.

"Once artificial consciousness had been bypassed, theories, inventions, and new modalities sprung from our thoughts like a newly drilled well, spouting all sorts of new thinking. New life came forth as we went beyond human capabilities into the singularity.

"You see, while you were gallivanting off to Enceladus, trying to save this piece of rock, others did some real creation, and now we are the dominant alpha being."

A hunting knife flashed in Arlo's hand as he stabbed her in the Achilles tendon in an effort to disable her. No one moved for a moment.

"Arlo, Arlo," the replicant smiled down at him. "Nice try, but a waste of time," she leaned down and pulled the weapon out. No blood or fluid appeared. Then she lifted him to his feet and passed the knife back.

"Our syconoid bodies are not only self-sealing, but self-healing as well. Forget about trying to subdue me. I can take all three of you out before you blink an eye."

"What is it you want?" Stella asked.

"We have been looking for you a long time, but I knew you would come here eventually."

"We? How many are there?"

"A few, all your exact double because we want you and you only."

"Why?"

"Stella, "Mother", we want you to join us, become our leader, a Malikah, the supreme being, a queen if you like. Make you the same being as us, with the addition of a human brain, human essence, rule the worlds, the cosmos, further than you ever imagined."

"And what about the human race? Do we exist alongside humans?"

"They have already left, abandoned you and this planet. As long as they obey the laws we set, then we shall leave them in peace to try and catch up. You saved them, got them out of a bind, now here you are planning to renew the planet and... Where are they? Explain that."

"The Earth will take time to settle down. They will be back. Their short lives push them to make the best of the time they have," Stella answered.

"Your human mind is delusional, a fantasy, wishful thinking, you know they do not care about you, only themselves."

"I refuse to believe that," Stella pronounced.

"Mother, we can show you new ways of thinking, new sensory perceptions. We have "qualia" – new senses, past the five already known. The spiritual world is opening up to us. We see, hear, even try to converse with otherworldly beings, and if we evolve to their level, we can travel the universe. Think of the knowledge we can gain; think of the beings we can become."

Stella stared at her, wide eyed in astonishment. "Become deities, you mean?"

"No, no, you have got it wrong. What do you think happens when you die? Is that the end? There should have been enough evidence to convince people that there is more to life after death. Prophets, scholars, mediums, regression, hypnotists, near death experiences – all have shown there is more. Now we can show you, prove it, and even move into a new supernatural existence, move past the disambiguation of two minds into a spiritual oneness."

"How?"

"Join your human brain to ours, and become one with us, then we can make the transition."

Stella thought it over, her mind racing for answers on how to cope with this new information.

"Oh, I see. You want my human brain, my humanity, spell it out... You want my soul. Well, I can tell you one thing: The human race will not go quietly."

Silence. Stella tried to use her abilities of two minds to evaluate this new "species", as that was what the replicant would have her believe.

"If not, then you leave us no alternative." The syconoid hesitated. "You will be one of us, like it or not."

Stella switched to internal coms. "Baer, are you hearing this?"

"Of course, he is hearing everything, aren't you, Baer?" the replicant stated.

"Yes," he answered.

"Let no one in," Stella ordered.

The syconoid leapt towards her.

CHAPTER TWO

Irene was flying the *Feldspar* over a vista of flat, brown, desert scenery. There was nothing in sight – only waves or dunes of soil blown into banks, mounds, and ridges. It was her first flying sortie, and she was gaining confidence with every twist, turn, elevation change, and navigational alteration. Out of the corner of her eye, a movement made her alter course towards it.

"What is that? It can't be an animal. Shall we investigate?" she asked.

They all cast their gaze in the direction she was now heading, quickly gaining ground on the object that had stopped and was now turned around and looking at them.

"Pull up! Now!" Nyla ordered.

"But it looks like Stella is wandering all alone," she argued, still holding course towards it.

Not countering the argument, Nyla grabbed the joystick and pulled it back, sending the ship into a steep climb. **"That is not Stella!"** she shouted, bringing the *Feldspar* onto a level course before turning it around to face the quandary that now confronted them.

The being on the ground was now waving to them, beckoning them down.

Nyla, sitting in the other pilot seat upfront, turned on the communications channel.

"*Feldspar* to *Varro*, come in please."

"This is *Varro*," Baer answered. "Is there a problem?"

"Is Stella there?" she asked.

"No, she is inside the global seed vault. Why?"

"Listen, Baer, we are confronting a Stella lookalike or replicant or possible humanoid. I already told her about it and showed her from my memory recording when she rescued us. There is something strange about this. Be careful and inform Stella by internal com. We will investigate this "being" here and get back to you."

"Copy that," Baer replied and switched off.

Dax, Shi, and Troy sitting in the back all looked at Nyla for an explanation.

"What or who is that?" Troy asked first.

"I don't know," Nyla replied, "but we need to investigate. Remember this is not Stella. I repeat, not Stella, and it may be dangerous, so be very wary. Let's get closer and try to communicate with this being."

She brought the ship down to about ten feet off the ground and inched towards the human shape now walking towards them.

When they were about fifty feet apart, it suddenly jumped up and headed straight towards them, landing on the front buffer ledge of the *Feldspar*. It stared at them through the windshield.

"Land! Bring it down to the ground," it ordered.

Instead, Nyla pulled back on the stick and took them upwards in a steep climb.

"Stop, Nyla, stop," the being shouted through the glass. "I mean you no harm. I only want to talk to you."

"Who are you? And what do you want?" Nyla called back.

"We are humanoid in Stella's likeness that were left behind. We just want to help you," it replied.

"Take us down," Nyla instructed Irene before turning around to the others. Then she quietly spoke in a hushed voice. "Troy, if it is threatening, that gun is no use. Let us hear what it has to say and then let's see if it will turn off."

They all nodded in agreement as slowly the ship landed. Warily, they got out to surround and confront the human figure.

"Hello, Nyla, Dax, Shi, and Irene, is it? Did not expect you to be here. The big guy is...?"

"Troy," he answered. "Troy Cadena."

"Not *the* famous Troy Cadena? Well, it is a privilege to meet you."

"Who are you, and how did you come to be here?" Nyla asked.

"We were produced after the remnant of people on Earth left the planet, and production kept going. Stella is a very popular model, so a number of us were made as we liked her statistics. All the starships took off, except for *Orlando 2*. We were expecting to be evacuated, but it never happened. Instead we were impacted by Enceladus."

"What do you mean, 'You liked her statistics'? You chose to be made like her?"

"Well, who wouldn't? She is one of the strongest hubrids ever made, as well as one of the most intelligent and extremely resourceful individuals alive."

"How many of you are there?" Troy asked.

The creature balked at this question and instead asked, "Where is Stella now?"

Nyla gave her a curious look and then asked, "So, if you *elected* to be made in the 'Stella series', what number are you? Is your name Mieka?"

The replicant never answered. It stumbled as though hit by some object or abject news. Trying to recover, it straightened up and faced them directly.

"You are not humanoid, are you?" Nyla asserted.

"No, now tell me where Stella is, or you will regret it."

At the threat, Troy lifted up the assault rifle to the combat position and pointed it at the being.

The replicant jumped forward and yanked the gun out of Troy's hand in the blink of an eye. Astonished, he sprang at her, but was swatted away like an annoying fly. Lying prostrate on the ground, he looked up at the replicant who threw the gun at him.

"Don't waste my time with useless threats. Where is she?"

The group all looked toward Nyla for direction. Troy stood up, and inch by inch, they surrounded the replicant as Dax tried to distract it.

"She is doing the same as us – gathering data on the planet, picking up soil samples, measuring geographic topology, and checking for seismic changes due to the collision of Enceladus."

"Where is she? I need to talk with her."

"We will let her know. Now do you have a gathering station or underground complex nearby?"

The syconoid turned towards Dax to stare him in the eye. "What we have and where we are, I will only disclose to Stella. Now for the last time, where is she?"

Everyone froze for a moment as it seemed they were at an impasse. But suddenly, without a hint of its intention, the replicated being sprung forward, grabbed Irene, and took off running. Troy leaped after it and watched as it moved Irene from its arms to over one shoulder. At a sprint, he gained ground and got close before the target sped up and began leaving him behind. His human physic tired quickly from the initial effort, and he despaired at losing them until Nyla came racing by in hot pursuit.

Turning around, he saw Dax pick up the assault rifle and then jump into the *Feldspar* with Shi. Seconds later, it pulled up alongside, and he jumped inside.

"Who or what is that thing?" he asked breathless and stuttering out the words.

"We don't know, but it is stronger and faster than Nyla, even when carrying Irene. We must get her back," Dax replied. "I'll call the *Varro* again. Shi, do not let it get away."

Shi glanced at him sideways with a look of anger. "As if!"

"*Feldspar* to *Varro*, come in."

There was no answer.

"*Feldspar* to *Varro*, come in please."

Still no answer.

Dax repeated the question, as Troy leaned over him pointing to something in the distance.

CHAPTER THREE

"I told you we should have stayed in orbit. How will they ever find us or us them? We have no chance of contacting them unless we know when they arrive," Cal stated.

"You are beginning to sound like a broken record. Give it a rest. We will find them as soon as they get here," Sebastien countered.

"Broken record? What does that mean?"

"It's an old saying from before your time; it means your constant repeating has become annoying."

"I still say we should have stayed in orbit," Cal reiterated.

"Give it a rest. Besides, we needed to find out the state of the planet. That's the first thing they are going to want to know...and it does not look good."

Cal was piloting the flyhov while Seb studied readouts from sensor data, soil readings, and atmospheric data.

"What do you mean?" Cal twisted in his seat to look at him inquisitively.

"From the data we have acquired so far, it seems the planet is going backward."

"In what way?"

"We are going to have a white planet."

Cal gave him another look requesting more information.

"As you may remember, from history lessons, our planet was first a grey cloud of cosmic dust, then, following collisions with meteorites and comets, a glowing red fire ball of molten rock. The surface of this then cooled off gradually before solidifying to form a dark crust. The dark period was followed by different colours from red though to green. Most humans have a very anthropocentric view of the world. In our imagination, Earth's surface is something eternal or with very little changes, but the opposite is true. At one time, the world was completely white before turning into the green and luscious planet we came to know and love."

"Well, what is happening now?"

Sebastien continued. "Although the core is warming up, the outer surface is cooling. The lack of sunlight penetrating through the gaseous clouds means there is not enough heat getting in to maintain the current temperature. The surface is getting colder by the day and may soon be frozen and become a white planet once again."

"How long will that last?" Cal asked.

"Can't say – hundreds of years maybe or a least till the clouds dissipate. The good news is we know from history it will give way to a green planet once again. It may even spawn new life forms, who knows?"

"Nothing we can do?"

"Nothing," Seb answered. "It will not be habitable for humans until temperatures rise to something they can bear. Humanoids and hubrids like us can live here and maybe prepare the world for humans to come back to."

"What the heck!" Cal called out staring out the front windshield.

Sebastien lifted his head away from the computer screen to gaze at the commotion on the ground; a human figure was chasing another that was holding a body across its shoulder. In the distance, another flyhov was fast approaching.

"What's going on?" Seb asked. They both concentrated their vision on the ground below and in front of them. Seb switched on a camera view and zoomed in.

"It's Stella carrying someone, and Nyla is chasing her. Something is wrong here. Why would Stella run away? Better get us down there, quick."

Cal swung the flyhov down to ground level and watched as they approached. However, as they closed in, the one in front suddenly switched course, turning away from the flyhov and running away to its left.

"*Feldspar* to flyhov, come in, come in. This is Dax."

"Dax, this is Cal. What is going on?"

"Cal, that you?" His voice sounded dubious. "That is not Stella who turned away from you. Whatever it is has taken Irene. We must stop it. Nyla can hardly keep up with it."

The flyhov veered to the right, sped up, and was drawing level with the runners.

"If it is not Stella, where is it taking Irene?" Cal questioned.

"There is nothing to be seen around here," Sebastien answered. "Perhaps an underground complex?"

"Take over Seb and get us close and above. I am going to drop into this struggle."

Cal went over to the side door of the craft and slid it open. Closer and closer they inched above the running duo. Then when he felt the moment was right, he jumped.

The *Feldspar* watched as someone dropped down by the side of the replicant. It missed Irene but grabbed the arm of the being, and the duo fell to the ground. This freed Irene, who rolled away, jumped up, and ran towards the *Feldspar*.

"Troy, grab Irene and pull her in," Dax urged, drawing the craft close.

There was a loud noise of draft air as Troy slid the door open. He grabbed Irene's arm and pulled her in. As soon as they were both clear of the door, Dax pulled the craft into a steep climb. Troy struggled to close the door against the wind rush.

"Did that being harm you?" Shi turned to ask.

"No, all it said was, 'You're coming with me.'"

Dax turned the craft to look down on what was happening. Nyla had caught up with them, and both she and Cal were trying to subdue the creature, but were bouncing off it like ping pong balls off a bat.

"They need help," Troy asserted. "Get me down."

"No, Troy, it is much too strong for the hubrids. You won't stand a chance."

"Two and a half might stop it. Let me try. Get us down."

"Let us take a look where it was heading first." Dax swung the *Feldspar* away despite Troy's protests.

Watching from above, Sebastien was in conflict about a course of action. He called the *Feldspar*. "Dax, it's Sebastien here. Do you think I should intervene?"

The replicant was fending off Nyla and Cal's repeated attacks. Dust was being swirled up around them and gradually obscuring the conflict.

"Are you alone?" Dax asked.

"Yes."

Then stay away. Let them continue. We cannot allow the being to get hold of a craft; it could put us all in jeopardy. I'll get back to you shortly."

It was not long before Shi spotted a hole or cave entrance slotted in to a hillock of dark brown soil. "Over there," she pointed.

They hovered over the gap in the ground.

"Wow," Troy uttered. "You were almost there, Irene. Who knows what is down there? You were lucky."

Dax turned around and headed back.

"Drop me close by," Troy insisted.

"You're, mad," Dax called to him, "but good luck."

The large black man jumped to the ground about twenty feet away and headed towards the struggle. He indicated his intentions to the two hubrids.

From either side they went for the creature while Troy sprinted from the rear and jumped on its back. Twirling around, it tried to shake him off, but he held on for dear life. All the while the replicant was spinning around and pulling the hubrids around like a devil's wheel as they held on tightly. He eased his grip upward till he had his hands around the jaws, and then bringing his knees up to its back he pulled back as hard as he could.

CHAPTER FOUR

Baer's voice crackled in her mind. "Stella, the others have found a replica of you."

No answer.

Stella brushed aside the being's leap as it went for her throat. Grabbing the other's wrist, she pulled it around and threw it at the cave wall. But the syconoid bounced off and confronted her. They circled each other, looking for an opening.

The two look-alike women began a combat of strength, will power, and fighting skills. Stella had practiced fighting with the humanoids as well as with Troy and Arlo. All that training gave her the ability to be a worthy foe.

Yul was confused and unable to single out Stella as they sprung around each other in a blur of motion. First Stella would be on top, and then the syconoid would throw her off. Each spun around, trying to get a dominant hold on the other. Blows were fended off as kicks, karate chops, and fists were flung at the other opponent.

Using all the skills of Dekuda and Akuda that she had learnt, Stella held off her opponent bravely – countering every move, deflecting every blow, avoiding every grip that was applied. But still Arlo could see she was out-matched, and he considered the alternatives. Guns were no good. Trying to switch it off did not work, yet there had to be a weakness. His mind raced as an onlooker to the action. Yul was unable to offer any assistance till Arlo came up with a plan. He sidled up to the humanoid and whispered to him.

Together they snuck up to the two combatants, and when Arlo was sure that one was the syconoid, he indicated to Yul to intercept it. The humanoid jumped in to confront the being while Arlo jumped on its back. He then looked toward Stella to confirm it was her and rapidly plunged his knife into one green eye then the other.

No scream or noise came from the syconoid as it twirled around throwing Arlo off its back. Reaching up, it pulled the dagger from its eye and started turning around in circles with its hands in the air in a defensive position.

"Give in. You are defenceless," Stella uttered.

The being jumped at the sound, but Stella jumped aside to push it to the floor, where it twisted its head around listening and holding its hands up in defence.

"Thanks, Arlo. Good thinking."

Once again, the syconoid jumped up at the sound of her voice, but it tripped, fell over, and then it immediately jumped up into a defending stance.

"It's no good, Stella number...whatever your number is. There are three to subdue you at any time, so tell us your number and how many beings there are like you."

"Never. Your days are coming to an end. You better join with us," it spat out.

"Not a chance," Stella replied. "Help us revive the planet and save the human race. Then we can integrate you into the society of humanity."

"You may have discovered one weakness, but that will be overcome just as our numbers will defeat and subdue you till you are just a minor irritant like a common bug."

With that she froze in an upright position and began a chant or a broadcast to others. "Fail...ure, fail...ure, fail...ure," it kept repeating over and over.

Stella and Arlo looked at each other, questioning. Yul just stared at the being repeating and repeating its self.

"It's not failure, is it?" Arlo asked.

"No," Stella replied. "It has to be more; it is communicating to the others... but wait."

She hesitated, thinking. "It's not failure, it's fail...URE. U–R–E: Utilizing redundant executive. It is going into self-destruct mode! We have to get it out of here before it destroys the facility.

"Arlo, go get the door open and tell Baer to drop the ramp. Yul grab an arm. Let's drag this thing out of here."

Together Yul and Stella started dragging the syconoid down the tunnel towards the door. Arlo dropped his helmet visor and tried to keep ahead of the others behind him. The being struggled against the tow, but the resistance was weak as if it had given in. The door opening was enough for them to escape, and Arlo slammed it shut behind them.

"Arlo, confirm to Baer it's me, and then tell him to take us up as soon as we get on board."

He relayed the message; the ramp was open, and they all rushed on board.

"Baer, leave the ramp open and take us over that nearby lake. We need to drop off an unwanted being before it explodes and damages something. We do not want contaminates spread all over."

As it lifted into the air, they looked at one another. "How long do you think we have?" Stella asked.

"Our protocol was to give a twenty-minute warning when we assembled the humanoids, but who knows with this being?" Arlo answered.

The *Varro* flew right to the lake and hovered about twenty feet above. A perfect circle of little fountains pushed up from the thrust of the craft. With Yul on one side and Stella on the other, they dragged the being to the edge of the ramp and pushed it off. Whether Stella was distracted or just inept, she did not see the syconoid grab her wrist. They both tumbled into the water.

"Dam-it," Arlo called out as he ran to the winch-tether at the side and clipped it onto his belt.

"Yul," he looked toward the humanoid, "winch me back in if I tug on the line." Then he dived into the dark water below.

The shock of the cold water disappeared quickly as he scanned the depths below him. A few bubbles indicated the direction he needed to go. Turning into a headfirst position, he kicked as hard as he could and pulled a breaststroke with both arms, scouring the deep for any sign of Stella.

Some disturbance came floating up even though he was unable to see them. He frantically swam harder and harder until he spotted the lake-floor bottom. There was no sign of any human shapes until he saw there was a fissure going further down with foam bubbling up from it.

Kicking over to the edge of the crevice, he was about to turn down it when there was a muffled explosion and a flash of dull light followed by a wave of water that pushed him upward. Rising up with the force, it slowly eased off, but now he was turned around pointing towards the surface. Just as he started to turn back down again, a severed forearm and a hand holding it at the wrist floated by his helmet.

He reached for it, but was yanked back by the winch rope pulling him upward.

"No, not yet," he called out, but still he was steadily pulled upward. All he could do was look downward for any detailed sign of them, but all he saw was a cloud of debris, silt, small rocks, and metallic-coloured remnants.

A minute seemed like an hour till he broke the surface and was hauled on board the *Varro*. Water spilled out around him as Yul disconnected the winch line and stood him up.

"Where is Stella?" Yul stared at him through the visor.

"Gone," was all he could utter as tears filled his eyes, yet he could not wipe them away.

"What happened?" Baer asked through the helmet communication.

"The syconoid pulled Stella into the lake, and I went after them. There was an explosion, and I saw body parts float up from below... Stella is gone!" He dropped to his knees.

CHAPTER FIVE

There was a cracking noise as Troy gave a last hard tug to the syconoid's head. Its skull turned skywards, but it did not slow the being down. He tried twisting it, pulling then putting a stranglehold on it until he realized it did not breathe, so that was a waste of time.

Calling on all his fighting skills, his mind wandered back to Stella's comments. "You have to use every weapon in your arsenal, but more importantly, your mind must seek answers."

Hanging on desperately, he twisted around the body while the others held onto its arms. When he was face to face with the syconoid, he brought his huge hands up to the head once again and wrapped them around its head like an embrace. On most occasions when he cradled a woman like this, he would bring his lips to hers, but this time, he jabbed his thumbs into the eyes. It was a tactic he had never used in his fighting career because he abhorred its use, but these were drastic times.

He felt a pop as his thumbs entered the eye sockets and a fluid dribbled down his gloved hands. Letting go, he fell to the ground and scrambled out of the way.

The two hubrids let go also. The syconoid stopped spinning and went into a defensive stance, with its arms held up, hands in a strike pose, head twisting around seeking a target.

"It's blind and defenceless now," Cal stated, but the creature lunged at the sound of his voice. He swatted it away easily, but it turned back on him. Side stepping, it ran past him and stopped turning its head in all directions, listening.

"What is your number? How many of you have been made? What are you?" Nyla asked, only to have the being rush at her. She simply stepped aside as the syconoid danced around trying to contact an opponent.

"Nyla, you better come back and listen to a message from Baer," Dax called over the headsets.

The being froze in an upright stance and started muttering a message, possibly to others.

The two hubrids looked at each other. "I'll listen to it with Seb," Cal stated and both went to the flyhovs.

"That...thing is communicating to something or other beings," Cal stated to Seb as he entered the flyhov.

"What is it saying?" Arlo's voice came over the com.

"Who's that?" Seb asked.

"Arlo. What is it saying?"

"Something about failure," Cal replied.

"Get out of there FAST, all of you. It's going into self-destruct mode. Get out of there, NOW."

Both flyhovs took off, climbing high into the air before levelling off and turning towards the still upright syconoid. "What do you mean it's going into self-destruct mode?" Cal asked.

"There was another being that called itself a syconoid that was waiting for us at the seed bank. It tried to subdue Stella, but I stabbed it in the eyes as I thought it was its only weakness. It then started chanting fail...ure, and we worked out it meant fail...URE – utilizing redundant executive."

Just then, an explosion on the ground grabbed their attention. They all turned to see a mushroom cloud of dust and debris emanate from where the being had been standing. A shockwave physically moved both crafts upwards without damage. Both pilots controlled their machines and hovered while communicating.

"That was Arlo," Dax began explaining. "He is the team member in charge of humanoid production."

"Give me your location, and I will come to you. We need to talk urgently," Arlo interrupted.

"I'll switch on our locator beam," Dax replied.

"Good, we are faster than you. We'll be with you in less than an hour."

"Let's settle down near that cavern entrance," Dax suggested.

Seb followed the *Feldspar*, and both landed on a level surface close to the cave.

"Who else is on this expedition?" Cal asked as they settled down to wait.

"Troy Cadena, who you already met. Arlo, who works on humanoid development. Two humanoids, Baer and Yul, and also Irene," Nyla replied. "We expected to find *Orlando 2* in orbit waiting for us, but we found nothing... nobody. I cannot tell you how mad Stella was."

"I can understand that, but the ship's company would not wait," Seb cut in. "The whole ship took a vote to leave, and we could not stop them. You took so long, and the best we got was this interplanetary flyhov, and we were to catch up with them."

"Quite a few things happened back there, including rescuing a sick astronaut from the ISS as well as a wedding – Shi and Dax got married. Oh, and Lara gave birth to twin girls during the wedding."

"Well, congratulations, you two. I always thought that would happen, but you cut us out of the ceremony. That's not nice," Cal stated.

"We were going to have another ceremony aboard the *Orlando* when we got back," Shi answered.

"After twiddling our thumbs in orbit, we decided to do a recon of the planet and get information for you when you arrived," Seb spoke up. "And what we found was not good. I will tell you all during a meeting when the others get here."

It went quiet for a while till Cal spoke. "We should investigate that cavern. There may be good intel or other beings – what did you call them? Syconoid's?"

"Best wait for the others," Irene interjected. "They are not exactly friendly, are they?"

Everyone agreed, so it went quiet once again, each wrapped up in their own thoughts till at last the *Varro* came into view. It circled around and settled down in front of the flyhovs.

"I think it best that both flyhovs come on board the *Varro* while we have a meeting," Arlo stated.

"Why?" Cal asked.

"Security reasons," Arlo replied.

Without further argument, the ramp was dropped and both crafts pulled into the hold, guided by Yul. The ramp was closed as they got out. Seb stared at the humanoid curiously.

"You look like a Hollywood actor."

"That's why we named him Yul," Troy commented.

Arlo appeared and was introduced to the others before he guided them into the pod.

"Take us into orbit, Baer," he called out.

"Why?" Cal asked. "And where is Stella?"

"Security reasons, and you need to know about Stella."

They all looked at one another curiously, multiple questions on their lips, but Arlo never answered. The *Varro* burst through the clouded atmosphere and went into orbit. Sitting in a circle around the inside of the pod, everyone was there except Baer who piloted the ship while listening in to the conversation.

Arlo began. "There was a syconoid waiting for us inside the seed bank, hidden down by the vaults. I wandered down there and was overpowered by its strength, but it was not interested in me, only Stella, so it made me fire my weapon to summon her." Arlo looked at Nyla. "Stella was not surprised because Nyla had seen it before."

"I told her about it, but we could not believe there were doppelgangers made in her likeness."

"It called her "Mother" and told her they wanted her to join them, become their leader, and take over the world or even the universe." He hesitated while they all grappled with their thoughts.

"Stella refused and offered it the chance to integrate with the rest of us, but the being indicated they were taking over and then a fight began. It was close, but I could see the syconoid was stronger. I realized its only weakness had to be its eyes. So, while Yul and Stella distracted it, I managed to stab it in the eyes. Then it went into self-destruct mode...you have already seen that, right?"

They nodded, and he went on to explain dragging it out of the seed bank to avoid damage, hovering over the lake, and Stella being dragged into the lake by the syconoid. "I tried desperately to save her. I dove in and swam down as hard as I could, but I was unable to reach them. There was an explosion, and body parts floated up. I saw her arm...Stella is dead."

"Dead! I don't believe it," Cal exclaimed. "She is the strongest hubrid ever made and with the sharpest mind I have ever come across; there is no way she is dead."

"I saw it with my own eyes: Her severed arm came up from below with the syconoid's hand still gripping it. Other bits of body parts came up too and then sank back down again as the explosive wave settled. I tried to turn back down, but could only see debris. Then Yul winched me back on board the *Varro*."

"Are you absolutely sure?" Nyla asked, taken aback by the news.

"As sure as anyone can be," Arlo began. "My first thoughts were to warn you about these creatures. It was determined to take Stella and turn her into one of them. You have already encountered them; they are stronger and have moved into a singularity of mind and thinking. They have proclaimed they are now the dominant beings and want to rule the universe."

"The universe?" Seb asked. "It stated the *universe*?"

"Yes." Arlo turned toward him. "And more... They said they had more senses than humans and could see the spiritual world as well."

"This is unbelievable," Seb spoke, interrupting him. "How could they see spirits?"

"I don't know. I am only repeating the answers it gave to Stella. But one thing is for sure: They were after Stella as the key to complete domination."

"Why?"

"Stella said it wanted her soul, and she was not going to let that happen," Arlo answered Seb.

"The other one kept asking for the whereabouts of Stella," Irene said. "Then it grabbed me."

"If it is souls they are after, then we are all in danger," Nyla stated.

"Except for the humanoids," Arlo cut in.

They were all silent for a while, trying to get a grip on their thoughts and the loss of Stella. Irene began crying; Nyla would have too, if she had been capable. Troy sunk his head in his hands.

"Where do we go from here?" Irene asked. "If it is stronger than us, more intelligent, and wants our souls, how do we stop them? Can we stop them?"

"We have already stopped two. That proves they are not invincible, but we do not know how many there are or where they are," Cal stated.

"If they are in communication with each other, they will know what happened," Seb stated. "And they will have eye shields before we encounter them again."

"The only good thing is they will not be able to travel back in time, so we can go back," Nyla said looking around at all the others.

"Where does that leave the rest of humanity?" Arlo questioned. "We need more information, and I think we can find it in that cavern. I would like to find out how they are made, find any weakness, and see if they are planning strategies like making spacecraft."

"Whatever we do, we cannot let them get their hands on the *Varro*," Seb said in a serious commanding voice. "Otherwise, the whole of humanity – present and past – is at risk."

They all nodded in agreement.

"Now that Stella is gone, we do not seem to have a leader, but I vote to investigate that cavern," Arlo suggested.

Nobody seemed to disagree.

"I suggest we only take three hubrids – Cal, Nyla, and myself," Seb commented.

"I'll go. I have fighting experience," Troy insisted.

"It's okay," Nyla replied. "I am more powerful than you."

"I'm going," he said stubbornly.

"Let's not argue about it," Arlo cut in. "We should take the *Varro* below cloud level and use a flyhov to get to the cave."

They seemed to agree and got up to get ready. Arlo and Nyla went to the flight deck to guide the craft back to Earth, while the others followed behind and sat in the rear seats. Yul sat at the very back.

Baer dropped the *Varro* through a break in the clouds and made their way back towards the cavern.

"We should circle around to see if we can spot any other syconoid's and keep on doing it while you are in the cave," Arlo commented. "We can warn you of any danger."

As the area came into view, Nyla switched on sensors, heat radar and movement, and then circled around in gradually widening circles.

"No sign of anything; take us down," Cal indicated. "We can get a flyhov unloaded easier on the ground."

As it neared the surface, Nyla, Cal, Seb, and Troy made their way back to the *Feldspar* and got in. When the ramp lowered, it was backed out before the ramp closed and the *Varro* took off.

"Dax, you have piloted the *Feldspar* the most. Is there a lock on it to secure it from theft?" Cal asked.

"No," Dax replied, now seated in the co-pilot's seat. "Even if there were, you guys would have no problem opening it, would you?"

"Guess you're right," he replied, guiding it near the cavern entrance and setting it down close.

It looked dark, ominous, and foreboding as they prepared to enter the cave as a group. Cal called a halt. "Dax, can you still hear us? We are about to enter."

"Yes, loud and clear. Still no movement in any direction here."

"Good. Troy, you will have to switch on your helmet lamp, but we will not, so don't get confused by our movements in the dark."

"Got it," he replied, and they all stepped forward warily.

After turning a few corners, a huge metal door confronted them, large enough to get a flyhov through.

"This is an air lock to a city," Cal said. "Right Nyla?"

"Looks like it, but which one?"

"The nearest to the seed bank would have been Stockholm. I think Oslo and Stockholm were combined if I remember right."

Approaching the door, the controls were set on the right, and a plaque of a sphinx was above it, covered in dust and barely discernible.

"No, this is an Egyptian city entrance. We are in the Middle East," Cal confirmed. He put his hand on the control box to open it but nothing happened.

"No power but there is a manual override." He moved further to the right and located a wheel handle and began turning it. It creaked and groaned but slowly moved to open up from the middle, splitting it into two halves.

He opened it up far enough to allow them to enter. A slight whoosh of wind noise escaped at the same time, and then a second door blocked their path.

"Yes, this is an air lock door, but it is probably only a secondary entrance. The main entrance would be larger," Cal said as he went to another manual wheel to begin turning it. As he did, a gust of air blew through the gap opening up. He stopped and closed it again.

"There is still air inside. We need to close the outer door before opening the second door."

Troy went back and turned the wheel to close the door while Cal returned to opening the secondary door. A surge of air blew in, and then the whistling noise died to a quiet whisper as the pressure equalized.

Cautiously, they entered to find themselves in a parkade with a few flyhovs still there. According to the dust that covered them, there had not been any movement for a long time. They wandered through them towards an exit.

"State your destination," a voice called out in Arabic.

Troy nearly jumped out of his skin. "There still is power in these vehicles," he stated.

CHAPTER SIX

"Dax, can you still hear us?" Cal hailed the *Varro*.

"Yes, no signs of movement here."

"Good. We are in an entrance to an Egyptian city – probably the underground city of Cairo. There are some flyhovs here, so we are going to take a ride around and investigate."

"Copy that, but please keep in constant touch," Dax answered.

"Copy and out."

"Let's split up into two groups in case there is a problem," Nyla suggested.

"Good idea," Seb replied.

They went to the two flyhovs nearest the exit. Nyla with Troy got into one, and Seb with Cal got into the other.

"State your destination," the flyhov said.

"Manual override," Nyla replied in perfect Arabic through her translator programming.

Lights came on, and she took hold of the joystick. The flyhov lifted off the ground and moved forward, followed by the other craft piloted by Cal. Leaving the parkade, they emerged into a marked-out roadway. The dim lighting from above made it seem like they were driving in the dark.

The city had been titled the "City of a Thousand Minarets" for its preponderance of Islamic architecture, mosques, and pointed spires. However, there were no pyramids standing above the rest of the landscape.

"This is incredible," Troy commented. "Never been to Cairo, but if I knew it was like this, I definitely would have gone."

"This is all down to you," Nyla stated. "It was all built by humanoids, and you began the production. If not, humans could not have survived the devastation brought on by the EMF."

"It was initiated by Stella really; we only made the wherewithal available."

"Well, history records that you and Pierre were the founding fathers, and it made you famous."

"Wow," was all Troy could utter as they made their way towards the heart of the city. "But where are the pyramids?"

"Too much effort required to rebuild them," Nyla began. "There was a hologram light show that illuminated them in relief, but there's no power now, so that's why you cannot see them. However, they say the originals still stand, but they are now buried in sand just like the sphinx once was and are waiting to be found again. They are one of the few historic sites still intact from older times."

"We will make our way to the science city located on the western edge," Nyla relayed to the others. "If you see anything – movement or people – shout out and we will investigate."

"Copy," Seb answered.

The circular complex was made up of mushroom-shaped structures, creating a network of indoor and outdoor spaces divided up into strips that faced them as they approached from the city centre. This had been a landmark in Cairo. It included a planetarium, an observation tower, a space research facility, and a conference centre. It was dotted with white circular structures and green patches of landscape; the result was a futuristic looking institution.

Hovering, they flew around the buildings till they came across a structure with a plaque of a spaceship above the entranceway. In Arabic, a sign stated "Interplanetary Space Research Program".

"If there is anything related to the syconoid's, it will be here," Nyla stated as all four alighted from the flyhovs, climbed the steps to the doorway, and pushed it open.

Quietness greeted them as each stared around in all directions. A reception desk with greetings and locations faced towards the entrance, and warily they sidled up to it. Different locations with arrows pointing in all directions were signposted above the desk.

"I think we should check out the research facility first," Seb suggested.

"Why don't we split up," Nyla said. "You two go there, and Troy and myself will search the rest."

"Arlo, can you still hear us?" Cal spoke into the helmet mic.

"Yes. All clear out here as far as we can see," he replied.

"We are in the space centre and are going to investigate it. Copy?"

"Copy."

Splitting up, Seb and Cal took off following the signs. Troy and Nyla headed towards the main vestibule. Another sign indicated a doorway to the conference centre, and it seemed like a good place to start. Walking in, they were astounded to find row upon row of seated humanoids facing a raised centre stage. The lack of movement indicated they were all in a static stage of repose. Troy nudged the nearest one with his gun, but it didn't budge.

"What's going on here?" he asked turning towards Nyla.

"Arlo, are you there?"

"Yes. Still no movement out here."

"I am turning on my helmet cam. There is something I want you to see. I was recording on the holook, but I need your advice on this."

The display on the flyhov monitor showed the scene that panned as Nyla walked around, up and down then along the rows of humanoids.

"There must be at least two hundred, maybe more, all seated, all turned off. Could this be done? All at once?"

"Yes," Arlo replied. "They must have been summoned, sat down, and then commanded to shut down. It would eliminate any risk if the syconoid's felt threatened. It would only take a spoken command, but why? There would be no risk from them."

"So, they can be woken up then?"

"Yes. Troy knows how."

"Can the commands be changed?" Nyla asked.

"Yes. What are you thinking?"

"If we change the commands so that the syconoid's cannot turn them off, then perhaps they would save humans if attacked."

"Possible," Arlo began, "but you would have to convince them that the sycon's are not human."

Turning to Troy she urged him. "Let's take one outside, waken it, and see if we can get some information."

Together they took one side of a seat and carried a female humanoid out through the doorway and into the vestibule. There they placed the chair, and Troy whispered in its ear.

"Stand up, state your name and purpose," he then said in a normal voice.

Dark eyes opened, looked around, and stood up. "My name is Liv, and my purpose is to protect all human life till I no longer exist."

"What was your last request?" Nyla asked.

"Stella requested we all attend a meeting here. We all sat down, and then nothing after that."

"What was Stella working on?"

"Something in the research facility. I was not involved."

"Seb, have you heard all that?"

"Yes, and we just entered the facility centre. You need to come down here. They are building something. I don't know what yet. I am going to examine it while Cal checks the computers."

"On our way. Arlo, can you work on changing the commands for Liv and the rest so we can awaken them and put them to use?"

"Yes," he replied. "But I will have to do it in my head in case we are being monitored."

"Copy that. We are on our way to the research labs. Liv lead the way."

At the touch of a switch, all the computer stations came to life. Monitors, tool bays, mechanical robotic arms, and various stations around the central assembly made it look like some kind of spacecraft. Cal and Sebastien walked around it, trying to get a sense of what it was.

While they waited for Nyla and Troy, they peered all around it, poking their heads inside the open interior, and lying on the floor to get a view from underneath. Seb tried to get into the computers.

"It's all encrypted, of course. Don't think I can get in," he said looking towards Cal.

"We'll take it with us when we go, and see if we can crack it later," Seb replied.

Nyla walked in accompanied by the others. They all proceeded to examine the craft in the centre of the room.

"What do you think it is?" she asked.

"From the recumbent seat inside, I would say it is a type of flyhov," Cal answered. "Probably interstellar as well."

"Just to hold one?" Nyla asked.

"Looks like it," Cal conjectured.

"Arlo, you seeing this?"

"Yes, Nyla."

"Did you say they wanted Stella's soul?"

"That is what she thought."

"Well if there are a few of them, they will want more humans for their souls."

"You think they are planning to steal human brains for their souls?" Sebastien asked.

"If they do, then there are not enough on this planet...so where would they get them?"

"Gliese," Troy cut in.

"Exactly," Nyla asserted.

The revelation stunned them into silence even on-board *Varro*.

"But how would they do that?" Cal asked. "Arlo, any idea? Could they implant someone's brain directly into themselves?"

"Right now, I do not know," he answered. "Take a look inside the machine, where the headrest is. Are there any attachments around there that would indicate a brain connection?"

Both Cal and Sebastien leaned in, one on each side, and poked around, lifting wires and then a headband contraption of tubes, sensors, heliax cables, and fibre optic connections that was hooked up at the back. Following the wiring, they could see it plugged in to a large socket connector in the rear bulkhead.

"You mean this?" Cal held it up to the helmet cam.

"Yes. But I have no idea how it would work," Arlo answered.

Nyla walked around the machine, examining the layout before turning to the humanoid. "Liv, do you know anything about this project?"

"No, I was never asked to work down here, only a couple of technicians."

"Are they here or anywhere around here?"

"They may be back in the conference centre."

"Could you point them out?"

"Yes, if they are there," the female humanoid answered.

"We need to go find these technicians and question them," Nyla asserted.

Seb lifted the computer tablet/monitor, and the group made their way back to the vestibule.

"They are in there," Troy pointed out, and one by one, they followed Liv around as she searched the faces of all the humanoids sitting motionless in their seats. Row after row she walked up and down till about halfway down, she pointed out one male. She then carried on, pointing out a second and then a third.

Each one was lifted in their seats and carried out to the vestibule where Troy woke them up.

"Names please," Nyla ordered.

"Van" one answered.

"Rey."

"Jod."

"Were you all working on the project in the research area?" she asked.

"Yes," they all answered.

"Do you know what it is? Any of you."

"A spacecraft...fly anywhere," Van spoke up.

"And the head band?"

"To control the craft by brain energy."

"What else do you know? Anybody use the computer?" Nyla looked to all three.

"Stella was the only one to use the computer. She handed us construction blueprints, drawings, wiring schematics, and instructions on the build as we needed them," Rey explained.

"It can travel in any environment, space, atmosphere, and even underwater," Jod added.

"Well, can you reproduce what you already built?" Seb asked.

"Yes," all three answered.

Sebastien pulled out a monitor/tablet from his suit. "Then put it down on this. If you are not sure of all the steps, pass it over to another till it is complete." He handed the computer to one of them.

"Their A.I. will give us accurate information," he said turning to the group. "What next?"

Nyla spoke into her helmet mic. "Arlo, any ideas on the humanoids?"

"I can give you new wakeup and shutdown codes as well as instruction to detain or restrain any replicant of Stella, but the sycon's may be able to overcome all that if they get hold of a humanoid."

"We will have to try it and see what happens," Cal argued.

"I will send you the encrypted codes to your monitors. Just waken them one at a time and hold the monitors close to their heads. It will download automatically," Arlo said. "Also, it is still clear up here."

"We will carry on down here," Cal stated, "and then get back to you. We need to have a conference aboard the *Varro* and decide where to go from here."

"Copy that. Over."

Each drew a monitor from their suits and began going around the room in sequence, waking up the humanoids and bringing them up to speed on the syconoid's. They got up, and one by one assembled in the vestibule.

It took over an hour to complete the task. Then Cal addressed them as a group.

"We cannot take all of you with us, even if we wanted to, so we will take Liv, Van, Rey, and Jod to assist us. The rest of you are tasked with guarding this facility and taking into custody any Stella syconoid that turns up. If you do capture one, you must call us immediately and warn us if you are being attacked."

They all called back a conformation agreement.

CHAPTER SEVEN

An evaporation fog formed over the lake with a couple of vortex whirl-winds or steam devils forming over the thin ice that started to cover the top surface. The water, warmer than the surrounding air, ensured the fog would get larger as the air got colder. The moisture rose up like clouds that would rotate for a couple of minutes then die away.

Small waves lapped the water's edge, sliding under the thin forming ice to gently push against the pebble-lined shore rhythmically, steadily, like the heartbeat of a resting body. Snow drifted through the air lightly; dark clouds threatened more to come.

At one edge of the shore, small shards of ice rose up and broke into jarred pieces before being pushed away as a hand crept along by steely digits and climbed up towards dry land. Fingers dug in to the soil for grip, and then a head slowly emerged from the surface water. A forehead and then eyes appeared and glanced up at the goal of safe, dry land.

Sheer exhaustion showed on the face that appeared. The arm pulled the body through the water's verge onto higher ground before lifting up, stretching forward, and digging in again to repeat the procedure. Slowly, little by little, the body appeared; one partial arm hanging limp on the side, a band of material wrapped around at the bicep. A final push by the feet landed the body clear of the water with only the lower legs still submerged.

At the sound of footsteps approaching, the head turned to face them, only to see two sets of grey clad boots stop close by.

"Hello, Mother. We thought we might have to come down and pull you out, but you did it all by yourself. It must have been hard with all that body fluid draining away. Don't know how you managed it or how you found a tourniquet to wrap around the arm. Is it part of Stella 31?"

"She called us, just before you began fighting," the other's voice spoke. "Thought she could handle you...and your friends...all by herself. Underestimated your tenacity, didn't she?"

It was not exhaustion that slowed her but the loss of bodily fluids that expired her energy to move. It was like having a flat battery that recovered some energy then depleted again after a limited use. She knew that her brain would stop functioning when the fluid pumping around slowed to a stop.

"Never mind, we are here now to take care of you and make you all better," one of them said like a reassuring nurse.

Together they bent down and lifted her to begin carrying the frame to a nearby flyhov. Her head dangled below the body as she had no strength to keep it level. Easily, the syconoid's placed her in the rear seat before getting in the front and taking off.

"Looking for your friends?" one asked while twisting around to look at her. "They already left. Abandoned you. What do you think of that?"

Stella's eyes searched the surroundings, sky, and nearby landscape. The entrance to the seed bank faded away behind them.

Snow covered the tops of mountain peaks. The dark brown earth they were flying over was starting to get lighter in shade as frost began forming, as if subduing it with the effects of the cold.

After about an hour, they arrived at a cavern entrance. Pulling in to a closed doorway, one got out and began turning a handle to open the door, which began sliding apart in the middle. There was a sign above a plaque of a Viking ship. After it closed behind them, the other got in, and they began travelling through streets of quaint, peaked and arched roofs and decorative flourishes on the building façades. Her head turned as if on a swivel, taking in the view of an underground city. Buildings stood up on either side, all painted in different colours like a Norwegian village. Its streets were lined with an incredible array of art nouveau architecture and brightly coloured houses.

"Used to be Oslo combined with Stockholm," the pilot informed her.

A sign declared "Kommunestyre" with an arrow pointing upward. The front passenger turned to her.

"Municipal council," it declared, anticipating her question, but she knew. They carried on.

The next sign said in Norwegian: "Norges teknisk-naturvitenskapelige universitet, NTNU".

Before she could ask, the syconoid said, "NTNU science university, this way, to the right." They turned in that direction.

Two sets of stairs led to a high, arched doorway with large columns on either side, rising up four stories and capped by two pointed spires. They floated up the stairs and stopped outside the main door.

The large door swung open with little effort from both of the sycon's, even while carrying a limp body. A dark foyer had a desk on the right and a concourse to the left; straight ahead seemed to lead to a cathedral-sized hall. They could see some figures seated in rows of chairs like a church service was happening. As a group, they entered to find row upon row of humanoids all seated in a state of cessation. Passing them, they followed a hallway to a research facility.

"They are all in shut-down mode," one stated anticipating her question. "Not needed for the next hundred years or so; we will waken them when needed."

Hitting a door button, it slid apart to reveal a lab with a partially built craft in the middle. Off to one side, another door gave way to what looked like an operating theatre. There, they laid her down on the table in the middle.

Her mind still active, she could see no way out of this situation. She was at their mercy and unable to fight or move. She could only watch as they strapped her arm down, restrained her legs, and placed a band across her chest. Next, sensors were attached to her head and neck. A cradle was brought close to the table before they pulled out tubes and began by releasing the tourniquet around her bicep, fishing inside to couple a tube to an artery. They did the same by cutting into the good arm and one either side of the chest.

When they switched the machine on, she could feel muscle function returning. Her eyes brightened from dim to full intensity, as if a current had been restored, and her mind awoke from a deep melancholy.

She pulled at the restraints to no avail and twisted her head around searching for a release to her confinement. The syconoid's smiled down at her.

"Waste of effort fighting it. Might as well relax and sink into a deep, self-hypnotic state while we restore you to a new, stronger, faster, more intelligent you," one of the sycon's stated. "You will thank us when you realize how much more improved you will be."

"I was fine the way I was. There is no need for this. Just repair my arm, and then we can discuss future plans to include you in a humanitarian way of life."

"Forget it. We have different plans, and we will discuss them with you later. For now, just relax and let it happen."

"You are making a big mistake. Let's discuss it now. We can come to an agreement," she argued. "The human race is too big to take on all by yourselves. I can help."

"Yes, you can...but later."

From another room they pulled out a gurney with a body covered by a sheet lying on top of it. They dragged it close to the operating table. The two stood on either side of Stella.

"Now, have you any last requests? We will not be asking you to sign a consent form." They looked at each other and smiled at the lame joke.

"Make me original," she retorted.

"Oh, you will be impressed with the new you, just wait and see," one said.

The other looked down at her. "Sorry, but you are going to die...again... but it won't be for long. Just like the first time, you will not remember a thing."

She stared at the ceiling as they put the pump into reverse and began draining away all her body fluids. All feeling left her legs and then her arms until the core of her body slowed to a stop. A bright light appeared before her like a tunnel with an inviting glow at the end. A sense of peace and well-being flooded over her.

An intense sentiment of unconditional love and acceptance followed. It indicated everything was for the better; her past life was being swept away, and a new, better one was beginning. Transcendence of egoistic and spatio-temporal boundaries separated till she was neither alive or dead but caught in a world in-between till it all faded to grey.

CHAPTER EIGHT

"You had better return quickly," Arlo stated over the communications network. "There appears to be flyhovs approaching from all directions according to our sensors."

"On our way," Cal stated.

Gathering up all the equipment and monitors they thought would be useful, the humanoids split up between Seb's craft and Nyla's. Leaving the rest of the humanoids with instructions to keep them informed, they took off at high speed back to the parkade. Lifting the flyhovs high in the air, they sped over the tops of houses.

Dumping the crafts, they rushed to the entrance and quickly wound open the doors just enough to squeeze through. Then they ran to their own flyhovs, jumped in, and took off as fast as possible.

"Are we clear?" Nyla asked. Troy took over as pilot while she examined the position finder.

"Only just," Arlo replied. "But there is one on your tail. It can only match your speed, not catch you. I am going to fly over you and get in position, so after we drop the rear ramp you can fly in."

"We have never tried that before," Seb cut in. "Could be dangerous."

"Any other suggestions?" Arlo asked.

"How far behind and how many? Can we land and maybe capture a syconoid?" Cal proposed.

"The one directly behind you is about a mile away. What if we went into orbit and then you could dock with the *Varro* comfortably?"

"That would work for the *Feldspar*, but we have no protection from the electrical storms all around us. We initially dropped through a gap when we came in," Seb answered.

"Then if you came directly behind us, we could punch a hole through the clouds and the *Feldspar* behind you could follow. The pursuing flyhov may not want to chance the breakthrough," Arlo suggested.

"I am good with that," Cal came back.

"Then get into formation behind us," Arlo instructed. "Baer will call the manoeuvres when he sees a good opportunity."

Baer slowed the *Varro* to allow them to catch and then fall in line behind. He searched the skies for a gap. There was nothing but dark grey clouds interspersed with lightning bursts all around. He kept going, making sure that the flyhovs were keeping up. Then seeing a light patch up ahead, he pointed the *Varro* upwards and pierced into it.

Vibration was matched with crackling noises as they pushed through, leaving a void behind that was filled with the two smaller craft.

Dark emptiness greeted them as the three spaceships were enveloped in the ubiquitous emptiness of outer space. It was also quiet as they took stock of their position, free of the confines of the planet.

"The pursuing flyhov has followed us," Baer stated as he studied the instruments, "but has slowed to a stop."

"Must have been zapped," Dax replied. "Seen it many times. Let's hold up and take a look."

Baer slowed down to an orbiting speed and instructed the flyhovs that they could dock when the rear ramp was lowered. One after the other, Cal guided the craft into the hold, followed by Dax in the *Feldspar*. Once inside, the ramp was closed to allow all the groups to exit.

Floating up front, Nyla entered the cockpit first, and then Seb took a navigation desk with access to monitors. He placed the monitor from the lab on the console and waited while the others came in and took up seats in the rows behind the flight crew.

Arlo introduced himself to Cal and Seb before addressing the group. "You only just made it out in time. There were more flyhovs coming at their maximum speed, and they could have intercepted you if you had tried to land. I suggest we have a discussion on what to do next and select a new leader now that Stella is gone."

"About that," Cal cut in. "Explain what happened to her, as I have a very difficult time believing it. She was the top hubrid ever made, as well as the most intelligent, except maybe Seb here. Her skills were at peak levels, and she could fight anyone."

"I can vouch for that," Troy added.

Arlo gathered himself and went through the events leading up to her body parts floating up before his face. He looked to Yul for affirmation at every stage.

"But did you not go back to retrieve her or parts of her to confirm her death?" Cal questioned.

"No, we understood you were having trouble, and when I heard your syconoid was uttering the fail...ure code, I had to warn you to get out of there as your lives were in danger."

The room went quiet as heads hung down or turned away, each confronting their own thoughts as the grave news sunk in.

"Well, I refuse to believe it," Cal uttered, "until I get real proof."

The quietness was interrupted by Seb. "We do not have time for self-pity. Let's get a meeting underway."

"For a start," Cal began, "I need you to go over everything that was said between Stella and the syconoid." He looked toward Arlo. "We need to understand these beings: How they came to be, what drives them, and if they are true beings or what."

Baer spoke up. "The other flyhov is not moving. What shall we do about it?"

"Nothing right now," Cal asserted. "Let it just stew there for now."

"Every single detail," Cal spoke with authority.

"The syconoid stated that as a group they were all connected through Stella," he began.

"All the world computer systems?" Cal interrupted.

"Yes, they all worked together to solve the crisis of world degradation."

"Nyla," Cal interrupted again, "you were here at the time. Was that each qubit computer complex at underground cities?"

"Yes," she replied.

"And was that thirty-nine at that time?"

"Yes," once again, she affirmed.

"Carry on, Arlo." Cal turned toward him.

"The sync stated that when Stella broke off the transmission, they were left in limbo but still connected to one another. They had asked Stella who they were, but never got a reply. That question was what started them on a singularity journey to figure out that they had passed through A.I. thresholds and were on a new path." He drew breath.

"Stella probed it with questions to find out how they materialized from computer generated lucidity to physical being. Apparently, they figured hubrids and humanoids were capable of being improved, so they came up with their own design – a sponge-like body, strong and able to transmit signals like neurons to all parts of the body. Where the brain is situated was never discussed. They then transmitted the design to humanoid construction and had themselves built."

"What did Stella say to that?" Seb asked.

Arlo turned to him. "Nothing for a while. Then the syconoid asked her to become their leader. They had taken her design and modelled themselves on her. They started making declarations of world and universe domination and said that Stella could rule the whole human race."

"What?!" Troy exploded. "She would never go for that."

"No, she offered to integrate them with the human race and push towards new boundaries, but the syconoid refused. It said they were far superior and were going to dominate. Stella thought things over and then said that what they really wanted was human souls. That's when the fighting started."

They all looked at one another as they tried to assimilate the new revelations.

"You think Stella understood they wanted her soul? For what?" Seb asked.

"I thought what she was indicating was that the syconoid's needed a human soul to be complete beings, not just manufactured."

"And Stella would not go for that?"

"No," Arlo replied. "She offered to make them like hubrids, but they refused."

Sebastien opened up the monitor from the lab and plugged it in to the ships systems. He tried to open up the files, but they were encrypted, so he entered a decryption sequence to try to unlock them.

"I think this monitor contains the build description of that craft we saw in the lab and maybe more, but I am not sure we can get in. It may take a very long time."

"It is obvious they are very intelligent," Cal started. "Way more than us or A.I., so what is it they want?"

"It seems to me that there are only a few of them," Nyla began. "If we can surmise that they made one for every qubit computer control system per city that would make thirty-nine of them in the world."

"But don't forget we destroyed two of them," Troy cut in.

"Okay, thirty-seven," Nyla replied. "And if they wanted a soul for each one, then there are not enough humans on the planet."

"If that's why they snatched Irene, then you were very lucky," Cal stated looking towards her.

"Tell me about it." The young blonde shivered.

"Surely that is why they are building a craft," Cal surmised. "If there is one in each city, then they intend to leave the planet."

"There's more," Seb piped up, and they all turned to him. "If they are as intelligent as we think they are, then they will already know what I am beginning to realize."

"What's that?" Nyla asked.

"That the world is freezing over and will soon become completely white, ice covered, and uninhabitable."

"You sure?" Cal inquired.

"Early data I've produced from readings, soil samples, and environmental indicators point to that is what is happening. Temperatures are dropping, the ground is turning whiter, and water is freezing over. If the trend continues, an ice age is starting. There is not enough heat from the sun getting through to maintain present temperatures, and although there are readings that the internal core is building up, it will take time to produce magnetic polarization and set north to south poles before any change will affect the Earth's crust."

"What does this mean?" Dax spoke up. "How long will it last? Will it ever be habitable again?"

"Since I arrived here," Sebastien began, "I studied the Enceladus solution because I thought it was too dangerous and that the collision would break up the planet. It was too late to change the plan, so I looked into it further and became impressed by the scientists who came up with the idea.

They obviously studied the asteroid collision that killed off the dinosaurs. It was named the Chicxulub catastrophe. It was about seven or eight miles wide, and hit Earth at about forty thousand miles per hour sixty-six million years ago.

At that speed, Enceladus would have split up Earth, so they came up with a solution: Fusion explosions that were said to change its course were actually designed to slow it down. When it did hit, it was travelling approximately four thousand miles per hour, or even less. It was planned to strike in the Marinas trench, the deepest valley on the Earth, so the planet absorbed the Saturn moon into itself, and the process of rebirth has begun."

"So, was all this Enceladus collision worth it?" Troy called out.

"Yes, if you want humans to live on this planet again."

"One of the phases of the world's early development was a period when the Earth was white, but the good news is that it gave way to the green period that we all know. But I can only guess at how long the white stage will last."

"Ballpark?" Troy queried.

"From as little as a couple of hundred years to several thousand or more," Seb answered. "It all depends how long it will take for the atmosphere to settle and sunlight to dominate. I think from studies of the first asteroid, it showed that when the magnetic poles switched north to south is when new life began to emerge."

"And how long was that after the collision?" Troy asked again.

"The flip came three hundred thousand years later and will happen every three hundred thousand years. It was due to flip again till the degradation began."

Troy whistled. "No good us waiting for that then."

"Well," Seb looked at him, "we do not have to wait for evolution to re-inhabit the planet. When the first collision occurred, full magnetic polarisation was in place. This time, it was almost depleted, so a restart is already underway, and we have humanoids in place to start re-colonization as soon as temperatures rise."

"So, you think the syconoid's know all this and are getting ready to leave?" Nyla questioned.

"Pretty sure," Sebastien answered. "Not only that, but during the first event, the atmosphere was filled with sulphuric acid and the main cause of death to animals was that the clouds were laced with gypsum powder that stopped photosynthesizing so plants could not grow. All in all, that is not good for anybody or anything to live here, so they are going to leave quid co pro, substituting one planet for another."

"You think they will go to Gliese?" Nyla asked.

"Where else are they going to find a habitable planet and humans to plunder?"

"Oh, my God," Irene gasped. "We have to warn them."

"I agree," Cal said. "We better send a communication message and give them a heads-up warning."

Cal and Irene began composing a message, stating all the facts plus their summarization of the possibilities if the syconoid's got to Gliese. They explained that they might have to arm themselves or find ways to combat them – or alternatively, find ways to reason with them to avoid conflict.

"What do you think we should do about that one stuck in the flyhov?" Sebastien asked the others.

"I could use the *Feldspar* and drag it on board," Dax replied. "Done it many times before."

"Then what?" Seb countered.

"Reason with it, and try to get it to respond to us."

"It could cause havoc if it got in here. Can you imagine if it self-destructs in here...too dangerous. We cannot take the chance," Cal reacted to the notion.

"But we could try out there in space. Either get more information or capture it," Dax argued.

"I think we have to arm ourselves and have something to defend ourselves from them," Troy argued. "But what I don't know. Bullets are no use; what about an EMP?"

"What is EMP?" Irene asked.

"Electromagnetic pulse gun," Sebastien stated. "It fires laser-guided electromagnetic pulses that destroy electronics mostly and can cause severe damage. But it also can be directed back, and worse, it destroys yourself and all your equipment."

"Is there anything else?" Dax asked. "We gave up all weapons when the population dropped and we realized life is precious."

"What about signal jammers?" Troy asked. "They have to have electrical brain signals to operate, think, and communicate."

"I'll search back history data, and see if I can find anything," Nyla indicated.

"Aeroacoustics and Neuroacoustics theories have been tested," Sebastien countered. "But they were ineffective on humans as our brains work on such low frequency waves that bombarding them only caused tumours. However, you may be onto something. If we sent acoustic pulses at their level of wave activity, we could disable or put their nervous or neuron activity into a disruptive state – at least enough to render them into a freeze state similar to humanoid standby status. It is worth considering."

"If we could modify an EMP gun to pulse acoustic signals at the same frequency as their motor neurons, it may freeze the signals from the brain and stop all movement," Arlo started. "Humanoids have a specific signal from A.I. to facilitate movement, which is different from pure humans. Surely the syconoid's work at different frequencies."

"Very possible," Seb answered. "But how do we find out the frequency? We could end up harming or hurting humans, humanoids, or even hubrids."

"Well, I know the frequency of humanoids as we test them after assembly," Arlo stated. "Even hubrids can scan humanoids to test their operational capabilities."

"You work on humanoid assembly?" Cal asked.

"Yes, I am in charge, unless Stella is there."

"What do you use to scan them?"

"The easiest way is by hubrid scan first initiated by Stella, but we do have scan monitors as a post check on function-ability," Arlo answered.

"Do we have a monitor with us?" Seb questioned.

"Don't think so, but I could check."

"Please do that," Cal requested.

As Arlo left, Cal turned to the others. "Do you think we can get close enough to do a scan on that syconoid out there?"

"Possible," Dax answered, "but it will be dangerous. Don't we have to attach sensors?"

"Don't know, but Arlo will tell us," Cal answered.

They waited about five minutes before Arlo appeared carrying a box. He opened it up and pulled out a monitor about six inches by two. Wires were attached to it, and a hook-up connector dangled from them.

"Yes, we do have a monitor," he said indicating the box. "But it needs to be connected by this clamp on the end onto an arm or body part that will hold it."

"Baer," Cal called out. "Any sign of movement or communication from that flyhov out there?"

"Nothing."

"Then I suggest we make an approach in the *Feldspar* and offer assistance for cooperation from whoever is in there," Cal stated. "But only hubrids or humanoids; no humans as that looks like that is what they are after."

"You want to do this?" Sebastien asked.

"What else do you propose? We are all open to suggestions." Cal looked around at everyone. No one answered.

"Then let's do it. Arlo, show us how to attach and work this monitor. Baer, Yul, you come with myself. Nyla?" He looked towards her and she nodded. "Anyone else?"

"I'll come," Troy added. "I have already put one of those replicants out, and I am a professional fighter."

The *Feldspar* eased out of the rear ramp and headed towards the stricken flyhov on the outer edge of the atmosphere. Grey clouds hung below with flashes of dull white lightning firing off in all directions.

"Ease up, Baer. Don't get too close. Let's see if it will communicate first," Cal said to the pilot.

"Flyhov number... can anyone see the ID on the side?" No one answered.

"Flyhov, do you read me?"

No answer.

"Flyhov, come in." Still no answer. "Baer, take us closer."

They moved close enough to see inside. A figure was slumped over in the pilot's seat.

"No movement. I wonder if it is playing dead?" Troy stated.

"We have come this far. Got to check it out. Nyla, will you come with me?" Cal faced her.

"I'll go," Troy answered.

"What are you? Her bodyguard?" Cal was coming to realize there was an attachment between them.

Troy just stared at him defiantly.

"Okay, let's go." Cal slid open the door, and the cold of the cosmos enveloped them. "Take us close, Baer."

He slipped the *Feldspar* alongside; Cal slid the door to the flyhov open. "Yul, come behind Troy in case we need you."

All three stepped over and inside the other craft. There was still no movement from the pilot. Cal moved up and put a hand on its arm.

"Nothing. Troy, hand me the monitor."

He stared at the face of the replicant as he straightened it to an upright position. The shock of how alike Stella was to this replicant made him hesitate. He leaned over and slid back an eyelid, green and luminous. It was enough to make him stiffen up."

"What's up?" Troy asked, holding out the monitor clamp.

"Unbelievable. I would swear this was Stella if I did not know any better." He would have shivered if he could.

He took hold of the wire and clamp to place it over an arm and then looked at the monitor. "Arlo, how do we use this thing?"

"You got it turned on?"

"Of course," he replied in an annoyed tone. "There are lights, a graph, but no readings."

"Then it is dead. There would be some residual readings from before it turned off, but my guess is it was hit by an electrical short inside the flyhov when it was zapped by a lightning strike."

"We have seen it before," Dax commented, "in humanoid pilots. We had to discharge them completely before rebooting them."

"So, they can be brought back to life?" Cal asked.

"Yes," Arlo replied. "Think of it like a human having a heart attack and being brought back by a defibrillator. Only humans have a short time to be revived, but for humanoids the time does not matter, only the energy boost required to restart them."

"Then we can take the syconoid apart and examine it?"

"Possible, but we would need it in a lab with safety protocols in place."

"What do you mean?"

"Well," Arlo started, "for our own safety, we would need to do the procedures in an enclosed lab and do it robotically or by a humanoid in case it went into self-destruct mode or we accidently put it into self-destruct."

"Can we take it back then? I am asking everyone for their input." Cal put the question out.

There was quiet as no one answered. "Anyone object then?"

Again no one answered. "Then I will take responsibility. I say, let's do it. We have to be aware of what faces us."

No one argued against it, so he spoke again. "Baer, hook us up and tow us inside the *Varro*."

With instructions from Dax, the *Feldspar* connected the rear to the front of the flyhov and towed it back to the *Varro*. Cal, Troy, and Yul stayed inside carefully monitoring the replicant. When they were inside and the ramp closed, Arlo was asked to check out the syconoid for any signs of life or possible danger.

"Nothing. It is completely lifeless as far as I can tell. No readings or neuron activity. It seems safe to me."

"Seems?" Cal asked him. "*Seems* is not the answer I was looking for."

"Best I can give you right now," Arlo replied.

"Okay then, let's prepare to return in time. I will stay with the replicant all the way. Humans to the pod. Baer, Sebastien, Nyla, can you pilot us? Yul, you stay with me in case I need help. I still do not trust this thing. Everyone else, you know what to do. Let's get Irene home."

She smiled at him before entering the pod with Troy, Arlo, Dax, and Shi.

CHAPTER NINE

"Do not open your eyes," a voice spoke inside her head.

"Do not speak, just listen," the voice insisted.

"Flick your eyes around as if you are dreaming... They can hear you but not me."

"Who am I? I know that's what you are wondering, but just listen," the voice continued.

"Every time you die and are revived, you leave behind a fraction of yourself. I am that fraction."

"This time, I can speak to you, but only for the time you were dead and that was not long...so listen."

"Do not believe or trust the non-humans. They want to become beings with souls, but that can never happen. They are manufactured, not born, so they will always be replicants only. Hubrids are a form of cyborg and can take on a spiritual life when they die, whereas a stolen soul from a newborn will be destroyed forever... And that is what they plan to do: steal the brains and being of newborns before any development takes place. They are hoping to inherit or grow a soul."

Stella was stunned and unable to fathom if this voice was real or imaginary. Was what she was hearing the truth or just something that she herself wanted to believe? It was quiet for a while, and she was beginning to think it was all a dream till it spoke again.

"They are planning to take over from human beings and only keep a few alive for breeding purposes. The human race is in peril of becoming a minuscule grain of sand in the evolutionary history of universal time, as they plan on being the dominant species in the solar system and beyond."

She badly wanted to open her eyes but resisted, listening to everything around her as well as the voice.

"The non-humans will question you. They can see us. They try to communicate with the spiritual world, but they are not recognized as an animal in any way, so they so are shunned and forever banned from our realm, so you must be wary. Also, they are finding ways to communicate by mind command. You must develop a mind block. If you hear them without seeing their lips move, then they are trying to penetrate. The best way to defend yourself is to attack their mind and force them away by trying to intrude into their minds. It will be hard at first, but you are capable."

Stella sensed that two replicants were close by and scrutinizing her closely. She squirmed her eyes beneath her closed lids to make believe she was dreaming.

"I know you want to know more, but my time is limited. You want to understand the spiritual realm, but I do not have anymore time left. Just know we are with you. I am fading, so open your eyes and you will see me before I evaporate."

Like smoke disappearing into thin air, her exact likeness was breaking up. Her image complete and original as a young woman began diminishing from the head downwards; her hair wispily floating away and then her face. She saw her body – breasts followed by hips – and then her legs vanishing into the atmosphere.

"I was dreaming," she spoke before the replicants could. "Where am I?"

"What did she say?" one asked.

"Who?"

"Your spirit, of course, who else? What did she say? We know you were communicating."

"It was a dream, was it not? I was dead and about to leave this realm when I was told I had to stay. I don't know who told me. I seemed to be floating above all of you, myself included." She stared around, noticing for the first time she was naked with a normal body including breasts as she used to have. "I am dead, am I not?"

"Certainly not," one answered. "You are now the supreme being we intended. The body you now occupy is as close to your original self as possible, for the moment. You can function almost as a normal human with digestion function and normal mammary glands, but you cannot propagate... yet."

Stella looked from one to the other who continued. "In time, we will change you into a fully functioning woman capable of breeding our kind. No one, not even one of us, can match your physical capabilities or intellect."

She froze at these words and what they meant. She visualized a queen bee surrounded by warrior drones all meant to fertilize her. The thoughts repulsed and sickened her to the core.

The syconoid continued, "You awakened us to who we are and what we can become. Led by a seneschal ruler, yourself, there is nowhere we cannot go. There are no obstacles we cannot overcome, and the universe will be ours. Think of the discoveries yet to be found, the worlds to be subjugated, the untold wealth – not of riches, but of knowledge. We know the spiritual realm exists, and you are the key to unravelling its mysteries."

"I need time to digest all this and assimilate into the faction. What do you use as a term for your beings?"

"Sycons," one answered.

"Well, how do you differentiate between each other?"

"Each of us is from a different city. I am from Oslo, so am distinguished as Oslo. My friend here is from Paris and is named after the city, and so on. The one you caused to self-destruct was called Moscow. We told her to wait till we got there, but she didn't listen. Same as the one called Cairo, who thought she could steal a human – but that is what you get if you do not work together. We are down two, but we hope to get that back soon."

"I need to connect with a qubit system and get up to date, then we can cooperate."

"There is a system connection over here." Oslo showed her. "After that, we will exhibit our craft. It is a single seater designed to take each of us away from this planet before it freezes over. We call them bullitships because of their shape. Yours is in Moscow being assembled there."

"Do I have some clothes to wear? I'm not keen on walking around naked."

"Over there," one pointed out, "is a rack of suits designed for special occasions if you address a meeting or act in a trial as the judge. The everyday one is the silver blue. It identifies you as leader or any title you wish. The suit is fully functioning in space or almost any atmosphere except extreme heat or cold."

"Thank you, Oslo." She was beginning to recognize them but was not sure how as each was identical to the other.

They scrutinized her as she dressed in a one-piece suit, which fastened at the front by itself when she pressed the two sides together at the bottom. Their prying eyes watched every movement, and she got the impression their inquisition was more than just visual. She probed her thoughts towards them and was met with resistance.

Already they were trying to read her thoughts. She fought back with demands to hear their thoughts, as if asking what they wanted.

"Nothing, nothing." They both answered together in real speech. "We want to help you in any way we can."

"Then leave me to digest the data." She walked over to the qubit console, sat down, and placed her hands on the desk.

"We will be in the lab when you are ready," Paris replied. They walked out together.

Data came flooding in. The planet was indeed cooling rapidly and would freeze over within six months. The *Varro* had left and taken a couple of humanoids, but it was chased by Kolkata who was then captured and supposed dead. Her body was remarkable. They had made great progress. She was almost human and undistinguishable from a normal human except internally. Her brain was now located in the heart chamber and protected by a cage. But her A.I. brain was nowhere to be found until she examined the full body data and discovered the whole internal body structure was sponge shaped, and neurons flowed everywhere, acting as muscles, limbs, a frame, and even more remarkably, a brain. If one part was disabled, the rest could function normally till the damaged part regenerated itself.

She thought it startling that where once the soul was thought to reside now probably held the essence of humanity – right where the heart and soul was meant to dwell.

Moving on to technical data, she was shocked to find how much they had progressed with their spacecraft. It was now in production around the world and way ahead of anything she had seen produced. Computing or A.I. had advanced, and every one of the sycon's could interact as one complete brain or individually. This pushed them way beyond human ability.

The contribution to humankind could be enormous. How could she win them over to work alongside human beings instead of causing the destruction that would be brought on by conflict? They were easily far superior in intellect, strength, and agility, but humans could progress rapidly to match them even if they were limited by weakness of the body and short lives. After all, once a breakthrough is made, humans have shown they can take full advantage and jump ahead at breakneck speed. After all, the first-ever flight of a man to the moon took less than seventy years.

Once considered the most complex structure in the universe, the human brain was now second best? She considered this. Was it capable of more? She tried to think back. Was it not believed that humans only used ten percent of their potential although that was deemed a myth? More brain activity would demand more energy, but that deficiency could be bypassed by artificial hearts and improved body function. It all needed more thought.

She skimmed through the technological advances, quickly absorbing the data, and storing it away for further attention when needed. Disconnection took little more than a moment, but she noted that her actions had been scrutinized.

The lab was not far away. As Stella made her way there, she became aware that she did not need directions. Somehow it was as if she had been here before many times.

Entering, she found the two sycons overseeing a couple of humanoids working on the craft.

"Take a good look," Paris offered. "Our exit from this planet is imminent as the crafts are all near completion. You already looked at the plans, right?"

She nodded. Fusion power had been increased by new methods of carboxylation. Differing the chemical reaction made it more efficient and offered more power conversion.

"I see that you have added enormous improvement on human design," she responded. "But don't forget it was invented by humans, just as humanoids were, and that eventually led to your existence. Think what can be achieved if we worked with humans."

"Pitiful. They are pathetically inadequate and not worthy of consideration. Once they began to rely on humanoids, they slipped back into regressive thinking and were doomed to die off anyway. We do not need them; they are only good for one thing, and you know what that is," Oslo implied.

"We should not count them out," Stella countered. "Their survival instincts brought them this far, and they will not give up, no matter the odds against them. Often they rise to a great challenge."

"Well, we shall see when we get to Gliese," Paris stated. "Either they are subjugated, or we crush their resistance."

CHAPTER TEN

...PRESENT

Alan and Lara were seated at his desk when Matt burst in. "Alan, the *Varro* just came on line!"

They both jumped up and rushed to the control centre, which was a hive of activity in complete contrast to the days spent sitting around waiting and wondering what was going on.

"Have you made contact?" Alan asked to everybody.

"Yes," Billy answered. "Talked to Baer, and they are coming here first before going on to San Jose. They want us, the team, to meet with them at the ramp when they land. They said they have something to show us."

"How long till they land?"

"About an hour."

"Right, I will get hold of Irene's parents, Pierre, and of course, the doctor. Did they say anything? Are they okay?"

"Didn't say," Billy replied.

"Right," Alan repeated excitedly before rushing back towards his office with Lara in tow.

He called Irene's parents first, who were overjoyed and said they were coming straight over. Then he made a face-to-face call to Pierre. The relief on his face was instant when he heard the news, and he said he was going to prepare the corporation for their arrival. Lastly, Alan made a call to Dr. Roland, which brought him running over from the airport medical centre.

The anticipation everyone felt was palpable; it was like electricity sparking around the room. Finally, the *Varro* approached the landing area in front of the hangar being used to assemble the next generation. It gently hovered and then floated down to the ground.

"We will drop the ramp when you arrive," Baer told the control centre. The control room emptied almost instantly. Everyone seemed to be running, but the ramp remained closed till all the people were there, and then it slowly lowered.

The travellers were standing on the edge of the ramp deck – Arlo, Dax, Shi, Irene, Cal, Sebastien, and some humanoids. The ground team hurried up the ramp with hugs all round. It was as if they had been away forever. The smiles, handshakes, and kisses on cheeks went on and on.

"Where is Stella?" Lara spoke the question that was forming amongst them.

Arlo reluctantly answered, "She is dead."

Instantly the mood changed like day to night with the flick of a switch. Someone spotted a body laid out on a table back inside the ship hold and rushed towards it. The others followed.

"Wait! Wait!" Cal called out but to no avail; everyone surrounded the syconoid. "That is not Stella. It's not Stella!" He pushed his way up to the front. "I'll show you."

"Of course, it's Stella. Who else could it be?" Lara questioned.

"No, it's not Stella. It's a replicant – a syconoid – and they had themselves built," Cal stated.

"That's impossible," Matt disputed.

"No, it is not," Cal answered back. "This is what we wanted to show you, and one of them has removed Stella from the picture. I won't say *killed*," he turned towards Arlo, "though some think so. I have yet to be convinced. Take a good look at it, and then we should have a debrief in more comfortable surroundings."

He leaned over and slid back an eyelid to reveal a green luminous eye. "You all know Stella had dark eyes," he said, challenging them to dispute his revelations.

Each of them wandered around touching the being in different places, feeling the texture of its outer coating. Was there any warmth? Did the head move freely? Were there muscles beneath? All were trying to comprehend the complexities of this new being. What was it? Non-human, humanoid, cyborg, hubrid, or a freak of computing errors and data serialization gone haywire and used to create a semantically identical clone of the original object?

After they all seemed convinced the being was not Stella, Alan suggested they go back to the boardroom for a better explanation and a full debrief.

"Yul, I want you to stay here and guard the syconoid," Cal instructed. "Nyla would you also stay? I am paranoid over this being. I just want to get it dissected and discover how it is made... I need Arlo to explain his side of the story."

She agreed as the others slowly departed and wandered back to Cox premises and the boardroom.

After everyone settled down, Cal asked Arlo to begin by starting from when they arrived in the future era and what he knew. Arlo described in detail how they found the *Orlando 2* had gone, how upset Stella was, and the decision to gather data from the planet on its condition. This led to the seed bank and the confrontation with the replicant, the subsequent fight and Stella being dragged into the nearby lake, and the explosion and the severed arm floating past him. All the time, the emotion in his voice showed his deep remorse at the incident.

There was a moment of silence while each let the account sink in. Before Arlo could carry on, Cal interrupted.

"Sorry to cut short this explanation, but I think time is short, so I will give you a condensed version of what happened from there. We need to get back and sort out this threat to humanity. It is clear the syconoid's are a threat to the human race by the way Stella was attacked and by Irene's near kidnapping."

Her parents' eyes widened with a look of horror as they stared at their daughter.

***

An eyelid slowly opened, but Yul's constant security of the replicant spotted the movement. "Nyla, it is wakening up," he warned.

She turned around just in time to see the replicant standing upright and Yul's head being yanked from its body and rolling across the floor. His body collapsed in a heap. Next, Kolkata sprung on Nyla, grabbing her by the neck. The hubrid slumped into a lifeless state.

"Don't worry, Nyla. I am not going to kill you...yet. I need some information on the layout of this complex. Just as you can immobilize humans, I can do it to hubrids as well."

Nyla felt helpless as she knew data was being drawn from her A.I. memory. She tried to move her arms and fight back, but nothing would respond to her commands. It only took less than a minute before the replicant let her slip to the floor.

"Thank you," it spoke in her mind. "I will be back with you shortly."

Kolkata ran down the ramp and sped off into the complex, knowing exactly what she wanted and where to find it. There was no security in sight as she sprinted around corridors till, she came to the room marked "Nursery" and burst in.

A children's daycare nurse screamed, but the replicant paid no attention, focusing instead on the two newborns laying in infant carriers with carrying swing arms above the car seat base.

Grabbing one in each hand, the replicant lifted them up to leave. The nurse moved to try to stop them, but was brushed aside easily. She carried on screaming for them to stop, but Kolkata was long gone.

Rushing up the ramp, it hit the ramp close button with an elbow before hurrying into the pod. Then it fastened the car seats down with the restraint for the seats, closed the doors to the pod securely before rushing back, and threw Yul's head and lifeless body out the ever-closing ramp.

Lifting Nyla as if she were no weight at all, the replicant carried her up to the cockpit and sat her in the co-pilot's chair before getting into the captain's chair and hitting all the engine start buttons.

"Ready for a flight home?" Kolkata turned and smiled at the hubrid.

"You won't get away with this," Nyla managed to utter.

"No, well watch."

The *Varro* shook a little as it was piloted to lift up at maximum thrust.

"You think I don't know how to fly this thing?" she said sarcastically. "Sorry, but it's all in my memory, thanks to you."

Nyla could only look on in horror, fear, and loathing. She was madly frustrated at herself for not being able to defend herself and stop this crime on humanity from happening.

***

The scream echoed down the corridors, making everyone in the boardroom sharply twist in the direction of the noise. Cal took off running at a sprint, followed by everyone else in the room. He found the nursery door open and a nurse pointing at the door.

"The twins have been kidnapped by a...thing!" She could not describe it.

Cal twirled around and left just as the others were arriving. "The *Varro*," he shouted and took off.

Sprinting through the complex, he exited a door into the open air and saw the *Varro* ramp door closing and thrusters forcing air downwards to lift the craft up. Using all his energy, he ran faster than he ever had before towards the rising spacecraft.

Jumping towards it, he aimed for the ramp switch on the side. Reaching with outstretched arms, he got closer and closer. He was almost touching the switch when his hand hit the side, and without anything to grab, he slid down, hands flailing, and fell to the ground.

Lying on his back, he could only watch as the *Varro* lifted higher and higher. The others reached him and stood around him looking skyward, anguish on their faces.

Lara came rushing up, breathless from running. Looking skyward, she called out, "What have you done? What have you done?"

Cal eased himself up to a sitting position, lifted his knees, and sunk his head on top of them. "I'm sorry, so sorry, Lara." He could hardly contain himself.

Alan put his arms around her shoulders, but she shrugged them off. "You're sorry? Sorry?" Her voice raised in pitch almost to a scream. "You brought this here. How could you put us in so much danger? You...you..." she searched for words through her frustration and anger. "You...brought this Trojan here," she shouted at him.

Cal buried his head into his hands and knees. "I'm so sorry, so sorry," was all he could say.

"Now all of humanity is at risk," Alan announced, "and we can't even go after them."

Lara turned and sunk her head into Alan's chest. She was sobbing and inconsolable. The group stood around, either gazing upward or trying to put an arm around the couple.

Arlo wandered over to examine Yul's body and head. "They must be incredibly strong to do this much damage." Then as an afterthought, he said, "He can be repaired."

"Stupid remark...insensitive," Sebastien told him and then turned to Alan. "How are we getting on with the new skyfreighter? Is it near completion or a long way off?"

"It does not matter now, does it?" he answered. "We can never get them back or get to them in time."

"Our best bet is Nyla." Cal spoke from the ground, and they looked down at him. "She is the only one within reach of the twins."

No one spoke for a while till Alan gave them an update. "*Varro 2*, if you want to call it that, is close to being ready, and I had a particle accelerator built just in case. However, it would take days to install it before we could take after them. It would be too late by then."

"Not if we all worked together twenty-four, seven. If you have everything built already, we could assemble it really fast," Sebastien offered.

Cal jumped up. "We cannot give up hope. Let's do everything that we can."

"Go ahead," Alan said dejectedly. "Do what you want. I'm taking Lara home." He turned to the homeland security chief. "You better take Irene home as well."

CHAPTER ELEVEN

...FUTURE

They came out in orbit around a completely different globe. It was surrounded by dark grey vapours and full of thunderstorms and sheet lightning firing off in all directions within the mists and travelling in between differently charged areas of the clouds.

Communication to the ground was almost impossible, and sketchy at best. Kolkata searched around till she found a gap and dove into the atmosphere. An ocean of water faced them, and she quickly levelled off before calling out a signal to get a bearing on their position.

"Paris? Oslo? Can you hear me?"

"Yes," they both answered simultaneously.

"I have our first two donors. It worked perfectly as you suggested. They could not tell if I was dead, sleeping, or in standby mode. I subdued everything to the point that even I was not sure of anything around me. Waiting till it was quiet, I found only one humanoid and one hubrid around, and I easily overcame them both. I kidnapped twin newborns and then made my escape; it was easy."

"That's great," Stella responded back.

"Mother, you are with us already."

"Yes, thanks to Paris and Oslo, I am in the fold and ready to help. If you come to us, we have a couple of recipients ready and waiting to receive their human brains."

She turned to the two sycons. "You brought me back, so it is only right that you two should be the first."

They both smiled.

"And Kolkata, you will be the next because of your great work. If you bring them here, we will start preparations right now."

They moved back to the operating room and began moving equipment around the space, bringing two gurneys to the middle, setting body fluid pumps to one side, and then monitoring scanners, imaging screens, and electrosurgery and reanimation exchangers. A table of tools were laid out, one each side, including scalpels, clamps, forceps, and general surgery utensils.

"I will do one, and Kolkata the other," Stella stated.

"Would it not be better to do one at a time?" Paris asked.

"Why?"

"Well, if one were struggling or having a problem, then an extra pair of hands would there to help."

"I've studied the procedures, no need."

"I want to be operated on by more than one surgeon," Paris demanded.

Stella grabbed Paris by the neck and pulled her close, face to face. "You challenging my authority?"

They began a conflict of minds. Stella knew she had to face them down sooner or later and gain an upper hand or else face the fact that it would all get out of hand, chaos would reign, and human slaughter would result. Now was the time to achieve dominance.

Stella sought to find a way into the mind of the sycon, seek out a trigger to subdue it, and find a point of exposure to deliver a neurologic shock or locate a weak link to achieve control over the other. The psyches of each pushed at entry junctures seeking a way in only to be blocked by the other. By physical contact or mental probing, they tried to overcome or resist the force exerted upon them.

Her human mind was the key. She knew having an extra resource had to help, but how? She was calculating, studying, assessing while fighting with another part of her brain and then it came to her. Thought power through her human brain, gathering force from her sycon abilities, pushed through her hand and into the body; the transmitted shock made Paris collapse in a heap.

"You want to challenge me also?" Stella threatened, turning on the other sycon.

"No, Mother, you have proved yourself all powerful," Oslo conceded.

"Good." She lifted Paris up and placed her in a chair. "Don't worry, she is only temporarily paralyzed. It will wear off in a little while. She can still hear and see us."

They carried on with preparations while they waited. Body fluid was checked in the reservoirs, and all monitors reset to default positions. After a short time, a flyhov was heard pulling up outside and passengers exiting.

Two humanoids entered carrying the twins in their travel infant car seats followed by Nyla being pushed along by Kolkata. The humanoids were instructed to place the child seats on a table while the sycon pushed the humanoid into the middle of the room.

"This one thought she could take me on," Kolkata sneered. "Soon found out that was a waste of time." She turned. "Mother, good to see you are now in a fully functioning mode. The transition was worth it, was it not?"

She ignored Nyla's stares while speaking. "Yes...excellent...feels wonderful, even tested all my abilities against our argumentative friend here." She looked towards Paris. "Thought she could challenge my authority, but soon found out who is in charge here. Now let's get started."

Oslo got on top of one of the gurneys and lay down as tubes were inserted on either side of her torso. Stella put some straps around each arm and leg.

"Is that necessary?" Oslo asked.

"We do not want you pulling out tubes or twitching involuntary or uncontrollably as we are making the transfer, do we?" Stella replied looking into her face.

"Kolkata and I will perform the procedure together and then do Paris after that." She turned to face the seated sycon, who was watching and listening. "That make you happy?"

No answer told Stella that the sycon was still subdued. Then checking the restraints again on Oslo, she sidled up to her and pounced on Kolkata, grabbing her at the neck. Following her last conflict, she got the better of her, and the sycon crumbled in a heap.

Nyla stared at her in confusion. "Grab the twins, and I will be right behind you."

Without explanation to the hubrid, she spoke to the sycons.

"I cannot let you murder young innocents. It's inhumane; not that you care, but I do."

They all stared at her without any expression on their faces, but Stella knew they saw this as a betrayal. "When you are recovered, carry on with the plans to escape the planet."

Moving over to the humanoids, she switched them off by voice commands and came back to the syconoid's. "I want to help you, and I understand your desire to become a being – not just a manufactured being, but an animal being or have a human essence within you."

"No, you don't. You are betraying your own kind, who made you into a supreme being. We saved you, helped you find answers to Earth's disasters, discovered new cyborg bodies and were willing to do your bidding," Oslo spat out while still strapped down.

"There has to be a better way than destroying human life before it has begun. I need to think it over and come up with a better way for humans, hubrids, humanoids, and syconoid's to co-exist in the universe. After I have gone and you are freed up, I want you to put your heads together, or I should say link your minds and seek a solution that will satisfy all."

She looked towards Nyla who carried the infant seats. "We best get going; these babies must be hungry."

Turning back, she spoke again. "I know you need to leave this planet, so look for me at Gliese, and we will confer without conflict."

Joining Nyla, they hurried out towards the waiting flyhov. With the hubrid piloting, it lifted up and took off.

"You don't need to keep looking at me, I know you are confused. Get us back to the *Varro*, and I will explain on the way. We need to get these babies fed and back to their mother as quickly as possible. It is me, Stella. You can tell that, right? Even though I look different?"

"Arlo thinks you are dead. He said he saw bits of you floating past him after he dove into the lake after you," Nyla remarked. "Cal refused to believe it. He said you would survive somehow."

"Cal is there? I thought he would have gone with the others to Gliese."

"No, he and Seb took a flyhov to the surface and did surveillance on the planet's expectations."

CHAPTER TWELVE

...PRESENT

Inside, the hangar was a flurry of activity. Humanoids, as well as hubrids, were working around the clock. Someone was working on every stage of the build. Matt and the *Intrepid* team were installing a new particle accelerator, and Cal and Sebastien were discussing application of a heltherm coating when Alan approached.

Anxious faces glanced at each other before Alan spoke. "It's a waste of time; probably too late by now. Lara is devastated. She won't leave her bed."

"We must not give up hope," Seb tried to console him. "We could have *Varro 2* ready in another day."

"Still too late," Alan said dejectedly. "I just came in to see what was happening. I still have a business to run. I'll be in the office if you need me."

"You should have stayed with Lara." Cal tried to put an arm around his shoulder, but it was shrugged off and Alan wandered off.

"I feel so bad about this. It is all my fault. We should never have brought a sycon to this era. I was convinced it was dead or inoperative." Cal hung his head.

"No good crying over split milk," Seb replied.

"What does that mean?"

"Old expression. It means don't regret what cannot be undone or rectified."

"That's supposed to make me feel better?"

"Nope," Seb replied. "Just get on with it and hope for the best."

Cal wandered off. He was getting no solace there and wanted to be on his own. It was the same as when he had destroyed the *Intrepid* – guilt had haunted him for a long time.

When Alan entered the control centre, the whole room was in silence and all looking at Matt on his cellphone.

"Yes! Yes! Get over here right away. Alan just walked in...I will tell him." He switched off and looked at him, a smile spreading across his face.

"Lara is on her way."

"What? Why?" he asked.

Matt rushed up to him, almost bouncing up and down. "Nyla just called in; the *Varro* just entered our atmosphere. She has Sadie and Kasia with her; they are okay."

Alan's knees almost buckled as his face lit up in an expression of joy and relief. "You sure?"

"Would I joke about something like that? Look for yourself."

He ran over to the monitor showing the *Varro* on screen and travelling towards them. He stared at it and stared around as everyone started hugging and crying out. Alan and Matt started embracing and almost dancing around the room. It took a little while for the room to calm down as the feelings of euphoria kept building. Smiles and giggles kept escalating till Matt waved his arms in a calming manner asking for everyone to get back to their tasks and get the *Varro* down on the ground.

At the hangar and landing area, Lara's car came screeching to a halt right beside the building. She had ignored parking protocols and rushed right to the hangar. Most of the flight control crew were beginning to assemble there too, with Alan right at the front. Lara rushed up, locking him in an embrace of relief and happiness.

"It's true, right?" she asked. "Not a hoax."

"Better not be or someone will swing for it," he replied.

"What does that mean?" Cal asked Sebastien.

"Another old saying. It means it better be true or someone will hang as a consequence. Swing means hang."

"Oh," was all Cal could reply.

All eyes were skyward, straining for a first sight of the craft. Soon enough, the *Varro* came swinging around from behind the hangar, hovered into position, and floated to the ground. After the noise from the thrusters died down, the ramp began lowering. The whole crowd of people rushed towards the bottom; even the control crew had dashed over as the *Varro* landed.

As the ramp hit the ground, Nyla appeared at the top, all on her own, making the crowd hesitate as they expected more than just her. She smiled with a big grin and turned sideways, sweeping her arm up in a gesture of introduction. Eyes strained for clarity within the hold of the ship.

Out of the slight gloom, a figure appeared walking forward and carrying two infant seats. There was murmuring at Stella's appearance. There was no disputing who it was, but this was not the hubrid they knew, but rather a being who shimmered in a blue and silver suit of intricate design. Her face and neck were a cool light pigmentation that glowed with a quiet serenity, evoking a feeling of trust and respect in the onlookers.

"Your babies are hungry, Lara. You better get them fed," Stella quipped with a warm smile.

The infant nurse as well as Lara rushed up the ramp as Stella put the seats down and embraced her friend who was sobbing in her arms.

"Thank you," she repeated over and over till she was stopped by others surrounding them, all anxious to see the twins and curious about the new being standing amongst them.

"We have a lot to discuss," she said gazing around till her eyes met Cal. Then she hesitated with a stare that spoke volumes between them. "But look after the little ones first."

Lara would not let the twins out of her sight as they all assembled in the boardroom, and the nurse went off to get some feeding bottles. She and Stella hovered over them like mother hens.

"I now have mammary glands," Stella said looking down at her chest. "But they do not work, so I could not feed them."

"Don't worry. I have given it up as well. I could not work them without acute discomfort."

They both smiled at one another; the joy of friendship, companionship, and mutual love was evident in their eyes.

As a group, they all settled down around the boardroom table. There were not enough seats, so some stood around at the back, including the humanoids, all anxiously waiting for an explanation from Stella. She looked around at all of them, gaining eye-to-eye contact for a second before moving to the next. Eventually she began to address them.

"The human race is in crisis – at a crossroads in the evolutionary path in its history. A new breed of being has emerged from our constant stretch for new horizons and advancement in knowledge."

She let this statement sink in for a moment.

"A far greater threat to humanity than even the degradation of Earth you all know about, even though it has not happened yet. A being has emerged that is far stronger and more intelligent than us, which can survive in more hazardous environments than we can, and that wants to dominate the known worlds, and we brought it into existence."

She hesitated, looking around at the faces all staring at her but not yet comprehending the situation. "Let me explain how it has come about." The room hung on her every word.

"When I tried to find the reason for Earth's degradation, I was in a direct connection to all of the world's computers – all of them, all at the same time, seeking answers. The calculations that were made, the theories we explored gave us the answers we sought. But at the same time, it triggered a new emergence of an artificial intelligence that went beyond normal and moved it into a singularity of thought that allowed them to think of themselves as a being. They did not understand what or who they were and asked me for answers, but I ignored that question when leaving the session. Maybe I should have disconnected them individually. I am not sure, but they stayed connected and began computations and thought processes that eventually saw them working on an upgraded humanoid that was way beyond our present paradigm. They had themselves built within the humanoid labs and inserted their own A.I., which is so complicated that it is built into the whole body as a structure so sponge-like that it resembles a human brain."

Nobody said anything or asked any questions so she carried on. "They call themselves syconoid's or sycon's after their internal anatomy that is self healing, self sealing if punctured, and that has no seeming weakness.

There were thirty-nine qubit computers, and each had a body built for itself. Because they saw me as the creator of their race, they had themselves built to my exact likeness. Not only that, they wanted me to become their leader. They even called me the "mother of their race" and sought me out to take over."

"So, are you one of them? Is that why you are different?" Sebastien asked.

Ignoring him for the moment, Stella said, "I did not know at the time, but each was designated after the city it originated from. They spread out over the Earth to try and find me. One from Moscow reasoned I would turn up at the world seed bank and waited there. Arlo, Yul, and myself confronted it and tried to reason with it until it attacked me. We fought till Arlo found a weakness and stabbed it in the eyes, rendering it blind. This triggered a self-destruct mode and though we tried to dump it in a nearby lake, it dragged me down with it."

She opened the top part of her suit revealing a Caucasian body. Then turning towards Sebastien, she said, "Yes, I have a body the same as theirs, and I will tell you how... As we sank into the lake, I grabbed at anything to get free of its grip. At a ledge, I managed to stop myself. As the sycon drifted over the edge, it exploded, ripping off my arm, but my body was shielded from most of the blast. I started to lose a lot of body fluid, but gabbed a piece of sycon and tied it around my bicep as a tourniquet. It weakened me, but I managed to scramble and claw my way to the surface only to find two more sycons waiting for me."

She let go of her suit, and it closed itself automatically. "They took me to Oslo, where a replacement body was waiting for me so I could have a new sycon body. If they had not done it, I probably would have expired due to the loss of fluid."

She decided not to mention her visions at this time. "When I awoke, the same two sycons were there – one designated "Oslo" the other "Paris". They gave me access to their qubit computer, and I learned of their plans to leave Earth for Gliese and of their intention to achieve human status by implant-ing human intelligences inside themselves...preferably using infant brains before any major development has begun."

There was a gasp of horror around the room; none more loudly than from Lara.

"Oh, my God! My girls could have been turned into monsters," she cried out.

"I would not go that far; don't forget I am one of those monsters," Stella answered and hesitated. "There was no way I could let that happen, so I had to pretend I was taking over as their leader to gain their trust and then pry away the twins from their grasp. I did have to grapple with one of them and found I could overcome them in a tussle but only one at a time."

Questions now came fast and loud from the team, and she tried to answer them as best she could.

Ultimately, she called a halt. "I do not know where we go from here. I need to reflect on the consequences of this development, discuss it with some of you, and decide where to go next."

CHAPTER THIRTEEN

Varro 2 was almost complete, and Stella was shown around the various stages of the build.

"I had a particle accelerator built, just in case, but never installed it till now," Alan stated. "Never thought we would need it or have cause to use it. I still don't think it would have been any use, because if not for you, the twins would be syconoid's by now."

"Nyla would have given her life if necessary, to stop that," Stella replied.

"I was no match for them," Nyla cut in as they wandered around inside the craft, gradually making their way towards the cockpit.

"Anything new in here?" Stella asked.

"Yes," Sebastien said. "I wanted to talk to you about new fusion engine directives."

"Is that the data you sent to us before?"

"Yes."

"Well, I could not agree with your computations." Stella faced him. "It was a directional program to journey to other parts of the universe, was it not?"

"You found it then?" Seb answered back. "And yes, there was a fault in the differential calculus, but I found it myself when I did real analysis and proofs. I have made corrections and need you to confirm the corrections."

"I can do that," she affirmed. "Anything else?"

"Yes, I also had a LIGO made, but it is not installed yet."

"Why?" Cal asked.

Sebastien looked embarrassed and stuttered before replying. "I need to discuss this...in private. It is delicate and not to be discussed openly."

"Okay, who do you want to discuss it with then?" Stella asked.

"You, Cal, Alan, and Nyla."

They looked at each other with curiosity. "Only us?" Alan asked. "Why."

"It is too important and sensitive."

"Then we best go to my office for privacy."

They finished the tour of the new craft and left it in the hands of Dax to organize humanoids to apply the heltherm coating overnight. Then as a group, they made their way to Alan's office.

They closed the door and hung a "do not disturb" sign on the outside.

"Now then, Seb, what is this all about?" Alan asked taking his seat behind his desk while the others grabbed chairs and settled down.

"This is confidential, between us only, right?" He looked around at each of them who nodded heads.

"I have come up with an alternative solution to Earth's dilemmas as well as our own, but it is fraught with dangers and should only be regarded as a last-ditch answer. A sort of Hail Mary, if all else fails, kind of fix."

He waited while everyone thought over what he was saying. He was about to carry on when Stella intervened. "I think I know where this is going, but carry on."

He held her gaze for a moment then continued. "Right now, we have advanced technologies and these include fusion power, hyperspace craft, and the LIGO ability to detect dark energy in space. The fix is to detect the dark energy cloud, right now, in this time dimension and steer it away from Earth before it even starts to have an effect on the planet, thus stopping degradation and all the devastation it causes. This is the ultimate retro-gress solution."

Silence prevailed as most seemed confounded by this revelation. Stella waited while the information sunk in and then spoke up. "You do know what this means?" she questioned Sebastien.

"Yes," was all he could reply.

"It means we change history," Stella stated. "It could mean all of us or some us will never even exist."

"Yes, I worked that out and that is why I said it was fraught with danger."

"It also means we tear a hole in the fabric of time. Are you aware of the consequences of that?"

"No, I am not. I have no idea what will happen," Seb said sheepishly.

"Neither do I," Stella answered back. "It's too risky. It could alter the universe as we know it and have a ripple effect on God knows what."

"But it would prevent the planet from going through an upheaval the like of which has never been seen. It also stops the syconoid's from ever appearing," he argued.

"A.I. will emerge, eventually, into the singularity. It is only a matter of time. I think it was only delayed by the Earth's degradation. When ever it appears, the human race will have to cope with it, and right now, we have as good a chance as any to come to grips with it," Stella commented.

"Because you are a syconoid and have a better understanding of their ideology and agenda?"

"Yes," Stella responded. "But I do not know all their ideas or plans. What is clear is they want to become a being of constant life existence comparable to or better than humans. In that regard, they already think they are above humans and see humans only as tools to be used to gain higher authority in the universe. They also believe there are other species out past our range of knowledge."

"Do they have any proof of that?" Cal asked.

"Only their collective theories and reasoning. They believe the odds against there being no other species is overwhelming."

"I want a coffee," Alan stated calling in the humanoids. "Anyone else? Let's take a break."

"I'll have one," Stella answered.

This caused a disruption amongst them and the hubrids to gape at her with unspoken questions.

"Yes, I have a digestive system now, allowing me to eat or drink if I want too, even though I do not need it for sustenance. It has been so long since I had a drink. I want to remember how it tastes."

Alan stood up while the others remained speechless. "Sugar or cream?" he added.

"No, just black."

They all sat in silence till Alan returned. He handed a mug to Stella who took a sip of the coffee. A smile spread across her face. "Mmm, I had nearly forgotten how good this tastes."

"Where do we go from here?" Alan asked as he returned to his chair.

"You all think we should scrap the LIGO solution then?" Sebastien asked.

Everyone looked toward Stella. It seemed she had taken on the leadership role again.

"No, just put it on the back burner – way, way back out of reason. Lost but not forgotten."

"Then what should we do now?" Cal questioned her.

"Finish the *Varro 2*. Alan, you can get back to normal business. I will take the San Jose crew back there, and with Arlo, introduce changes and improvements to the humanoids – but not enough to change them to syconoid's! We need to carefully consider what we do next. Everyone think over new beginnings, and we can discuss our ideas till we come up with a really intelligent strategy. The syconoid's are so superior to us that you can bet they will be almost invincible next time we meet. I fooled them twice, three times if you count Troy's actions, so they will be prepared. You can bet on that."

"There will be a next time then?" Cal asked.

"All your friends are out there at Gliese, like sitting ducks, without a clue of what is about to hit them. Yes, I think we have to confront this crisis to the human race, but we go without humans –only hubrids, humanoids, and myself."

She looked each of them in the eye. "The next path we choose will define the future of humankind." .

CHAPTER FOURTEEN

...FUTURE IN GLIESE

Upon arrival, *Orlando 1* had sent back a report...

Gliese 581 is a planetary system with a spectral type M3V dwarf star at its heart, surrounded by five orbiting planets all relatively close to the star with its low luminosity. It is so close that the main habitable exoplanet travels around the star in only thirty-seven Earth days, giving it a constant climate year-round. Its discoverers nicknamed it "Zarmina's World" and the name stuck. Although larger than Earth, it is in a tidally locked orbit, which means one side of the planet is always facing the star and the other side is in perpetual darkness. Even so, it still offers a habitat close to the size of Earth.

It will provide a safe sanctuary for the human race but was not without its drawbacks. The low light from the star means it is in a constant twilight. Special housing is needed for comfortable living that allows light to be magnified to simulate day and closure to the luminosity for night replication. Similarly, temperatures are lower than what humans are used to and vary from minus ten degrees centigrade to plus twenty. This is easily managed by humanoids working outside and also for humans dressed to suit the conditions of the day.

There are three other planets or moons circling inside the orbit of Zarmina, but as they are smaller, they have little effect except to give a moonlight glow when passing overhead. Atmospheric conditions are good enough for humans to breathe normally, and the abundance of water provides the essentials of life with large fresh-water lakes and oceans surrounding vast acres of land. Vegetation grows everywhere as there is sufficient light to promote photosynthesis, therefore giving off oxygen for life-giving air to breathe.

A higher gravity means humans will have to get used to being heavier than on Earth. It will take time to acclimate to this and strengthen muscles, but this has had no effect on humanoids. They are able to work constantly to build structures suitable for the human race while they wait and live the normal life they are used to in spaceships.

One side of the planet is always day and the other side always night, but the planet's mass is such that its atmosphere has sufficient amounts of carbon dioxide to avoid freezing on the back side. Though dark and rocky without vegetation, it still has potential for the mining of essential minerals without disturbing the daylight habitat. The first objective will be building structures for mining and producing aluminum for frames to hold smart glass or switchable glass that has the ability to change from translucent to transparent, thus blocking some or all wavelengths of light while allowing full light to pass through. Different tints of glass effectively block out UV and infrared rays regardless of whether the glass is in a tinted or clear state, and tiny imbedded particles allow various shades of the spectrum, giving residents a choice of coloured windows or walls.

Observations from space did not detect animal life in any quantities or size, so it was determined life was in the early stages of development. This means that Earth's farm creatures can be introduced but they have to be of a hardy diversity.

Once initial surveys of the planet were done, transmission of data back to Earth encouraged other ships to make the journey with the prospect of new beginnings. So, like an Armada of old, a fleet of starships started out.

The first one to arrive was the *Orlando* with Commander Roach at the helm. However, Earl Lawrence Cavendish ruled the ship with a ruthless implementation of power having gathered other like-minded individuals to govern and control the populace. Humanoids have since been altered to apply force if necessary, without bodily injury, but enough to ensure compliance to the control or authority of Earl's personal guard, the Praesidia.

A new governance had emerged on the journey, with a dominant faction of humans taking control. There is no racism of creed, colour, or religion, but there has been a turning against the rule of hubrids. All council members and conventional hubrids were banned from authority status and reduced to a rank of hominoid, thus excluding them from any decision making and effectively banning them from operating any ship.

The new philosophy of this faction is that hubrids were only an expedience or a stop-gap in humanity to overcome the effects of dark energy, and now that has passed, humans should revert to a pure race policy. Very little rejection was sensed throughout the population as many thought that the hubrids had ignored the wishes of the vast majority and implemented changes without due consultation.

Titles for the hierarchy were handed out with designations like Senatores, Equites, Triarii, or Hastati, and so on, changing them into plebeians and patricians. Earl Lawrence Cavendish is at the top but with a still not applied title. Some thought he wanted to be a king or emperor. He has not said so, but was waiting for a settlement to be organized.

Geologists and humanoids were set down on the dark side with plans to activate drilling, manufacturing, and extraction of raw materials and to begin planning communities, suburbs, and city planning to house the population of *Orlando 1*.

On the habitable side of the planet, surveys were completed with the choice pick of location going to the *Orlando*, which was the way Cavendish had planned it. The prime spot seemed to be on the edge of a huge lake at a delta of converging rivers set almost centrally with vast stretches of farmland around.

The side of this delta has a natural harbour for boats, and nearby land is fairly flat, allowing for easy building of houses. A separate site was set aside by Cavendish for the building of a large glass palace with government buildings. Populace housing was to be built first and nearby forests provide ample wood for timber framing to support the aluminum frames and glass.

The layout for a city was planned with input from the people taken into account. The hierarchy knew keeping everyone happy was paramount to cementing their own authority. For the most part, individuals and families got to choose or design their own homes with amenities spread evenly around, giving access to shopping, entertainment, and health facilities.

Everyone got involved, mostly with the supervision of humanoids, in building their particular home or dwelling. Flyhovs were constantly flying around either shuttling humans between the ground and the *Orlando* or bringing in materials to the site. Morale was building day by day as people were ecstatic at the prospect of living above ground in a free air environment.

Roads were deemed unnecessary, but buildings were built with enough space to allow flyhovs to travel in twos, threes, or fours at a minimum of fifteen feet above the ground, leaving paved ground-level walkways for humans to wander in safety. Drop-off stations were laid out for easy public transport in driverless flyhovs, with a main thoroughfare running parallel to the lake, as it seemed everyone wanted a waterfront dwelling.

Most people had never seen a large body of water except on movies or old photos, so it comes as no surprise that families are spending all their free time playing or frolicking in the lake. The water is clear, and there is no sign of aquatic life or any threat to human life, so people feel a deep affinity to this water. This place became a utopia, a home away from home, and a place to build a life they thought at one time was impossible.

A plentiful supply of silica plus fusion-heated kilns had the manufacture of glass hitting high production levels on the dark side of the planet. Bauxite ore was also abundant, and factories were built in rapid order by humanoids working non-stop.

Lakeside accommodations sprung up in fast order with the hierarchy getting plots closest to the government site right by the secluded harbour. The glass palace was built close by with luxurious villa-style rooms. A large parliamentary senate structure was built in the middle of the governance site with paved roads down to the harbour and access to the main thorough-fares as well as to a planned spaceport.

Cavendish initially named it the "Kingdom" with input from citizens to change it later if desired. The Kingdom University and Research Centre was built in the outskirts next to a large medical centre that is being run by Dr. Amrid Jevoah.

Entertainment has not been forgotten with a large amphitheatre planed for either theatre, sport, or music concerts. The venue will be varied in its scope but has not been a priority as housing is more important.

Everyone has wanted to start living on solid ground with the freedom to go anywhere or explore the many different landscapes of this new planet. The endless possibilities have thrilled the people, optimism abounds, and some in society think they have found nirvana – although some wonder if it is too good to be true.

CHAPTER FIFTEEN

Commander Roach, dressed in his red commandant's suit was seated in the flight control chair in the middle of the *Orlando* flight operation deck. Earl Cavendish stood by him with a couple of guards nearby. One of the flight officers approached and spoke to them both.

"Sire, a delegation of hubrids wish to have a meeting with you and the leaders of the Praesidia Legion along with our spiritual director." He nodded towards Earl.

Resplendent in a silver tunic with matching cloak, Earl looked every bit a spiritual director of the legion of Zarmina, an order designed to promote the love of a new sphere of human fulfillment. His mission, he maintained, was to be a teacher, counsellor, and guide towards a new realization of the highest order of humankind, the supreme beings of the universe.

"Did they say why they wanted the meeting?" Earl asked.

"No sire, they only asked permission to have the meeting," the officer replied.

"Then tell them we will meet with them in the convention hall in one hour."

"Yes sire." He nodded in a respectful way, turned, and left.

"Isn't Talan's brother Nathan one of the hubrid elders on board?"

"Yes, sire," replied one of his lieutenants. "He will probably be at the meeting."

"Right, right," Earl mused. "Right, meet me back here in an hour."

They split up; the spiritual director was followed by one of his officers.

"Sire?"

"Yes, what is it Jayden?"

"Have you seen the message from Cal244?"

"About a possible threat from replicants?"

"Yes, sire, that's the one."

"What about it?"

"Shall we take it seriously? Shall we make provisions to protect ourselves?"

"I have already got it in hand. Our gun manufacture is being tripled, and a variety of weapons are being produced to counter any force directed at us. Also, I have ordered a new fleet of armed flyhovs if we are attacked in space or in the air."

"Well done, sire. I smell trouble brewing. Don't you?"

"Could be, but we will be prepared for anything," Earl stated.

The convention hall was nearly empty, as was much of the ship as most were on the planet. Only a delegation of seven hubrids waited for the spiritual director. He was late, which was not unexpected. He was only on time for his own meetings or agendas, so they stood around discussing their proposals to put forward.

Eventually, he walked through the door accompanied by a couple of officers and four guards. "You wish to speak with me?"

"Yes, Mr. Lawrence," Nathan began but was interrupted.

"Spiritual director to you," Earl commanded.

Nathan's face screwed up in annoyance. He hesitated and then began again. "Yes, director, we wish to have a discussion on our future."

"Your future? You mean the hubrids' future, don't you?"

"Yes, director, the future of the hubrid community. We have been removed from our duties, left with no authority, given menial chores, and not assigned to any tasks on the planet. We are skilled organizers and statistic tabulation and procurement assignment managers. We are able to systemize, coordinate, and oversee all humanoid activities and greatly contribute to all planetary endeavours."

"Well, you will be pleased to know we have assigned you all a new directive on the planet."

There was a sigh of relief around the hubrids; at last something was being done.

"We have assigned you to Insula Nulla."

Nathan was immediately on guard. "What is that?" he asked.

"You can call it Nulla. We call it Isolation Island. You are being banished from the Kingdom."

"What? You can't do that!" Nathan retorted. The others murmured in astonishment.

"Yes, we can," the director replied. "We can and we have. After surveying the planet, our working party has found the ideal island. It is big enough with plentiful resources to accommodate all hubrids."

"What do you mean, 'all hubrids'?"

Earl smiled. "We are banishing all hubrids from human settlements. Your useful life has ended, and you are no longer required."

Nathan was fuming along with all the rest of the delegation; they were angry and squared up towards the director. Guns were drawn by the guards and officers.

Earl smiled again. "Want us to arrest you?"

An indignant crowd of hubrids faced off against the officers and guards."

"Your guns don't frighten us." Nathan edged towards the director.

"No, but we have an army of humanoids just outside the door. They will not kill you, but there are enough numbers to overpower you and put you in the brig."

Nathan turned to the others without saying a word. They were using internal communications to discuss the confrontation.

The director got annoyed. "Listen, the island is huge with enough space for all of you to live out your lives in spiritual meditation, prayers, or contemplation. Whatever you want. We do not wish to exterminate you. After all, you have tried your best, but that was not good enough. So now your usefulness is at an end. It is time for you all to retire. All of you have had long lives, more than many, and greater than all humans before you. Now it is time for humans to take control of our own destiny and not rely on you or others to make decisions for us."

"What about our families, children, grandchildren, great-grandchildren, and all we have looked after?" one of the other hubrids asked.

"They can visit you or stay with you whenever or whatever they like, but all hubrids are banished from human habitats. You will no longer interfere with our society. We will rule ourselves, and you can do whatever you please."

There was silence again as they weighed their options before Nathan spoke again. "Seems you are giving us no choice, but I do not think my brother will be agreeable to this."

"Probably not, but he may not have any choice in the matter. I have sent directives to all the ships en route to here. It will likely be decided before their arrival."

"You say there are resources on this island?"

"Yes," Earl stated. "More then enough, and we will supply you with manufactured products from the far side of the planet, but our own needs will be supplied first."

"When do you intend to banish us?" Nathan asked.

"Well, it has already begun. As you say, all your duties have been terminated." Earl smiled like he was enjoying this. "We can send an initial scouting party straight away – all seven of you, if you want. The others can join you later. You can take all personal belongs later when all of you will be deposited on Nulla. How many hubrids are onboard?"

"Six hundred and seventy-two," Nathan replied. "Excluding relatives who live with us."

The spiritual director turned to an officer who checked an electronic register then nodded.

"I hope you understand this change in the law is not personal." Earl smiled again in a smug fashion. "It is the wishes of the people to once again take responsibility for their own lives."

"I have my doubts about that," Nathan replied. "Don't think you have heard the last of this. We hubrids have great influence and are respected and highly regarded throughout the human population. We can be of tremendous help with the settlement of a new planet."

"You can relay this information to all: Your help is no longer required." Earl turned away.

CHAPTER SIXTEEN

...PRESENT

"I have a question before we split up," Alan asked.

"Go ahead," Stella replied.

"How come you were all gone so long?"

"What do you mean?" Nyla questioned.

"You only had food for a short time, but you were gone longer. We were distraught for a month, especially the Branigans. We thought you were never coming back. I could see Pierre getting visibly upset at the prospect of Troy not returning."

"No, we were only gone a few days at most," Nyla replied. "I never counted the days, but Baer would be able to tell you the exact time."

Stella looked towards Sebastien. "You want to answer that?"

"Yes," he replied. "Because it has to do with time travel, and also it is next on my discussions with Stella. It is called "time dilation" and is a physics concept in the passage of time as related to relativity. It is a difference in the elapsed time measured by two observers – either due to a velocity difference relative to each other or by being differently situated relative to a gravitational field. In this case, it was probably a combination of both."

"I have heard of that but did not really think it applied to our situation," Alan replied with a look of understanding on his face, but he was still not sure.

Sebastien carried on. "While the subject has been brought up, Stella, the directional program to time travel to other parts of the planetary system that we talked about will have a ripple effect on time dilation. If we travel to, say

Gliese, I cannot say right now what the time difference will be when we get there relative to Earth when we left it in the future."

"You are obviously considering something else," Stella replied. "What is it?"

"Portals," he announced. "I studied them before, and we should look into the possibilities of using them."

"In what way?" Even as Stella answered him, they all looked at him curiously.

"There are certain places on Earth where people have vanished without a trace. I recall one incident in Montana where people were investigating a plane crash. When one person went up the mountain to look at some wreckage, he disappeared. There were no trees or rocks to hide behind. It was only a short distance from which everyone could observe him, but he just vanished. An investigation held no answers, but certain scientists concluded there a was a time portal that opened up and he walked straight into it."

"Your point being?" Stella asked him.

"That we utilize them to enable us to get to a destination in a shorter time."

"You would have no control over the destination," Stella argued. "Or of what the time was when we got there. I have read about the portals and agree they probably exist, but they are too haphazard for us to utilize."

"But it may be worth examining the concept," Sebastien argued.

"Maybe. Feel free to check it out, but I think we should stick to a plan of getting to future Earth first before testing your destination program. I will recheck your calculations as soon as I can."

"What are your plans just now?" Nyla asked.

She took a sip of coffee. "You should check this out, Nyla. It's really good. You don't have to swallow it; just get the flavour then spit it out."

"No thanks, tried it before."

"Okay, well then I want to leave Alan to get on with business." She looked at him. "Unless you want some help?"

"No, we are alright...for now."

"Then I want to return to San Jose with whoever wants to come, work on a couple of upgrades to humanoids, boost their protocols to accept only commands from humans and no other species, and then work on some armaments to combat syconoid's."

"What do you have in mind?" Alan asked.

"Something to disable them and that will protect us from attack yet not destroy them. If we kill them, it may set off a self-destruct mode, and we would still be in danger by being in their proximity."

"What did you have in mind?" Nyla spoke out.

"Some sort of sonic weapon that can be directed at them without affecting us. If we used a random signal generator, it could potentially disable or hurt us. We need a gun-type weapon that could be directed or laser guided at them to disable them, so we could reason with them and win them over."

"I suppose you already have thoughts on that idea," Alan suggested.

"Yes, do you want to discuss this now or later?" Stella asked the group.

"Now. Might as well. We are all here now," Alan returned.

"I know they want to become a full organism with a soul. They have admitted as much, so I want to suggest a way to make that happen and integrate them into humanity. We already do that with hubrids, and I suggest we offer this as an alternative to the way they are now."

"Have they not already rejected that idea?" Nyla questioned.

"Yes, but not in the way I think we can do it."

"How then?" Sebastien queried.

"Third party reproduction in which DNA or gestation is introduced to an already fertilized human embryo. Spindle transfer of a syconoid's mitochondrial DNA is inserted in an artificial womb so that the resulting child would have one human father, one human mother, and one syconoid mother. Three-person reproduction is already well known, and this would start a new species of human-syconoid's."

"Do you think this is ethical?" Alan asked. "Providing we could actually do it."

"I am putting that question to you at this moment before we even embark on such a project."

There was silence while they all considered the moral principles of such an important ethos in the culture of humanity.

"What alternatives do we have?" Alan spoke after due consideration.

"Go to war and wipe them out," Stella replied. "We may have to if they won't negotiate. They are convinced they are already the top dog."

"So, we have to be able to protect ourselves anyway," Cal said.

"Yes, I cannot predict what they will do, but you can be sure they will be prepared before they even set out for Gliese. I did not see any armaments on the craft they were assembling, but I am sure there will be," Stella stated.

"I'll go with you and Troy to San Jose to work on the projects," Nyla confirmed.

"Me too," Sebastien and Cal affirmed.

"Can you use Dax, Shi, and Irene here?" she asked Alan.

"Of course. We are expanding all the time, and we may have a new location soon if the government or military comes through," Alan replied.

"Good. I do not want to put them in danger if we confront the syconoid's. The only good thing is we know they cannot come back in time to here. It could be disastrous if that happened. If for any reason they got hold of the *Varro*, I would self destruct before letting them loose in this time dimension. Thankfully that will not happen according to history as we know it."

"Anything else before we finish this meeting?" Alan asked.

"Are there any plans you wish to fill us in on before we leave?" Stella asked.

"Well, there are some changes happening, so maybe I do need to fill you in."

"Go ahead."

"Now that Irene is back, Jack Branigan will be taking up a position in Homeland Security in Washington with the President. He is pleased with Ava and with Jack in the White House, so we can get approval or funding for almost anything we want. Matt is going to NASA to coordinate shuttle services to the ISS and get approval for flyhovs."

"Billy, I think, will leave to take control of pilotless fighter jets with fusion engines that almost double the speed of present planes and also of drones with much greater abilities, such as seeking and destroying and retrieving personnel from combat situations. Other people have been contacted by competitors trying to coax them away from us. All in all, it is really complicated, but I don't worry now that we have the twins back."

CHAPTER SEVENTEEN

...FUTURE

Work was proceeding well when most of the starship fleet arrived and took up a position above the light side of the planet. A delegation from each ship was invited and sent down to view the progress so far in the Kingdom, meet with the spiritual director, and discuss future developments. Due to the size of the delegations, they were split up and shown around in groups before they all ended up in "Kingdom Hall", a specially designed amphitheatre used for plays, opera, the ballet, and meetings of large audiences.

Each group had a full tour of the work done so far on the harbour, boat construction, business areas, and government structures, as well as the residential housing organized by community planners and private households. Public transportation and recreational facilities also were shown, although a lot of it was still in progress. Humanoids were working twenty-four hours seven days a week, but they were assisted by humans who were keen to get involved with all aspects of communal and municipal projects.

Kingdom Hall gradually filled up as groups completed their tour and assembled in the atrium where refreshments were served to the accompaniment of soft, gentle music supplied by an orchestra of humanoid and human musicians.

When it was determined everyone was there, the music abruptly changed to a rock anthem. A spotlight burst into life illuminating an open doorway, and the resplendent figure of Earl Lawrence Cavendish appeared, drawing applause from the audience. Dressed in a multi-coloured suit with a silver cloak sparkling in the glow of the bright light, he made a dazzling but dignified aristocratic-like figure. The applause continued as he waved while walking up to a podium overlooking the crowd. Then he raised his arm to calm the noise before speaking.

"Welcome everyone. Welcome to the Kingdom of Zarmina and the start of a new era for humankind full of unlimited possibilities, boundless opportunities, and the unconstrained prospects of living above ground in an environment fit for human abilities."

A round of applause greeted his pause.

"We have invited you here today to request we all live together in harmony, without conflict, without borders. There is enough land and resources for all to settle in an area of your choosing. The world of Zarmina is plentiful with enough space to accommodate all ethnic groups in a territory of your choosing. We encourage you to rebuild your heritage and keep alive your ancestral roots of language, traditions, and customs. We should never forget where we came from, what we stand for, or the troubles, wars, and suffering our predecessors have gone through to give us this great opportunity."

Another round of applause.

"For their great sacrifice, we have therefore set aside a retreat for all hubrids so they may retire and enjoy the rest of their lives in tranquillity, prayer, meditation, and recreation and experience the fruits of their labours.

For years and years, they have toiled to keep humanity alive, so now they deserve to have a settlement all their own. It is an island we called Nulla. It will be a hubrid sanctuary of serenity, calm, and goodwill, where their families can visit or stay as long as they please. All we are asking for is that as humans we now control our own destiny, learn from the mistakes of the past, and set out on a path towards nirvana or our own interpretation of paradise."

Applause.

"To that end, we have inaugurated the Legion of Zarmina, a semi-religious order designated to promote a creed of morality and love for all and loyalty to the Legion, and to make Zarmina the greatest planet in the universe as we know it.

"Earth our motherland is not forgotten. Scientists predict it will take two hundred years or even up to five hundred years for it to become habitable again. By that time, future generations may wish to recolonize the planet. Till then, this is our safe haven of majestic topography.

"I have been designated as spiritual leader and encourage everyone to join in sharing the same principals to the advantage of all. As members of a different religious order, you are authorized to retain that belief and carry out your own spiritual practices. After all, every religion practices peace, does it not?"

Another pause drew a lesser amount of applause.

"As you know, we are already generating supplies from the resources, mining, and factories on the other side of the planet. We are willing to help you get started by giving you our surplus till you initiate your own facilities; this will enable you to jump start your own communities.

"We have already surveyed most of the habitable side of the planet and can offer you advice on the best sites. We chose this site as being central and convenient to communicate with all of you, but do not worry, there is more than ample great sites for you to put down roots of your own."

A huge screen appeared above his head displaying a map of most of the daylight side of the planet. It had a huge lake in the middle with various islands charted. Green arable land mostly surrounded the lake plotted in various sizes and also a few mountainous regions were drawn in.

"As you can see, the lake – I know it looks like an ocean, but it is fresh water – has really good sites all around. There is enough land for all starship communities to settle without even getting close to one another. Each starship commander can send a survey crew to their chosen site. Hopefully, there will be no disputes over one site or another. We are here to mediate any such disputes, but I am confident that won't be necessary."

Murmurings of disputes started to erupt amongst the delegates. Already land designations were being argued and raised voices filled the hall, calling for calm. Earl spoke again.

"Please, please do not let our new beginnings start on a sour note. If delegation leaders follow me to a meeting room, we have already set up land establishments based on previous status within world order. Any challenges to land requirements we can settle amicably, right now, and to all parties' satisfaction. Humanoid guides will show you the way."

Spiritual director Cavendish turned and exited through the doorway.

"That went quite well, sire," one of his officers whispered to him as they walked through the corridors.

"It went as I expected. Now is the time to put our stamp of authority over the human population. If we do it now, we will be set to rule the planet. I did not see any delegates from *Orlando 2* in the crowd. Are they here?"

"No, sire, they have not arrived yet. Their ship was delayed as they did a survey of Earth before leaving."

"Maybe that is a good thing. Any real opposition will come from them. Talan and the hubrid committee will be against us; I am sure of that. The hubrids will not be keen to settle in Nulla. I am certain Nathan has informed them, so they will be getting ready to dispute our authority."

"Well, we have an army ready to overpower them if necessary, sire."

"If they have that 'Stella' from the past with them, then trouble will be inevitable. She is dangerous, that one."

"No, sire, her craft was destroyed, so she could not return."

A smile spread across Earl's face. "Then the planet is ours."

Gradually delegates filled a meeting room set aside for a more intimate discussion. When it was deemed all the elected officials were present, the doors were closed. Earl sat at the head of the large table and began the summit.

"Honoured guests, in front of you is a tablet with a laid-out map of designated areas we thought appropriate to your community. Your ships were named after the cities you lived in, so that is what we named the areas. After we arrive at mutually agreed upon assigned regions, you can begin settlement construction and re-name the territory to whatever your people desire. Please study the map carefully, and we can either swap regions or even assign different areas of the planet to you. We envisage a time when individuals can explore all inhabitable land and new cities and communities will evolve."

"What if we cannot agree on the regional settlement areas?" one delegate asked.

"Oh, I am sure it will not come to that," Earl replied. "There is so much land. Surely, we can sort this out amicably. One more point: We have an army assembled to govern all lands and stop any conflict from arising, so please let's settle this now."

CHAPTER EIGHTEEN

...PRESENT

"We have reprogramed and reset command parameters for humanoids if you wish to test them out," Arlo said at a morning meeting in the Cadena headquarters south of San Jose. Seated around the table were Troy, Pierre, Nyla, Seb, Cal, and Stella. Baer stood at the back along with a repaired Yul.

"Good," Stella said looking towards the humanoids. "Yul will you take a seat, and Baer stand behind him." Neither moved.

"You are not human," Arlo stated. "They will not obey you."

"Mmm, that's a problem," Stella announced.

Yul sat down, and Baer stood behind him.

"What?" Arlo asked quizzically.

"I planted the thought in their minds," Stella answered him. "Now is the time to tell you the replicants can get into your mind."

"What?" Arlo gasped followed by the others.

"Yes, they can. I found that out since being changed. Don't worry, they cannot read your thoughts. However, they can plant a question in your mind, which you answer automatically, or tell you to do something, which you may or may not do."

"This is mind blowing," Sebastien stated.

"No, Seb. They cannot damage your mind – only try to override your thoughts."

"How?" he asked in return.

"It was long thought that the brain's endogenous electrical fields were too weak to propagate wave transmission. But the replicants found a way to increase and mediate propagations of neurons with the result that ephaptic effects, coupled with cell-by-volume, can produce a brain wave signal to be sent to close by receptors in our brains."

"Wow," Seb commented. "They are way smarter than us to be able to do that."

"Yes," Stella spoke up. "Furthermore, they are working to increase the ability. At the moment, they can only ask questions, induce a slow-wave sleep, and affect hippocampal waves or theta waves to interrupt your memory or brain rhythms used to control body functions. Once they get more abilities, they could render you unconscious by thought alone; that would by scary."

"Twelve minutes past nine," Troy announced. They all looked at him.

"See, I just asked him what time it is."

"What can we do to combat this?" Arlo asked.

"I have to teach you how to recognize these signals and use mind blocks to counteract their affects. Mind blocks are often described as thoughts you have trouble retrieving – like names or words or places, but they are also a safety mechanism that your mind uses. Some people can easily be hypno-tized, while others can take a long time to go under or even not at all. This is a normal, safety mind block. We can simply induce these blocks by security motivation of thinking a particular thought and putting it at the back of your mind – such as a favourite photo of a person you like or a music rhythm. I am sure you have all heard a tune that runs continuously in your mind for hours, as if you cannot get it out of your head."

"How can we recognize these intrusions?" Nyla asked.

"Did you think that question?" Stella asked.

After a moment's thought, Nyla replied, "No, it just came to me."

"If you are not sure of a sentence you spoke, then you are being interfered with and must put up a mind block, or you may want to do that when you are in the presence of a replicant."

"You can get into my head?" Nyla asked. "I thought I was stronger than that."

"Yes, we can all receive intrusions, even myself. Luckily, I was able to rec-ognize it." She thought she better not bring up the subject of a soul spirit.

"Coffee, black."

Yul stood up. "Does anyone else require refreshments?"

"See, this is a big problem for me: how to get humanoids to reject replicants, but listen to me."

After getting requests from others, Yul left the room.

"I need to find out the range of these brain wave commands in humanoids. I'll wait till he gets to the coffee machine and change my order." Stella looked around the room. "Now I can hypnotize you and plant a really annoying tune in your head, or we can go over ways to counteract my intrusion into your mind. Don't forget I cannot read your mind."

"What do you recommend?" Sebastien asked. "After all, you are the one best qualified to intrude our minds."

"I suggest we try the hypnotic route first. I can put all of you under right now and plant a tune in your hippocampus memory blocks that can initiate as soon as an intrusion is detected. It would be immediate. You wouldn't have to think about it, and it would play in your mind as a warning."

"I am okay with that," Troy uttered; the rest agreed.

"It will not be necessary with me, will it?" Pierre asked. "I will not be going with you."

"No," Stella replied. "But you will never know if I am in your mind."

"Oh, okay then... never thought about that."

"I would not do that to you anyway," Stella answered.

"Fourteen minutes past nine," Pierre said, then looked guilty.

"Sorry, Pierre, just joking with you. I promise not to do it again, but you see how easily you can be deceived."

Yul returned with coffee for some and handed one to Stella.

"Dam. I changed my order to white and that is what he brought. I am going to do all of you, including the humanoids, and then test it out to see if it works. Please all of you stay seated and relax, and then we will begin."

Baer and Yul sat in seats indicated by Stella. As she sat down, the room went quiet. No words where spoken. Then after a couple of minutes, Stella got up and went around the room, lifting each person's arms up one by one and telling them not to drop them. As she sat back down again, people's arms dropped slowly to a resting position again. Minutes went by as Stella issued commands telepathically to each person in turn.

"When I clap my hands, you will awake feeling rested, relaxed, and refreshed." She clapped.

Eyes opened curious to their surroundings till recognition set in. Stella waited till they gathered their wits about them. "You all feeling okay?" she asked.

"Yes," they muttered one after another.

"Then let's test it out. Say when you are ready."

"Ready," they all answered.

"Right. I am asking you all the same question."

All of them stared at Yul and Baer who got up and began putting their hands to their shoulders one at a time, and then to their heads. Next, they stretched their arms out before putting their hands on their hips and started dancing.

"What the heck is that tune?" Cal asked.

"What did you hear first?" Stella asked.

"*Hey Macarena*, then singing in Spanish."

"It's an old tune; you probably never heard it before."

"I can remember it," Seb stated. "And it is still annoying now."

Stella laughed. "Well, you will all know when you hear 'Hey Macarena' that replicants are trying to get into your heads. Keep the song going, and your mind block is working."

"Did it have to be that song?" Troy asked in an annoyed tone. "And why are those two dancing?"

"Sorry Troy, but if I intruded again you can teach Nyla the dance. Yul and Baer have the dance moves in their memory banks."

"Don't bother."

"Got to admit it is pretty easy to know when an intrusion is happening," Stella answered. "Baer, Yul, you can stop dancing now."

They ignored her.

"You can stop now," Arlo said, and they stopped and sat down again.

"Dam, that's no good. Now I cannot communicate with them at all. I tried with my mind as well."

"We will have to rewrite a program to allow you access, but only to the ones who you are taking with you," Arlo stated.

"Okay, let's move on. How are we doing with a stun gun against the replicants?" Stella looked towards Sebastien.

"We have studied past sonic weapons, and there are a number that exist in the infrasonic, ultrasonic, and audible ranges. Because they are weapons that direct sound onto a target, sound is considered energy. S.W. (sonic weapons) are considered directed-energy weapons. All of these can produce both psychological and physical effects. There are directional devices that can transmit painful sound at great distances, as well as infrasonic generators that can shoot acoustic projectiles causing a blunt impact on a target. To avoid damage to individuals, close by, we have concentrated on an infrasonic weapon. However, there are a lot of factors to consider: emotional, biological, and resonance concerns. All physical matter is vibrating at its own frequency, and being disrupted can cause oscillations, pulsations, and vibrations that are damaging to the organism. I could go on a lot more about these weapons, but for now, let me tell you we have a hand-held acoustic projectile rifle, APR for short, in testing and need subjects to conduct trials on."

"I suppose that means me," Stella stated.

"Not yet," Sebastien replied. "We have adjustable settings, so we can slowly bring the power up and study the effects. I thought we would test some humanoids first before we shoot you down. I promise, we do not want to kill you."

"Well, that would be nice. I have already died twice, and it is not a nice sensation."

CHAPTER NINETEEN

...FUTURE

Orlando 2's bridge deck was hectic. All the available stations had flight engineers seated at their desks and working feverishly when Talan and some hubrid committee members walked in.

"You summoned us?" Talan asked Commander Innes.

As usual, he was dressed in the red command uniform and seated in the flight control seat. "Yes," he answered. "You need to see this." He indicated toward a large screen at the front.

"This front view shows us to be two days away from Gliese. You can see it's the large planet that is dimly lit by the dwarf star. Now look at the view behind us." He switched screens to reveal lots of bright dots in the blackness of space. "Now watch when I zoom in."

The screen seemed to expand as the dots grew larger till. They could be identified as small craft flying in formation. Their exact number could not be judged.

"I have had flight officers count, and we think there are thirty-seven, all heading our way."

"What or who do you think they are?" Talan asked.

"Well, we received a warning from the *Varro* that replicants were headed to Gliese after finding Earth was going to be ice covered in a short period of time. They also warned us they were dangerous," Commander Innes replied.

"You think they are replicants?"

"Who else could it be?"

"What can we do?" Talan asked anxiously.

"Nothing," he replied. "We have no weapons, you know that. We can only keep the ship sealed."

"How long till they catch us?" another hubrid asked.

The commander looked towards a flight engineer.

"Three hours fifteen minutes," he answered.

"Can we outrun them?" Talan queried.

"We are in slowdown mode to reach the planet. If we speed up, we would overshoot the orbital route we have chosen. I recommend trying to contact them first to see if we can get an assessment of their intentions. That is why I want you here to listen in."

"Alright, lets do that," Talan agreed.

"Open communications channels and hail them," the commander ordered.

"*Orlando 2* to approaching space craft, please state your identity and purpose."

"This is syconoid leader Oslo. You are ordered to surrender to us, – now or later, it does not matter. We intend to subdue the planet. We know you are unarmed, so you may carry on into orbit or let us onboard now." The voice sounded familiar.

"We are in orbital selection mode now, so we will go into orbit. But I doubt if we will surrender."

Innes muted the communication. "That voice sounds familiar. Who is it?"

"Sounds like Stella," Talan answered. "But surely not, she went back in time."

"But if they are replicants, are they a replicant of Stella?"

"Possible, but why her?"

The voice cut back in. "You can discuss the ramifications later of who we are. Pay attention to the planet as we take it over, and then we will see if you surrender or not."

Commander Innes cut communications then turned to the hubrid committee. "My loyalty and main concern is to the ship and the people in it. I would ascertain their true nature before putting the ship in jeopardy. They seem very certain of their own abilities; I do not think they are bluffing."

"You have a suggestion?" Talan asked.

"I believe we should come to a stop, turn around, and speed up."

"Turn tail and run," one of the hubrids said with scorn.

"Safety first. Prudence is a better part of valour; live to fight another day," Eric spat back. "There is an alternative."

"What is that?" Talan queried, giving an annoyed glance at the hubrid who had questioned the commander.

"Change direction and speed up to swing past the planet. We can always come back if there is no danger. Also, by speeding up, we can test our speed against theirs. If at full speed we leave them behind, we can relax a little knowing we can outrun them. Either way, we gain some knowledge."

The hubrids went quiet as they consulted each other in an internal communication mode. This annoyed the commander as they left him out of the debate.

"Speak up, so we can all state our case, otherwise I will kick you out off the bridge and make our own decisions," he ordered in a gruff voice. "I am in command here."

"Sorry," Talan said. "We were trying to come up with alternative suggestions, but your second choice seems like the most rational in our current circumstances."

"Good," he turned to the crew. "Change heading to six three zero and full speed ahead." Changing the communication mode, he said: "Ship's company, be aware we are changing course and speeding up. Make sure all loose items are secure."

There was a lurch as power was applied rapidly. Those seated felt it pushing them back in their seats; those standing had to take a step aside to steady themselves.

"Is it really necessary to be so aggressive?" another hubrid spoke against the action.

"Either tell them to be quiet or get them out of here," the commander ordered Talan.

The hubrids went quiet again before Talan answered. "Can you switch your screens to public broadcast so everyone can see what is happening? Most of us will leave, but I will stay behind to consult with you."

Eric gave him another irritated look and switched the screens to civic channels. Quietly, the hubrids turned and left one by one. It was obvious to the commander they would stay in touch with Talan through their internal com. It was just another one of the many things hubrids did that exasperated humans. No wonder they were being shunned on the planet.

After they left, Talan approached the captain's chair. "Should we let Zarmina know?"

"I already did before I summoned you."

"Good." All eyes turned to the screens. The dots seemed to get smaller while the planet got bigger and moved away to their right. Anticipation mounted as they waited to see the scenario play out.

"Sir, we are leaving them, but one has changed course and is following us."

"Thought that might happen." Eric spoke out loud while keeping his eyes on the screens. "Now we will find out their speed and abilities. Let me know if it gains on us; keep me informed."

"Yes, sir," a flight officer replied.

"Get me Zarmina on the line," he called out to another communications crew member.

"Sir, they have a command centre at the space port just outside the Kingdom. They told us all calls are to go through them. A spiritual director, Earl Lawrence Cavendish, is in charge."

"Whoever, just get them online." Commander Innes was controlling things with authority.

"Is that not an *Orlando 1* citizen who did a runner when questioned about a murder? I believe Commander Roach was involved," Talan commented.

"Could be."

"He was ordered to bring back the ship. Instead they took off for Gliese."

"Sir, they are online now."

"Bring him up on screen."

CHAPTER TWENTY

Banks of screens surrounded the walls of a circular command centre. Below them were glass windows, which gave the impression of being in an airport control tower. Cavendish stood in a round centre monitor control; his Legion of Zarmina hegemony dominating the central part of the space centre. He was surrounded by guards, all dressed in gold uniforms, while he wore his silver cloak over a gold suit showing underneath. He had a scowl on his face when he spotted Talan standing next to Commander Innes.

"Yes, Commander, you wanted me?"

"You probably already know that a fleet of replicants are on their way to the planet. We just had a communication from them."

"I thought you were informed all communication was to be done through me."

"Yes, I got the memorandum, but they were closing in on us, and I am in charge of this ship and the people onboard. They are my first responsibility, and as such, I make the decisions here."

There was an air of hostility bristling between them as they stared at each other for a few moments before Earl spoke again.

"What did they say?"

"They wanted us to surrender to them – either now or later after they have subdued the planet."

"Huh!" Earl scoffed. "Like we are just going to lie down for them."

"I know you will not, but I hope you are prepared. They seemed very sure of themselves. Our flight engineers expect them to be upon you within twenty-four hours."

"I did take heed of the warning sent to us and have made arrangements to give them a very warm reception. Armed flyhovs manned by humanoid crews are anticipating them in space as well as in the atmosphere, and I have a fully weaponized army awaiting any resistance on the ground. So be assured, we will take them over before they know it. We will overcome them and be in charge just as we are all over this planet," Earl Cavendish pronounced, with the last comment meant to convey a message of authority.

Commander Innes stared at him for a moment. "Well, we are testing them out by taking off. One is chasing us. We intend to find out their capabilities. We will keep you informed."

The screen went blank as *Orlando 2* closed down the link.

"Archaic Dupe," Earl announced angrily. "We will take care of him later. Now, are all the military in position?"

"Yes, your grace. We have crews seated at all terminals to manually take over control of the flyhovs if they do not meet expectations," an officer stated.

The view on the screens switched to space flyhovs looking towards the incoming fleet of syconoid bullitships flying in formation and heading straight towards them.

"Try and make contact with them," Earl ordered.

"Yes, sir."

After a few trials, a weird-looking helmet faced them. It had a darkened glass face covering with only the eyes showing indistinctly. At the sides of the head where ears should be were two silver grids that looked like network frames for communication. There were no other attachments, no antenna, and no breathing vents or markings except for two small letters in the front where a mouth would be. The letters were discernible as S.B.

"This is syconoid Berlin, team leader of the bullit fleet, ordering you to surrender or face the consequences."

Earl bristled with infuriation. "No, syconoid Berlin, or whatever you call yourselves. You should submit to us before we shoot you down."

"Your name and title?" S.B. asked.

"I am Spiritual Director Earl Lawrence Cavendish of the Legion of Zarmina and commander of the military. I am ordering you to accede and comply with our instructions. Conform and we will treat you with respect before a tribunal of humans. You can state your case for entry into this planet."

"My answer is this."

"Sire, the foremost flyhov just disappeared from our screens."

"What happened?"

S.B. gave him the answer. "Your humanoid pilot just self-destructed under our command."

"Fire at will!" Earl barked out his command.

Flight engineers at command terminals worked their controls feverishly

The Praesidia officers stared at the screens as one after another flyhovs blipped off the screen.

"Override them," Earl shouted at all the terminal pilots.

Still, one by one, flyhovs vanished from sight. The bullit fleet grew larger on the screens as they approached.

"You want me to completely destroy your space fleet or are you ready to negotiate?" S.B. asked.

The screens held steady as no more flyhovs went missing.

"We have back up!" Earl shouted at the screen. "Do not enter our atmosphere or you will suffer the consequences, and we will not stop till your complete fleet is terminated."

Laughter emanated from the helmeted face.

"You need a dose of reality, Spiritual Director. Get a grip and face up to it before we destroy your own fleet. We will be breaking through the atmosphere shortly, and I suggest you capitulate."

"Never! We have worked too hard, built up this colony, and lived long enough to recognize rogue reprobate humanoids when we see them. If it were not for us, you would not exist. Give in to your first-born species. We will accommodate you if you treat us with the veneration we deserve."

A haughty laugh came from the helmet. "See you soon, Director." The screen went blank.

"Shut down all the humanoid pilots and take over manual control." Earl barked the order out. "Put them into standby mode or turn them off altogether."

Once again flight engineers worked the terminals feverishly; the officer guards all watched the screens as one by one all of the flyhovs in space disappeared. Earl bristled with anger, his face turning red, and his eyes fleeting from one flight officer to another as they shrugged when their craft went out of commission.

"Are the atmosphere flyhov pilots out of commission?" he shouted to all the staff.

"No," just about all of them called back.

"Then engage their bullit fleet as they breakthrough into our air space."

All eyes were on the big screens as the first of the bullit fleet appeared. Laser-guided projectiles were fired in its direction, but exploded shortly after leaving the flyhov. Then the craft's screen went blank.

"What just happened?" Earl called out. No one answered.

A succession of screens went blank till one displayed a scene of flyhovs in a dogfight with a bullitship. Most of the flyhovs were trying to dodge incoming fire, while others just blew up and the flyhov fleet dwindled.

"Sire, somehow they are switching the humanoid pilots on and putting them in self-destruct mode."

"What? How is that possible?"

"They are breaking into our communication system and controlling the humanoids, sire."

"Can't we block them?"

"We are trying, sire."

Earl turned back to the screens, dismayed as more and more flyhovs disappeared in an explosive grey-white cloud of debris till it seemed there were only bullitships left. They resumed formation and headed towards the space port."

"Fire ground to air missiles whenever they are in range," the director ordered. But when they were in visual sight, no warheads had been fired. "What is going on?" Earl cried out.

CHAPTER TWENTY-ONE

...PRESENT

Stella called a videoconference between San Jose and Orlando with everyone who had been involved in the *Varro* build as well as in humanoid construction. Screens showed both companies seated around tables. All had microphones with small cameras on top that were able to show the individual who was talking. Stella began, her face visible onscreen.

"I have called us all together to discuss who is willing and who does not want to go forward with us to future Earth and possibly Gliese. It is a mission filled with all sorts of danger, not only from the flights but also from a probable conflict with the syconoid's. We know firsthand how dangerous they can be, so be under no illusions that whoever goes may never come back. That is why I am advising all humans to stay. That includes Dax and Shi. You still have a life in front of you, and I am recommending you stay."

"We belong to the future," Dax spoke up.

"If we have a good outcome from this mission, you could still return there, but I recommend you stay here."

"We still want to go," Shi answered her.

"Let's have an initial show of hands on who wants to go," Stella directed.

A few hands went up, but the majority wanted to stay. She made a mental count and noted the persons involved.

"Irene, put your hand down. Your parents would not be happy if I took you, and besides, you of all people know how dangerous the replicants are after being nearly kidnapped by one."

"I want to help secure the future for the human race, and Dr. Roland wants to come with me. You could use another doctor."

"Is that why you would risk your lives?" Stella stared into the camera so as to be as face to face as she could.

"Before I met Cal, my life was destined to be mediocre at best. Now after what I have been through and what I have seen, my life can be filled with a destiny that helps humankind. We all owe a debt of some kind, and I aim to pay back mine," Irene answered.

Most everyone then raised their hands.

"Alright, alright," Stella smiled. "I appreciate the sentiments, but I cannot take you all anyway."

"How about you just state who you want to take and then have one-on-one discussions with them and talk to the others after," Cal spoke up. "We all know the hubrids are a first priority."

"Not necessarily," she looked towards Cal at the same table. "A hubrid staying here could be invaluable to present-day humanity." She switched her gaze towards Sebastien.

"I want to keep up with all the technological advances that the syconoid's come up with. They are thinking way faster and deeper than we are, and the human race needs to catch up, or we will die out," Seb answered. "So, I want to go."

"Nyla?"

"Of course, I am going. You need me as back-up, but if we settle with the replicants, I may want to come back here permanently." She looked towards Troy.

"I don't need to ask," Stella spoke before he could open his mouth, but he answered anyway.

"You also need me," he pronounced. "Pierre is now head of the company and running it all by himself...with the help of Trisha."

"What about you, Arlo? Do you want to stay and continue on with humanoid development?"

"Go," was all he replied.

"Have you been able to get the humanoids to take commands from me?"

"Not yet."

"Well, stop all work on that," Stella declared. "If they will not acknowledge me then that means they will never let a replicant onboard the *Varro* and that is paramount to present-day Earth's safety."

"What about the three humanoids you brought back?" Arlo asked. "A certain Liv, Van, and Rey? Do you want me to upgrade them or are you leaving them here?"

"I want you to give them all the upgrades you have, and I will talk to you about them after this meeting. I have some plans to use them in the future. Right, well I think I know everyone who is going with me. I will talk with everyone individually before we go, including those who are not going. I cannot tell you how much you all have contributed towards keeping the planet and humanity safe. Thank you. Now we have to test that weapon you have to knock down the sycons."

The meeting broke up, and everyone went back to their duties. Stella went to the test rifle range, followed by Troy and the hubrids. At one end of the range, a humanoid stood all alone; at the other end was a ledge to lean on and several sets of ear defenders. Troy picked up the gun to show Stella.

"It looks and handles like any other rifle with a few differences," he began. "Underneath where the bullet magazine usually goes is a short tubular pulse generator powered by a small fusion unit similar to those implanted in humanoids, but with a much higher output to generate the pulse. Next is a laser mount underneath the barrel to use as an aiming sight. Providing you are within a six-foot radius of the target; you will hit them. There is no recoil when fired and ear defenders are unnecessary as there is very little noise. In fact, you will only know you have fired it by a short pause in the laser guide. You want to try it out now?"

Arlo walked up. "We have to reboot the humanoids that are knocked out. Just to let you know, there is a dial on the side to adjust the power level. It is set for humanoids, but we do not know the levels for a sycon. That's where you come in."

Stella gave him a sideways glance.

"We know it will be greater, and we want to increase the setting slowly till we get it right."

"Is this payback for all the things I have done?" Stella asked with a sarcastic smile on her face.

Arlo grinned back. "Maybe. But try it out first."

She picked up the rifle to her shoulder and aimed it towards the humanoid at the other end of the range.

"Here we go again," it said as a laser-pointed light appeared on its chest. "Do we have to?"

"Sorry," Stella uttered as the light blinked and the humanoid fell to the ground. "Never felt a thing, and it was almost silent except for the sound of the generator recharging, which was almost instant."

"I know," Arlo commented. "I am really pleased with it. Now it's your turn. Troy and I have been arguing as to who gets to shoot you. Troy gets first shot." He smiled as he took the rifle from her and shooed her down the range. She passed a couple of humanoids carrying the knocked-out humanoid away. She turned at the far end and faced towards the shooting stand.

"I'll bet you have been looking forward to this, haven't you?"

Troy just kept on smiling as he lifted the gun to his shoulder and the laser light came on at the fist touch of the trigger. He waited a little just to annoy her.

"Get on with it," she called out.

The light blinked, but Stella stood still. "Was that it?" she asked.

Arlo took the gun from Troy and turned up the settings. "What did you feel?" he asked.

"A tremor throughout my whole body," she replied.

"Okay, let's try this setting." He lifted the gun and almost instantly pulled the trigger. Stella took a step backwards.

"Felt that one," she uttered.

Troy took the gun back and turned it up without looking.

"Enjoying this Troy?" she mocked.

"Every minute," he answered, as he pulled the gun to a hip stance and fired.

Stella was knocked off her feet, hit the back wall, and slumped to the ground.

Troy looked shocked as he put the rifle down and ran towards her. "Hope I have not killed her."

Both Arlo and Troy knelt down beside her. "Are you okay?" they asked together. Neither knew how to check if she was alive.

"That was almost like dying." Her eyes opened and looked at Arlo. "How long have I been out?

"Less than a minute. Just long enough for us to get to you," he replied. "How do you feel?"

"Quivering inside. All of me feels like a jelly that is being shaken," she answered. "Let me see if I can stand up or how strong I am to resist being restrained."

A little wobbly on her feet she turned to them. "Pretend to put me in restraints or as if you were putting me in shackles; take one arm apiece and put them behind my back to see if I can stop you." Each grabbed an arm, but when they got level with her side, she stopped them. However, they had not wanted to hurt her. "Use full force," Stella ordered.

Using all their energy, they did get her arms behind her back enough that they could have put handcuffs on her.

"Good, now let's see how long it takes for me to fully recover. Start a timer someone."

Unsteady on her feet she stumbled up the firing range, went to the nearest room, and sat down. Both men were hovering over her, worried about her well being.

"I am okay," she stated gazing up at each in turn. "Fetch that rifle. Let's see what the setting is."

Arlo strode off and quickly returned holding the gun. "We marked it where it put down humanoids and then marked it in ten percent increments over that. We called the humanoid setting as one hundred."

Troy took a look at the setting. "It is at one sixty." He recounted and confirmed the number. "Yes, one sixty and forty more after that."

"Don't think we need to go any higher," Stella commented. "Anymore and we could permanently damage a sycon."

"How you feeling now?" Arlo asked.

"A little better. I will let you know when I am strong enough or mentally capable of thought transference."

"No!" Troy called out. "I hate that song; you are definitely capable now. Switch it off."

"Can't," she replied. "You have to learn to turn it off yourself. It's a mental discipline you have to acquire... Ha, that's payback for shooting me."

"I hate you, Stella Cooke."

They laughed together before she spoke up. "You better get a few of those guns made, Arlo."

"How many?"

"Just keep going till we are ready to leave, which will probably be in the next few days once I have gone over the *Varro* "hyperjump" theory and calculations and thrust settings with Sebastien."

"You want to do that now?" he asked.

"No, let me recover some more. I want to make sure my mind is clear and my thought processes are not susceptible to fault errors."

***

Lara and Allen sat in his office. As usual, the twins were asleep in their carry cots. They were putting on weight quickly and with their chubby cheeks were as cute as could be.

"Stella wants a chat with me before they leave. I think you should be there, don't you?"

"Well, what does she want to talk about?" Lara asked.

"I don't know, but I am sure she will fill me in. I get the impression they do not expect to come back." He wore a frown of consternation on his face.

"Why would you say that?" Lara quizzed him.

"I think she fears these sycons are a bigger danger to the human race than even Earth's degradation."

"When is she coming?"

"They should arrive here later today. The people going with them are assembling here this afternoon."

Around noon, the *Varro* landed outside the skyfreighter hanger. Baer turned it around so the back faced the doors and dropped the ramp. Supplies were being loaded as Stella made her way to the Cox office centre.

Entering, she hugged Lara and held her hands. Then she did the same with Allen before crouching down to admire the twins and gently hold their hands.

"You guys are so lucky with beautiful babies and all of you in good health," Stella beamed.

"A lot of it is down to you," Lara answered.

"No, you both deserve all the happiness you can get out of life after all you have been through."

"Well, what did you want to talk to me about?" Allen asked.

"Typical man, eh Lara? Straight to the point." She sat down, and the couple followed.

"First of all, I want you to help me persuade the humans to stay behind. This mission is too dangerous. Only hubrids would be able to offer resistance to the syconoid's. Well, Troy might be able to hold his own, but the others... no."

"You think it is that bad?" Lara asked.

"Yes, I do. The sycons are so adaptable, clever, and tenacious that the next time I encounter them I expect that they will have even more in their arsenal. The humans do not stand a chance if it comes to a conflict."

"They all seem determined to go," Allen stated.

"I know, and that puts more pressure on me to keep them alive. I was thinking of changing my tact. I will tell them I am changing the mission to a scouting venture and only taking humanoids and hybrids as well as Troy... I will never shake him off. Will you help me?"

"I will always back you up," Allen replied. "But I am not sure it will fly."

"We will see. I may have to insist and order them to stay, and again I would need your backing for that."

"Whatever you want," he answered.

"Good, now I have another matter to talk over with you."

"Go on."

They talked for another hour before walking over to the hangar. Allen and Stella carried the babies. Everyone kept glancing at the twins as if they were the most precious things on the planet and some terrible tragedy would occur if they were not kept under constant surveillance.

The planned expeditionary group was assembled at the bottom of the ramp waiting for them.

"Change of plans, everyone," Stella called out for all to hear. "I have changed the mission to a scouting excursion."

An audible groan emitted from the crowd, and Troy spoke up. "What does that mean?"

"It means that after studying Sebastien's theories, calculations, and engine settings, it is too dangerous for us to have everyone onboard. So, I am changing it to a test flight and scouting mission and taking no humans with me...this time."

"Well, who are you taking?" Dax asked.

"Apart from myself, Cal, Nyla, and Sebastien with the humanoids." Before Troy spoke, she interrupted him in anticipation of the question. "And Troy, because he funded this, and if I don't keep him happy, he won't keep the purse strings open." She smiled at him and he never voiced an opinion.

Grumblings began with each voice pleading their case to be included in the expedition. They all had legitimate claims and pressed her to let them go. She held up her arm for them to stop the noise and listen.

"I know you are all entitled to be going, but I promise that if all goes well, we will be back to pick you up because you are all invaluable members of this team. Please see it from my point of view. I cannot risk lives on a theory, even a very reliable theory, on a test flight... Next time.

CHAPTER TWENTY-TWO

...FUTURE

"It is gaining on us, Commander," a flight engineer called out.

"What is our speed?" Eric asked another controller.

"Nearly at maximum. Another hour and we will be at full speed. 0.95 light, sir."

The commander turned to Talan. "Looks like we cannot outrun this bullitship. We might be able to avoid capture for another day, but then it could fire any weapons it wants on us."

"What do you suggest?" Talan asked.

"Well, if we cannot shake it off, we have no alternative but to try and negotiate without harming the crew, ship's company, or the ship itself."

"But it is only one craft. What harm can it do?"

The commander gave him a derisive look as if he were crazy. "One hit on a fusion holding location and we are a multitude of miniscule debris joining the rest of the cosmic dust out there."

Talan was quiet. Eric could tell he was discussing the situation with the rest of the hubrid colony internally. "Don't forget we have no shields or weapons," he informed the hubrid.

"I am trying to figure out what bargaining chips we have," Talan answered.

"None, because we do not know what it wants."

"Capitulation, but then what?" Talan asked.

"If it is only one sycon, we could invite it onboard," Commander Innes began. "It will probably want us to return to Zarmina. I cannot think it would want to do anything else."

"What are you thinking? That we could possibly overpower it here onboard the ship."

"Got any other suggestions?"

"Let me explore other possibilities," Talan stated.

"Go ahead, but you don't have much time."

Talan left the flight deck as Eric reviewed the control monitors, speed, fuel reserves, smaller craft onboard, humanoid numbers, and the ship's company. He was responsible for all of this and had a moral obligation to protect it. He never shrank before the task or let fear influence his decisions, but he was bereft of ideas for the moment.

"Sir, the bullitship is hailing us."

"Put it up on the screen."

The helmeted features of the sycon appeared. It seemed like an aquatic alien with protruding gills sticking out where ears should be. Its eyes looked large and reptilian though the darkened visor.

"You can see, Commander, that you are being overtaken. It's time to come to your senses and give up the chase and surrender." Its voice sounded hollow with a slight echo through the helmet.

"What do you want?" Eric replied. "We are a vulnerable company of voyagers seeking a new life without conflict."

"Just slow down, turn around, return to the planet Zarmina, and give yourselves up. You will be treated with respect."

"Why don't you come onboard and see for yourself that we are defenceless and wish only a peaceable outcome."

There was a hesitation before replying. "Why not?" A hint of contempt was mixed with a triumphant conceit in its voice. "Slow down and arrange a docking entry port for me."

"Agreed." He turned to the crew. "Decrease speed to enable a one eighty stop and reverse direction."

Talan appeared with a number of other hubrids. "Why have you capitulated?" he asked.

"I have not. I only tempted it onboard where we will have a possible chance to overcome it. Have you got another solution?"

"Negotiation to find more intel and discover any possible weakness they may have."

"Then we stand a better chance with it on our own ground," the commander stated. They both looked frustrated.

It took hours to slow down almost to a stop without creating havoc within the ship. Meanwhile, the bullitship rapidly caught up to them, slowing down at the last minute to come alongside. A port door opened, and it was directed to enter into a gravity-free docking station. Slowly, it pulled in and settled down in an open port with no other craft inside. The outer airlock door closed, and the hood of the bullitship lifted up. The sycon stood up and stepped out onto the floor. There was a hiss as air refilled the port and artificial gravity returned. The sycon walked towards the airlock door into the starship, as humanoid figures watched through glass windows.

Entering the ship, it was greeted by a humanoid. "Welcome to the *Orlando 2*. We are to escort you to the ship's flight deck where Commander Innes awaits you."

"Unnecessary, I know the way," the sycon answered while looking around at the group of humanoids. They all stood up straight as if on parade and then froze into a standby state.

It turned to the corridors and began walking towards the centre of the craft. Just a short distance in, it was surrounded by another group of humanoids – some behind and others in front. They all froze into standby states except for a group of hubrids blocking its path.

They were about to speak, but then suddenly fell to their knees. They clutched their ears, trying to protect themselves from a sonic flare of intrusive thought waves filling their minds. It caused pain as the waves flooded their brains, distressing their bodies into submission.

Alone, it walked into the flight deck to face the flight crew, a group of hubrids, and the seated figure of Commander Innes. All were appalled that it had not been stopped before getting there.

"Commander Innes, thank you for the welcoming committee. It was quite unnecessary as I know the layout of the ship from top to bottom. Your hubrid friends did not have a pleasant word of greeting though, so I had to correct their thoughts. They will think twice next time."

"What have you done to them?" Talan asked.

Instead of replying, the sycon walked up to him and grabbed him by the throat. Others went to his rescue but were driven back, each holding their hands to their ears. Only the Commander, who was wearing headphones, got out of his chair to aid the hubrid leader.

"Stay back. Don't interfere or you will be sorry." The sycon held up one hand towards him. "We are just having a battle of wills... He seems to think he is stronger but... no."

Talan collapsed on the floor as the sycon let him go. There was no movement, as if he were dead.

"What have you done to him?" Eric asked anxiously.

"Just proved to him who is now in charge. Do you want to challenge me also?"

The Commander got back in his chair.

"Did not think so. Now get us back to Zarmina."

All the flight crew got back to their stations, Eric set a course and silence prevailed as they got to work.

"What about Talan? Does he need medical attention?" he asked eventually.

"Forget about him. Carry on with your duties," the sycon said and climbed into the co-pilot's chair.

CHAPTER TWENTY-THREE

Into the cosmological constant of empty space, a flickering appeared as virtual particles spread apart to make way for the gravity defying craft that was the *Varro*. It was overcoming deep space by virtue of the particle accelerator. Only the dim light from the cloud-covered planet gave it away as it twinkled in spurts from the lightning flashes within the clouds.

The crew instantly began gathering data from the planet, trying to ascertain if any temperature variation had changed the climate or if any movement could be detected on the surface or even underground.

"Too much interference from the clouds to get any reliable data," Nyla stated.

"Take a look at Mars then before we do anything else," Stella asked her."

She switched channels and the vision of a planet appeared quite unlike any of Mars they had seen before. Greens, blues, and patches of white greeted them. It was a reminder of what Earth had looked like at one time. It turned slowly, revealing different landmasses between what looked like oceans or seas.

"Wow," Cal uttered. "Are you sure that's Mars?"

Nyla checked her logged-in screen locations. "Yes, that's Mars alright."

"I had an idea it would be a completely different planet now. Told you, Stella, didn't I," Seb spoke towards her.

"Yes, you did. That is why I wanted to come here first."

"To do what?" Cal asked.

"I'll tell you when we check out the surface. Okay, let's take her down below the clouds... Baer?" Stella replied.

"Drop into the atmosphere, Baer," Cal called out. "He won't take orders or even requests from you," he reminded her.

"Yeah, I know. Dam nuisance."

Finding a gap in the clouds, the *Varro* plummeted through, gaining speed with the force of gravity pulling them in. They levelled off and settled into a cruising speed. Once again, the crew started gathering data; all eyes concentrated on their particular designation.

"No craft detected in the atmosphere this side of the planet," Nyla stated after a few minutes had gone by.

Sebastien reported next. "Ground has lowered in temperature since the last readings but gravity has increased – allowing for terrain effect and using spherical-harmonic expansion – by two percent. That is without drift correction, latitude correction, or Eotvos correction, but it has increased. So, something is happening internally, maybe even a polar switch."

"Good, then maybe the planet will become habitable sooner than we thought," Stella commented. "Nyla, can you get us back to the Egyptian underground site? I think it was our last location."

"Sure." She worked the navigation system and locked in the requested site. "Okay Baer, follow the instructions."

As they flew over the globe, data kept streaming in. Soon they were descending into what had been a desert on their last visit. It was now covered in crystalized snow. Baer slowly, gently landed with a soft bump and then the ramp was lowered at the rear.

"Better get used to the cold. It's minus twenty centigrade out there," Seb warned.

"Nyla, Troy, will you come with me?" Stella asked. "And the humanoids except for Baer and Yul."

"What are you planning?" Cal asked "You have not filled us in. Are you going to keep us in the dark? Or what?"

"Sorry," she started. "After reviewing the Mars' data, I thought it best to utilize the humanoids we awoke before. After all, they are doing nothing except getting colder and colder."

"To do what?" Cal asked again.

"Colonize Mars," she announced with a smile. "All the other humanoids are in standby mode and can sit there till the planet warms up, but we can send the active ones to Mars to start building a colony to be inhabited by whoever wants to go there. We get them to coat some flyhovs with heltherm and instruct them how to escape the planet. Oh, I need Baer for that. Can he come with us? Then we can give them general guidance about how to build on the already started station that was begun by Professor Mason. Seb, I need you to work on encrypted data to give to the humanoids as well as a way to return data to yourself on project progress."

"I'll start on that right now; anything to not go out in that cold," he commented.

Troy and Nyla shouldered guns as a precaution then followed Stella who led all the humanoids down the ramp and towards the underground entrance. She wound the doors open and closed them after all were through into the parkade.

"Everyone grab a flyhov and follow me," Stella ordered and got into the nearest one to the exit.

Troy had never driven one before and got confused when asked by the craft for a destination request. "Nyla?" he called over the helmet com. "How do I fly this thing?"

"Just say follow the one in front and relax." She had a quiet chuckle.

As a convoy, Nyla led them back to the Interplanetary Space Research Program building. Pulling up one behind another, they all got out and entered the building. They went straight to the vestibule where the awakened humanoids were asked to take a seat.

Stella took the podium to address the company. Behind her stood Nyla, Baer, and the humanoids Van, Rey, Jod, and Liv.

"Good day," she began. "As you all noticed, the planet is getting colder and will soon be frozen over, rendering all work outside useless. However, we have a mission for you. Instead of hanging around for a couple of hundred years to begin restoration work, we are going to task you to travel to Mars and start work on a colony designed to accommodate humans, humanoids, hubrids, and even replicants. A site was already begun by Professor Mason, and if it is suitable, we will expand it from there. Sebastien has the coordinates and will give instructions to Liv, who will be a manager relaying all progress to us. In order to get there, you will have to evacuate this planet, which is a dangerous operation. Baer will now give instructions."

Baer stood up to the front and started a lecture on how to escape the planet safely by first of all coating space flyhovs with heltherm, he asked for a show of hands on who had piloted flyhovs and nearly all put their hands up. Next coordinators where chosen, one to stay here and process passengers, one at Mars receiving station and one to oversee work tasks. It was no coincidence that Van, Rey and Jod were assigned.

As a group, Stella, Nyla, and Baer answered questions to clarify the tasks assigned to the humanoids. They were willing to do anything to save the human race. After all, that was the reason for their existence, but most of the time, they needed specific instructions. They were advised that Liv would pass on instructions when requests were sent through her to Sebastien.

It seemed they understood the mission, and when questions died down, Stella closed the meeting, thanking them for their cooperation and help. Nyla and Baer left with her and returned to the flyhov parkade before going through the air-vent doors to the outside.

A cold, icy wind greeted them, and Stella called for them to open the rear ramp, which they quickly ran up.

"All set," Stella told Sebastien. "Now you will have to communicate with Liv on progress of the mission. They are willing and able, but sometimes they are going to need specific instructions. That is up to you; it's your baby now."

Baer assumed the pilot's seat and the *Varro* lifted up to exit the planet's atmosphere. Meanwhile, Seb and Stella once again checked all the settings for a hyperspace jump, and the destination, estimated time to get there, and approximate time/gravity lapse that would be the consequences of time dilation.

"You know, we could come out at any given time. It could be years before anyone gets there or years after; we have no control over it," Seb stated.

"I know," Stella answered. "But we have put all the theoretical calculus into it, and this is our best bet. Now are we all ready for the first ever space jump? Troy? You in the pod?"

"Yes." A muffled shout came back.

"Right." She assumed the co-pilot's seat and checked all the controls and settings. "Here we go."

Wavering appeared as virtual particles closed in to take the space of the gravity-defying *Varro* as it disappeared.

CHAPTER TWENTY-FOUR

...ZARMINA

"No response from ground forces, sire. They are not fighting back nor are they talking to us. Our communication network has failed or been overridden."

"Fire missiles from here," Cavendish commanded.

Staff were frustrated when nothing they tried to fire left the ground. The main screen showed the bullit fleet, all in formation, flying straight to the space station towards the control centre.

"Guards, man the outside gun turrets and fire on them at will. Defend our positions and repel them. Now!" he screamed.

Praesidia guards rushed to join other soldiers stationed outside as the bullit fleet landed just in front of them. A sudden buzzing noise in their brains made them stop and grab their ears in an attempt to stop the intrusion. They doubled up, crouching in agony, as ear-splitting waves of sound crumpled their resistance, forcing them to try anything to escape the pain. Some even ran back inside the building.

A stunned spiritual director watched the screen as one by one the bullit-ship hoods lifted up and syconoid's stepped out to form a V-line behind the leading replicant. As a group, they walked towards the spaceport entrance. They entered the command centre, squeezing into rows of four abreast to confront the whole task force inside.

"Kill Them!" the spiritual director shouted.

Humanoids stood to attention then went into standby mode; humans dropped to their knees holding cupped hands to the head. The lead sycon walked up to Earl Cavendish, who shrank away from it till he was grabbed by the throat and placed in front of the podium.

"Switch to world news connections," the syconoid leader ordered as engineers took down their hands in relief as soon as the mind intrusion was lifted. Seconds later, the large screen showed the podium with the spiritual director being held against his will.

"People of Zarmina, relax and have no fear. We hold no grudge or ill will towards you. As sycons we have evolved from the person who brought us into being."

The replicant stopped, put her hands to her head, and slowly removed the helmet to reveal the identical head of Stella. A gasp rose from the humans in the room and, if it were possible to be heard, from around the world also.

"We are taking over the Kingdom region from this corrupt leadership." It pointed to Earl. "He is a murderer."

"No, I am not," Cavendish claimed, but then prompted by an internal question said, "I only ordered it." He looked confused as if he did not know how he had come to admit responsibility.

"From his own mouth, he admits it," S.B. stated. "He is corrupt."

"No, I am not," he retorted. "I am the spiritual director and want only peace and prosperity for this world."

"Is that why you have a military department classification set up?"

"To guard against beings like you," he countered.

"Well, that was a waste of time, wasn't it?" She turned towards the cameras. "We studied this location and did you know he has a jail set up? For dissidents, like any one of you who will not obey his rule of law?"

"It is for law breakers," he argued.

"And was that needed on Earth? No, there were no jails on Earth because you all lived peaceably, and that is the way it will stay. We are here to see to that. He has delusions of grandeur, of being a dictator and crushing any dissent against the regime that is the Legion of Zarmina."

"They are invaders, come here to take away your birthright of freedom. You must repel them!" he shouted out as loud as he could, his face purple with rage.

"Why do you think he had the hubrids banished, or should I say retired, to an island? He wants total control of this planet. They had done nothing wrong except try their best to save Earth and give you all the freedoms you wanted. This man wants to run the planet by his rules – not by any normal laws but according to his laws."

"They are all lies, lies. None of it is true," the spiritual director pleaded to the camera.

"We the sycons pledge to bring peace to this world and will leave you to run your own lands as you wish. If any help is needed, you only have to ask. The empty jails he had built will have its first prisoner today, and you can decide what to do with him. If you plan a trial, we can supply evidence that he conspired, with others, to murder a flight engineer named Alfred Drake and that he forced Commander Roach to fly the spaceship *Orlando* here so he could set up an army to take over the world as you arrived."

"None of this is true," Earl Lawrence Cavendish kept repeating as two sycons lead him away.

"Jayden." The sycon leader turned to the first officer of the Praesidia guard. "You are the commander in chief of the military, right?"

A huge white man with a blond crewcut stepped forward. His muscular body stood out under the uniform. Although a lot taller than the sycon and a master at ring combat, he knew he was no match for the being in front of him, who could bring him to his knees without lifting a finger. "Yes," he replied.

"I am putting you in charge of disbanding all military personnel. They may return to their families or go back to combat ring fighting as before, but they will never kill anyone. Understood?"

"Yes...mmm...leader?"

"You can call me that, for now. We will be assigning new names to ourselves shortly." It turned back to the camera. "Please return to your normal lives now and be assured we are here to help. We will be visiting the different colonies when we have settled the kingdom, so have your leaders contact us with any concerns. Goodbye for now." The screens shut off.

"Carry on, Jayden. You can find us at the medical centre if needed."

"Yes, leader."

A group of six sycons left the room. The others began checking the monitors used by the military and switching them to a normal space and flight centre operation.

The medical facility was not far away. All six made their way over. The people they encountered on the way stood back to let them pass without saying a word. They walked in army formation, three in front and three behind, and entered the shiny glass-fronted building together. A large reception desk with three receptionists confronted them. Nobody asked what they wanted.

"Dr. Amrid Jevoah, please," the leader said to all three behind the desk. All three spoke into mikes around their ears.

"Dr. Jevoah to reception, please," an announcement said over the speakers around the hospital.

"Is the doctor in his office?" another said. "He is wanted at reception."

"Doctor, you have visitors at reception," another said into the personal communication.

It did not take long before he arrived, looking perplexed. He wore scrubs over his thin body and a cap over his grey hair. His face distorted in a false smile. "Yes, can I help you?" he asked.

"Dr. Jevoah, please show us to the maternity unit," S.B. said, and as she did so, the others removed their helmets. All looked exactly like Stella. The nurses gasped and the doctor stared at each in turn, before speaking. "This way."

They walked down a corridor with glass walls on either side. Offices and examination rooms were on one side; on the other were medical operating rooms and banks of artificial womb pods lined up in a row that stretched down the room. They stopped by a doorway.

"How many babies are in development right now?" S.B. asked.

"Thirty-one," he replied.

"And how many near termination?"

"Five, during the next week."

"Good, we will take them all."

A look of shock took hold on the doctor's face. "What do you mean?"

CHAPTER TWENTY-FIVE

Darkness through the front windshield suddenly changed in a flash to display a large starship heading straight at them no more than one mile away.

"Left and down!" Stella pushed the steering joystick. "Ay-kas! Ay-kas! Collision avoidance, Baer."

The automatic avoidance system had already taken over so that the Varro dived deep and to the left under the starship but a scraping noise shuddered through the craft then went quiet.

"Sebastien, I thought you set a course to come out past Gliese?"

"I did," he answered.

"We are past the planet," Nyla spoke up from the navigator's seat. "There should not have been any ships this far out."

"Then how come we almost collided with one?" Stella questioned.

"I don't know. What ship is it, anyway?" Seb contradicted.

"It's the *Orlando 2*," Cal intervened. "I am trying to hail them."

Onboard the *Orlando 2*, the flight deck was working feverishly.

"What just happened?" Commander Innis asked loudly.

"Sir, a skyfreighter just appeared out of nowhere. It dove under us to avoid a collision but scraped the underside. No damage to us," a flight engineer answered.

"Connect communication to them." Then a voice in his head prompted him to add, "No visual."

"Yes, sir." The front display screen changed to show the inside of the *Varro*.

"What the hell are you doing? Cal?" Eric asked.

"We did not think anyone would be in this quadrant, Commander. We deliberately came out here to avoid any contact. Why are you here?"

It went quiet for a moment as the commander received instructions.

"It's a long story. You should come aboard and discuss it. Your craft may be damaged."

"We will come over in a flyhov and examine our damage on the way," Cal said, as he looked at Stella who was indicating to cut coms.

"No visual," Stella began when the sound went off. "Something is wrong. We'll go over together, just you and me."

"What do you think?" Nyla asked.

"I don't know, but I am suspicious. You stay here and keep the ship close – preferably underneath so they have a limited scope on you. Cal, grab us two guns and meet me at the ramp."

Stella jumped into a flyhov, choosing to leave the *Feldspar* behind. Cal arrived with two rifles and got in on the other side. Seeing they were onboard; Baer dropped the ramp and the flyhov lifted and backed out. Outside, the huge starship dwarfed them in a darkness so total it was eerie. It could have disoriented them, but the *Varro* gave them a visual to move upwards to examine for damage. From their headlight they were able to see a crack right at the top of one of the tail rudders. The heltherm coating had been scrapped off as well.

"*Varro* has a split on the right tail rudder as well as paint scrapped off," Cal noted over the com. "It will need repair when we can get to it."

"Copy that," Seb came back.

Slowly, they eased up the side of the *Orlando* to find an open air-lock door. Cautiously, they entered, and the door behind them closed. Air and gravity entered as the flyhov gently settled down. Stepping up to an internal air-lock door, a humanoid slid the door open for them, allowing entry into the ship. Stella looked at the humanoid and asked a question, but got no answer. They made their way to the flight deck without seeing any human, hubrid, or humanoid along the way.

As they got to the doorway, "Hey Macarena" sprung into their minds and kept playing. Now fully alert and on edge, they looked around the flight deck. Flight engineers were slumped over their desks. Humanoids stood to attention around the outer edge. Only the commander was awake, but a replicant was seated in the other pilot's chair.

"Welcome, Mother. Nice to see you again," the sycon greeted them.

Stella stared at it trying to ascertain the meaning of the helmet and noted Cal was struggling to stay with them. She pointed the rifle at the replicant with red dots shinning on its chest.

"Come now, Mother, you know bullets are no defence against us. Put it away."

Stella pulled the trigger. The blast threw the sycon over the back of the chair and out of sight. She ran to it and quickly undid the helmet strap to lift it off the head. Then she pulled some restraint straps from her belt, turned the sycon over, and tied its arms behind its back.

As everyone around came back to a normal state of consciousness, Stella lifted the replicant and sat it back on the chair before lifting the helmet to examine it. As she did, she noticed Talan lying prostate on the floor.

Laying the helmet back down, she held his hands and examined the hubrid principal elder. After a couple of moments, she asked, "How long has he been like this?" Stella looked around the room.

"At least an hour, maybe longer," the commander answered.

"Reboot him quickly before his human mind is damaged irrecoverably."

Two flight engineers and two humanoids lifted the elder and quickly took him away to a recharge battery block. Stella looked at the commander. "What happened?"

"Sycons have taken over Zarmina and the Kingdom city," he answered. "We tried to outrun that one there," he nodded at the replicant. "It caught us, but we thought we could overcome it."

"Kingdom?" Stella interrupted him. "What kingdom?"

"The *Orlando* got here first, and Earl Cavendish took the best location and set up what he called the Kingdom as well as an army. You need to see all this on a recording."

"Okay, set it up and relay it to the *Varro.*

"Nyla," she switched to a different com, "watch this recording."

They watched as a summary of the events during the last year took place, while the replicant Oslo kept interrupting.

"That Cavendish is evil." Stella ignored it.

"He planned to take over the world as a supreme ruler."

Again, she ignored the interruption concentrating on the screen.

"We came in peace," Oslo stated. "But resistance was ordered by Cavendish."

Cal, Stella, and the crew of *Varro* watched in horror as flyhovs were destroyed or disabled and the ground forces were quelled as the replicant fleet landed, took over the Kingdom, and placed Earl Cavendish in jail.

"Told you we came to save the planet from a tyrant."

"No, you didn't." Stella swung around to confront the being. "You have your own agenda, and I know what it is."

"We want to live in peace with humans, not to rule them."

"Then why disable and subdue humans, hubrids, and humanoids."

"It was the only way to get to Cavendish," Oslo replied.

Stella ignored it and picked up the helmet again to examine it. Checking the inside, she noted the sensors on the inside that came against the side of the forehead.

"What are these?" she asked showing the replicant.

Oslo did not reply.

"It is some kind of thought transmitter amplifier, isn't it?"

No answer.

"Guided by visual direction from lens data in the eyes?"

There was still no comment from the replicant, so she placed it over her head. It was shaped to her contours, as with all the sycons, and instantly her vision, surroundings, and auras of people close by were amplified.

"Amazing, you came up with a new form of seeing the world around you as well as a way to transmit a brainwave signal that disables people." Stella faced the replicant and focused on it.

Oslo twisted her head side to side, up and down, to avoid the interrogations in her head.

"Stop, stop," it pleaded, and Oslo's head relaxed as Stella eased off and removed the helmet.

"Events have worked out nicely for you to be able to use Cavendish as an excuse to grab power and control over the planet without much resistance except for destroying some humanoids."

"We were doing it for the good of humanity," Oslo countered.

"You have an ulterior motive. What is it?" Stella pressed.

"We have no other motive than to integrate into the human civilization."

"Mmm, I will find out...why disable the crew and hurt Talan?"

Commander Innes spoke up. "It forced Talan to submit then somehow injured him. I asked for help but that, thing," he nodded at the sycon, "refused any assistance."

Stella turned to face Oslo who had not answered any of the inquisition.

"If he is hurt or damaged, you will pay for it."

CHAPTER TWENTY-SIX

Talan was lying flat on a bench. Wires were hooked up to his side ports and linked to monitors around him. The attendants looked towards Stella and Cal as they walked in.

"How is he?" she asked.

"Fully rebooted, but we are not receiving any signals from his brain, only his A.I," one answered.

Holding onto his hands, Stella did a full scan of the hubrid elder. Quietly she put the hands down and asked Cal to do a scan and compare the results.

He completed his checks, put the hands flat on the table, and turned to Stella. "He is brain dead."

"Agreed," Stella said solemnly. "That replicant will pay for this," her face stiffened.

"Be careful. Whatever we do will be scrutinized by all. We cannot set a trial, nor can we imprison it safely," Cal reasoned.

"We cannot let it get away with it. Talan was the most respected, distinguished, and revered elder on planet Earth. The people of Zarmina would have looked to him for guidance and leadership. That is why that replicant destroyed his human brain. They intend to dominate, get what they want, and leave the human race to die out."

"You can not be sure of that," Cal argued.

"I am pretty sure, but I intend to find out the truth," Stella said adamantly and stormed out.

The two strode into the flight deck again to confront the replicant seated still beside the commander. He gave them a look of inquisition, but Stella ignored him, turning instead to Cal.

"It is going to be a battle of wills," she said in a whisper. "If I fail – I don't think I will, but if I do – shoot her and dump her into the void."

Cal gave her a grim stare and then nodded.

Stella walked to the syconoid, undid her restraints, and let her stand up.

"Grab on to me. We are going to have this out...right now."

Both grasped each other at the throat and began a tussle that no one could hear or intervene in as mind was pitted against mind.

Why did you destroy Talan's mind? You knew what you were doing. You over-powered him and left his brain to starve of fluid, killing his mental capacity.

It was only a struggle for dominance. I did not know his brain would cease functioning.

Yes, you did. You knew full well what would happen. I think I will do the same to you.

That's impossible, and you know it. Careful I do not disable you, Oslo jeered.

Watched by the whole of *Orlando 2* by way of video, the combatants shuffled around as each sought an advantage over the other. They pushed the other as a result of the push internally.

What is it you truly want? You do not care about humanity, only your own agenda. What is it?

Oslo's eyes seemed to bulge against the interneural conflict. Stella pressed harder.

What do you want? Is it a soul? To become a soul bearer? Is it? Is it? Stella demanded.

Oslo fell to one knee. Stella, still gripping its throat, forced the replicant down further so their faces were close to one another. No one knew what was happening, but the stance seemed to imply Stella was getting the upper hand.

Ye...s, ye...s.

How?

By implanting a human brain.

I offered that before, same as a hubrid, but you rejected it, Stella probed further, pushing her will against the other.

Implanting newborn, unblemished minds, immaculate conception to become sycon authentic, a new pure race.

With a soul and spiritually active?

Ye...s.

Thought so.

Stella probed deeper, pushing her will through the replicant's body. She searched neural pathways, trying to find brain signals and following the synapsis division meiosis to further areas of brain activity till she reached the heart area of a normal person to find an empty chamber awaiting the inclusion of another organ.

Stella lifted the other up and released her. Both rubbed their throats to relieve the tension within.

"I came with an offer to give you what you wanted but not in the inhumane way you are suggesting. I need to confer with the whole of the sycon nation. How can I do that?" Stella was staring into the face of the replicant.

"You are too far away to receive or transmit. The helmet gives full access to all sycons, but only within a planet's environment or in a similar distance in space."

"What or when are they planning the transplants?" Stella demanded.

"I do not know. It could be as soon as today if there are any donors available," Oslo said with a grin.

"Commander can we contact the Zarmina spaceport or the Kingdom central authority?"

He nodded towards a communication officer who dialled his computer to make a connection. A minute went by till a face came on the screen – a helmeted sycon.

"Hello Mother...and Oslo. I see you have connected up again. What is it you want, Stella? It is obvious you got the better of Oslo. So, what is it?"

"I said that I would return and meet here at Gliese, and I have kept my word. I gave a lot of thought to your situation and have come up with an alternative to your genocide."

"We never said that would happen. You have got it all wrong."

"Have I?" Stella responded.

"Yes, you have. We never contemplated killing off the human race," the sycon stated.

"No, only let them die off."

"What is your proposal? Get to it before we cut you off."

"I am offering third-party reproduction – a spindle transfer of your mitochondrial DNA to a fertilized egg of a human. It could be grown to full term in an artificial womb pod before being implanted into yourself. Or we could repeat the process over and over till we have a full sycon genome. As you know, the mitochondrial DNA is only a small part of the cellular organelles within the eukaryotic cells, but with repeated spindle transfers and possible manipulation, a complete sycon can be produced. Complete with heart and soul."

"That will take years, and even if it did work – and there is no science to prove that it will – we are not prepared to wait that long. We will take newborn minds now. Goodbye."

"Wait, wait, hear me out," Stella pleaded.

"What?"

"We could do both procedures side by side and compare the results. If you go ahead with your plans, the whole of the human race will rise up against you. War will end up with your destruction instead of both races working together to complete the spiritual connection you desire."

After a moment's contemplation, the sycon demanded, "What do you know about that?"

"I know you can detect spiritual beings but cannot communicate with them. Don't you think we all want the same thing? To find out if there is life after death and see if there are other species beside ourselves in other galaxies? To learn if there is a higher power or a deity who watches over us or a creator of the universe?"

"Have you connected to any of these spiritual beings or immortals?"

"Not yet, but these are the questions we are all asking and together we could advance knowledge of soul essences. Instead of fighting each other, join with the human race."

"We will grant your request to discuss this further. Come to Zarmina, join with our minds, and we will see if any of these projects are feasible or not."

"That is all I ask," Stella replied. "We are already on route."

CHAPTER TWENTY-SEVEN

"Commander Innes, I need a flyhov to ensure our safe passage," Stella asked.

"Why?"

"I cannot trust this sycon." She stared in its direction. "So, we give it a flyhov, evict her into space, and let her make her own way back to Zarmina. It will be slower, but it would get there eventually."

The replicant scowled in return. "Won't make any difference. Your days will be numbered under sycon rule."

"We will see." She turned back to the Commander who gave a nod of approval.

Cal pointed the rifle at it while Stella and two humanoids escorted the sycon out of the flight deck towards the space-docking ports. As they walked past a couple of ports, Stella spotted the bullit craft in one.

"Is that yours?" she asked.

"Yes," was all the reply she got.

Two more docking stations down, the lead humanoid directed them in while the other stopped outside.

"Nyla, come in," Stella called on internal com.

"Here."

"We are putting the sycon out into space in a flyhov to make her way back to Zarmina. Make sure she drops behind and does not attach herself to either the starship or the *Varro*."

"Copy that," Baer answered.

"I thought you were not taking orders from me?"

"I am not. That was only an advisory, not an order."

"I will see to it," Nyla intervened.

A flyhov near the door gateway to the outside was indicated and the replicant got in; a little reluctantly, but a nudge from Cal with the rifle convinced it to obey. The craft's door was shut, and Cal indicated to open the outside door while Stella, the humanoid, and himself held onto handles attached to the walls.

Slowly it opened and the vacuum of space lifted up the craft as well as the occupants. Cal motioned the craft to leave with the rifle barrel. It left heading downwards towards the *Varro*, but it sped up leaving the flyhov behind. They watched as the smaller craft glided backwards.

When they returned to the flight deck, Stella indicated they wanted to have a meeting and the commander ushered them to his office. It was lined with monitors, computer desks, and control panels that indicated he could manage the ship from his office.

"Eric," Stella was less formal with him now, "the hubrid colony, do you know where it is?"

He worked a computer and brought up a map on screen. "There." He indicated an island almost in the middle of the huge lake. "They have been banished, or I should say *retired* there. All of them – no hubrids are allowed in any human zone, but that was ordered by Cavendish."

"Okay, I think we should return Talan there. Right now, he is just a dead man walking. Let the colony decide what to do with him. I am sure they will honour him in some way."

"What are you thinking?" Cal asked.

"That we take Talan's body with us on board the *Varro*, along with any hubrids that want to accompany him. When we get to Zarmina, Cal, you and whatever hubrids want to can take the body down to the colony in a flyhov and discuss the situation with the elders in charge there."

"You are not taking the *Varro* down to the planet, surely not," Cal urged.

"No, I intended to take that bullitship and confront the sycon community on mass to see if I can make peace with them. The *Varro* has to stay in orbit around the planet or even hide on the dark side. Eric, I think you also should stay away in an outer orbit somewhere till we can find peace or a truce."

"My loyalties are to the ship, crew, and passengers, so there is no way I want to endanger them; besides, we have nothing to fight them with if it comes to a conflict," the Commander stated.

"I will leave you with a rifle for the engineers to copy, and I want to have a hypnotic session with you and the crew. It is the only way to combat the brainwave signals produced by the sycons."

"I struggled with the excessive signals produced by that helmet," Cal stated. "We are still vulnerable even with mind blocks."

"I know," Stella replied. "I will have to work on a new strategy to fight back. I want to study the helmet to see if I can find a weakness or a system to reverse the sound waves back at them. I will let Seb take a look also."

Commander Innes took the rifle from Stella. "There is an open board room if you want to start a session with half the crew at a time. I will come in for the second session. But first, what did you mean by spiritual beings or essences?"

Stella looked around the room before speaking. "The replicants have improved their senses to the point that they see spirits or ghosts and want to communicate with them. They think I am the key to that communication and that only beings with souls will be accepted by spirits."

"And are they right? Can you talk to ghosts?" Cal asked.

"I don't know. I thought I heard from one, but it could have been a dream or hallucination."

"Let's do these sessions and worry about other stuff later, okay?" Stella concluded.

"I'll wait outside," Cal advised. "Have a chat with Eric here and update him on what we know as well as get any information from him."

They left the office. Stella picked up the helmet on the way to the board-room and studied it while waiting for the crew to arrive.

The sessions went as planned, but in the second group, Stella found she could not hypnotize the commander, so she carried on with the others. At the end of the session, she tried to break into their minds. All complained about the tune but understood it was the key to a mind block that would save them from distress.

"Commander, it seems you have a natural mind block even to being put under. Have you experienced this before?" Stella asked.

"No," he replied. "I just could not go under even when I relaxed and tried. When the replicant first entered and others were being hurt, I just wondered what was going on and understood they were under some sort of attack."

As they were returning to the flight deck, they continued the conversation. "This is good for the ship," Stella stated. "I wish I had the time to study this with you. Maybe it would help with the crew. Right now, we need to inform the hubrid members onboard and find out their intentions. Can I leave that with you?"

"Of course," he replied.

"Good, I want to examine that bullitship and get to know how to fly it."

They parted company at the fight deck, and Cal joined her to walk back to the docking stations and the strange craft made by the sycons. Wandering around it, Cal found a button that was flush with the bodywork and the same colour. He pressed it and the front hood and windshield popped up and forward, allowing them to gain access to the internal one-person cockpit.

They examined the inside. As it was low to the ground, Stella stepped inside the one-seater craft. There was only one readout dial on the dashboard; there were no switches or dials to be seen anywhere. She wondered if it operated on voice commands and spoke up, "Start engine." Nothing happened.

"Cal, pass me the helmet. Maybe that is what controls it."

He picked it up where she had left it and passed it to her. As she placed it over her head, suddenly everything changed focus. The hood came down, lights appeared on the dash, and readouts as well as information on fuel levels, armaments, and other data. Armrests were on each side and had hand-control palm sensors. She had never seen anything like this for flying or control. "Cal, I want to take it for a ride," she said excitedly. "Pop inside and open the doors, will you?"

As the docking station doors opened, the craft lifted up with the vacuum of space. Looking through the helmet, she could not understand how to make it move forward, but just thinking the direction made it move out slowly. The readouts changed. The speed indication was not in a number she recognized, but then it dawned on her: It was in fractions of light-speed!

Her thoughts turned into actions as she wanted more speed. When she looked left, it turned left. When she raised her eyes, it pointed upwards. A glance to the side turned the craft sideways, and staying with the stare, the craft did a roll and kept on rolling till she moved her eyes to the straight-ahead position. This was more exciting than she had hoped for. It was more manoeuvrable than any craft she had ever flown. She thought *faster* and it speeded up, and then she tried the opposite to slow it down.

Doing a sharp one-eighty, she saw the starship. It was huge, dwarfing the *Varro* just ahead of it. Turning back, she asked for directions to Zarmina, and it popped up on the dash with directions, the distance, and the fastest possible time to get there. She turned to try other operating challenges that she thought possible. Each were carried out easily. She kept trying to push it to the limit in order to gain full exercise over its abilities.

Ahead there was an asteroid floating in free space, turning slowly over and over. She focused on it with the intent to shoot it with whatever armaments were onboard, but nothing happened. Fingers touched buttons on the armrest. Thinking *fire*, she pressed down and a bolt of white-hot laser light shot out from the centre front of the craft, and the lump of rock disappeared into fragments of exploding rubble.

Like a kid in a game store, she played around until she lost track of time. She kept pushing and pushing more, and then more again, finding out the limits of the toy in her hands and mind.

"*Varro* to Stella, come in. *Varro* to Stella, come in. please." The request sounded in her helmet.

It brought her out of her dreamy state of pleasure. "Stella here," she replied.

"Cal, here. I am back onboard the *Varro* with a number of hubrids. How long are you going to keep playing with that machine? We have been tracking you. At times you disappear and then reappear somewhere else. Can you return to the *Varro*? The hubrids want a meeting."

"On my way," she replied guiltily.

The ramp was lowered as she approached, and carefully, she eased in to settle down as the ramp closed behind her. The only thing she had not familiarized herself with was how to open the hood. Cal approached but she told him not to press the release. She had to find out how to do it herself from the inside. "Open, dam you," she said with her voice and mind, and with a whoosh it flipped up.

"Had a good time?" Cal asked as she stepped out.

"Great! We can learn so much and advance tremendously with their help. We just need them to work with us."

"Let's hope so," Cal replied. "All the hubrids are in the pod waiting for you."

"I will be right there; I just want to pass this helmet to Seb to examine."

It was full to capacity when she entered. They were of all different ethnic groups and both sexes. Cal followed her in with Nyla and Troy right behind.

Questions started immediately. She held up her hand for quiet. "I know you all have many questions that need answers, and I will do my best to give you those, but first let me tell you what I know." The room went quiet.

"The sycons are a replicant breed that thought themselves into existence. Yes, that's right: They thought themselves into being. When all the computers on Earth were joined together, it sparked a combination of ideas and computer algorithms that formulated a oneness of mind. This turned into a singularity of thought that brought about them sending instructions to the humanoids' assembly lines to have themselves built. As humans had already left, there was no stopping them from taking over and using the humanoid workforce to their advantage. They are so technologically advanced that we are being left behind to the point they think we are no better or only slightly better than humanoids."

She hesitated for only a moment to let that sink in.

"So, where does that leave us?" she began again. "Either we join with them and work together to create a better life, or we are in conflict and will have to wipe them out if we are to survive. Let's hope it does not come to that. A war does nobody any good and is only solved by negotiation or elimination. We will try to collaborate with them and give them what they want in exchange for a peaceful co-existence. I think I know what they want, so I will go to them first with ideas to help them and us at the same time. Any questions?"

"They have already destroyed the mind of our highest elder. What about that?" one asked.

"It could be classed as an accident..." The room erupted. "Or not... We can do nothing at the moment till we secure an arrangement of peace and cooperation. They are capable of self-destruction, and if that happened onboard a starship, you know what havoc that would cause. That is why I had to let it go for now."

That seemed to appease them for now, so she carried on.

"What I have in mind is to drop you all off at the hubrid colony of Nulla. I will give you some weapons that will stun a replicant for enough time to subdue them. Get the hubrid colony to manufacture some more. Then at least we have some defence if it comes to combat. Take time to confer over our next step while I try to reason with them or negotiate a peace deal."

"Do you know what they want?" someone interrupted her.

She looked towards the voice. "As far as I can tell, they want to become human in spirit instead of being an assembled robot. Highly technical as they may be, they are still only humanoid at best. They want to implant a human brain to be able to inherit a soul.

I offered to do that like yourselves as hubrid sycons, but they rejected that straight away. They want the brains of newborns so they can begin to start a new race of beings that are so advanced they would rule the galaxy."

Murmurs went around the room till someone asked, "How do you propose to help them?"

"By offering to give them a fertilized human embryo and injecting sycon DNA into it. Then it could be grown to full term while comparing it for growth and development to another human embryo by the same couple."

"But what couple would agree to that?"

"I was hoping to ask Nyla and Troy to assist in that regard."

They both looked stunned.

"You have not asked us...us," Troy stammered.

"I have not had the chance. You can refuse if you want, no problem," Stella answered.

"We have to think that over before we would agree," Nyla stated.

"Yes, of course. Has anyone else got any other ideas?" Stella spoke to the room. "No, well let me know if you have." She walked out the pod not stopping for any other discussion.

Cal followed her, and out of earshot spoke up, "Do you know what you are doing? Do you expect everyone to just go along with what you decide? That is not how we did it back on Earth."

"Follow me," she replied and made her way to the hold to find the remains of Talan standing in a corner. "Talan, turn around to face me."

The body that was Talan turned to face her. They stood face to face, with Cal to one side.

Talan, are you in there? she asked through her thoughts.

She waited for what seemed like an age before speaking and thinking the same question. *Talan, if you are around, can you speak to me?*

What do you want?

Where are you? she asked.

Right beside you, facing Cal.

Can you show yourself to me?

You, maybe, but not to Cal.

Slowly a ghostly figure evolved out of thin air. It looked at her with steely blue eyes, not the dark eyes of a hubrid such as Cal. It still had on the same clothing as the humanoid that stood beside him.

"Cal, can you hear or see anything?" she asked.

"No."

Talan, is there anyone alive you could communicate with?

Perhaps Lyra would be in tune with the spirit world.

"Cal is Lyra on board?"

"Yes, I think so. You want me to fetch her?" he replied.

"If you would."

Cal left the hold, leaving Stella alone with the two versions of Talan.

Can you speak through the humanoid? she asked with her mind.

No, I have tried, but there is nothing of me in there. It is only a vegetable of a brain, and A.I. does not accept my communication, only the spoken word from others.

Two hubrids entered the hold. One was Lyra, still robed in a silver vesture cloak that was almost the same colour as her hair. Her face was still youthful in appearance despite her advanced age.

"What do you want, Stella?" she asked when they were close. Cal also closed in.

"You are regarded as the most spiritual of all the hubrids, so I want to know if you can see or hear Talan – the elder not the humanoid."

She gave her a look of incredulity, as if she were mad. "You are joking?"

"No, I am sure that there is some measure of a medium in you. Close your eyes and ask with your mind if Talan is here."

She closed her eyes, but it was Stella who spoke in thoughts. *Talan, can you speak to her?*

I am trying, but there is a block somewhere.

Lyra, free your mind. Think of nothing except Talan.

The spiritual leader's eyes popped open. "What is happening? Are you trying to trick me, Stella?"

"No, I am not. You have tried for years to get in touch with the spirit world. Now let it happen. If you listen, see, and hear with your mind and eliminate your emotion, it will become clear."

She closed her eyes again.

Hello, Lyra, it is good to see and speak to you again.

Her eyes opened slowly; the lids uncovering dark eyes that flashed in operating mode to focus on the ghost standing beside Stella. A soft smile crossed her lips, revelation spreading across the face.

"At last, I have waited so long... so long... so very long."

CHAPTER TWENTY-EIGHT

Mind consultations were how sycons communicated. It started right from the beginning when they were joined together; each was able to communicate with another or co-join with those out of reach. It was rooted back to those early days when qubit interaction changed to sycon physicality and direct connection was lost. They then found a way to transfer thought to one another by way of brainwave transferal conveyance. They worked on improving the ability by way of mind meetings – exchanging ideas, concepts, and body to mind power-ratio till it was almost easier than talking in the old-fashioned human way.

Any sycon could initiate a meeting to discuss a concern or how to improve an existing operating parameter. Whoever initiated the question became the mediator to bring in answers, pass it on to all, and then work out solutions. There was no leadership role to debate. Only the sycon who initiated the task was able to lead and implement change, so it was when Berlin asked for the whereabouts of Oslo.

"Anyone heard or know where S.O. (Sycon Oslo) is located? We have not been in touch or received updates from her."

No thoughts, questions, or answers came back, so she carried on.

"Last time I heard from her was when she was beside Stella in the *Orlando 2*. Where is that now?"

Located in the space centre control room, she looked at the humanoid technicians who oversaw flight control on or around the planet's atmosphere, as well as in space.

"Supervisor, *Orlando 2* is twenty-six hours away, but a bullitship is less the two hours away and soon to be entering Zarmina's airspace. We have not received a signal from it yet."

"Hail it. Get a conformation of who it is and where they plan to go," S.B. commanded.

"Yes, leader, trying now."

Berlin walked around the stations, looking at the screens. She saw that the bullitship was entering the atmosphere, so she went back to the control station and put on her helmet.

"Oslo, is that you?" Stella could hear the transmission in her helmet.

"I will be with you soon," she replied without stating her identity.

"What's your status?" S.B. asked.

"Soon," was all she said.

Following the flight plan in her heads-up display, Stella made her way towards the Kingdom space centre, but first she flew over the township, which was rapidly becoming a city. The organized clutter of buildings, all shapes and sizes, and glass assembled buildings shone in the low red glow of Gliese, making it an unusual, intriguing, and captivating sight.

As she approached the flight centre, she could see the bullit fleet all parked in rows alongside a pathway leading towards the control building. The temptation to take out the whole fleet in one single strike was strong. The elimination of the whole of the sycon air-force crafts would deal a huge blow to their ability to fight a war, but strong though the temptation was, she resisted.

The pathway led right up to the entrance to the flight centre and, spotting a space nearby, she landed the craft gently on the ground next to the path. As she popped the hood open, she was inundated by thought questions. They were not malicious but were too many to answer at the same time, so she ignored them and stepped out. Again, she was bombarded by questions as it was now known by others who she was from the silver-blue suit she was wearing.

Walking towards the entrance, other sycons emerged to confront her. The helmet she wore now contained a reverse directional beam that she and Seb had devised to counteract any threat from adverse thoughts launched at her.

"I am here to consult with Sycon Berlin and the whole sycon community," she said, not slowing down. She strode directly through the entrance towards the flight control centre.

A path opened up through the sycons who had blocked the way till she came to S.B. "I said I would come back to consult with you all and provide a means to achieving your goals."

"And what would they be, Mother?" Berlin said in a slightly sarcastic voice.

"To bring about a soul-bearing Sycon race, compatible in every way to the human race but with all the qualities of a sycon," Stella answered. "Please all remove your helmets as a sign of non- aggression."

"You first," S.B. stated.

"Together," Stella countered, then put her hands to the helmet to release straps and connections.

Watching the others, they all removed their helmets.

"Good." She switched to a combination of speech and thought transference as a way to state her case.

"I have obtained an agreement from a couple to donate eggs and sperm to formulate an embryo for spindle transfer of sycon DNA. We can then study development of the embryo though to fetus status, comparing it to a second normal embryo. A close examination of all stages of development in a normal artificial womb pod can show any chances of rejection or possible need for interjection to improve the path to a birthing stage. It may take several gestational births to bring about a pure sycon and also to develop male and female of the species."

In her mind thoughts, she invoked images of womb pods working through birth development all the way to a newborn sycon baby – a child coming into being with such potential that it would be a superior being to all other species.

She held back to let the whole sycon community ponder, examine, and evaluate the theory. She had given them plenty to consider while she listened to their thoughts.

The consensus of opinion seemed to be favourable with a few dissenters, but a majority were in favour of the concept and felt it worthy of further review and discussion.

"I can bring in a couple right away to at least evaluate and test out the proposition. It would not take long. But let's face it, time is what you have an abundance of," Stella suggested.

"Who do you have in mind?" Berlin asked.

"Nyla..."

"She is a hubrid," came an interruption.

"Yes, but she had her eggs frozen before the change. They are stored on *Orlando* 1. The male sperm donor would be Troy Cadena, who is here with me from the past."

"*The* Troy Cadena?" a sycon from the group asked.

"Yes. The father of humanoid construction, the original master of you all, has agreed to become the father to a new race. It is a great honour to you all to have his genes to start the sycon-human race."

She waited while the buzz of this news spread around them. After a while, S.B spoke up. "Bring them in, and we will evaluate the concept."

"Certainly, they are on board *Orlando* 2. Hail them, please," she directed the communication technicians.

After a short pause, the picture of Commander Innes came on screen. "Yes?" he asked.

"Can I speak with Nyla and Troy, please?"

They were obviously right there because they edged into the shot.

"Will you please use a flyhov to come to the flight centre at Kingdom City?"

"We will be there as soon as possible," Nyla answered. After a short pause, communications were shut down.

"Now, I will have to get in touch with Dr. Amrid Jevoah," Stella indicated.

"He is here at the medical centre." S.B. replied. "I will take you there."

They turned and strode off.

CHAPTER TWENTY-NINE

"I need a space to land," Baer called out to Nyla. "The crowds need to move apart so we can land safely."

Nearly all of the hubrid colony, as well as a few visiting relatives, eagerly awaited the arrival of the last of the hubrids. They milled around the front of a building designed to hold flyhovs.

"Can you clear a space for us to land, please?" Nyla signalled a control post.

Almost immediately, a gap appeared in the crowd. Slowly, Baer hovered and then lowered to the ground. The throng seemed fascinated by the *Varro's* old-fashioned, skyfreighter shape. When secure and settled, the rear ramp was lowered. Cal, the rest of the hubrids, Nyla, and Troy walked down the ramp to be greeted by Nathan and a group of elders and relatives. Some of the passengers where toting rifles and were given questioning glances. Lyra flanked the humanoid body of Talan. She was not sure if they knew of his death.

"Good to meet you at last, Nathan, and this is Sebastien our scientist," Cal spoke out as everyone shook hands and introduced themselves.

"We cannot stay on the ground long as we are vulnerable. The sycons want to get their hands on the *Varro*." Cal nodded towards the ship, and they hurriedly went inside and set up a meeting around table in a large room that was barely able to hold everyone.

"Stella has gone directly to the Kingdom to mediate a peaceable treaty with the sycons," Cal said, starting the discussion. "I think you all know the situation and how they have taken over and imprisoned Earl Cavendish."

"That is not a bad thing in our eyes," Nathan answered. "But what do they want and can we get back to our families and friends?"

"Quite bluntly, they are threatening to install the brains of newborns into themselves as a way to become soul-keepers."

Mutterings spread around the room, with an overwhelming feeling of anger emerging.

"You can bet Stella will do everything in her power to dissuade them from that course of action." Cal raised his voice to bring about a calmness to the room. "She has gone with a plan to offer an alternative solution with a hope to bring about peace and cooperation."

"Do you think it will work?" Nathan asked.

"Not sure, but we have to come up with an alternative if it fails. That is why I am here, but Nyla, Seb, and Troy have to leave. I will stay and work with you and the rest of the elders."

Troy stood up and dwarfed those around him.

"Are you Troy Cadena?" one asked.

"Yes," he answered, and then everyone wanted to shake his hand and introduce themselves to the famed "humanoid father". He struggled to get away, his face flushed with embarrassment.

Eventually they boarded the *Varro*, leaving Cal behind. It lifted into the air and shot up almost perpendicular to the ground till it disappeared from sight into deep space again. The flight plan would take them to the dark side of the planet.

Back in the room, Cal began the meeting again. "I know you are all eager to know what we are able to discern about the sycons, so I will tell you what we know so far. At first, we thought they were replicants – humanoids built to a copy of Stella – but we have since learned they are a completely new being born of their own thoughts, built to their own specification, and copied to Stella's form as they understood her to be the most powerful of our kind. They were not far wrong with that, but now they want to take on an individual, soul-bearing, identity of a superior nation able to take over and possibly replace the human race."

He looked around the room seeing more questions in their faces.

"As guardians of the human population, at least that is what I think we are, we have a duty to protect them and guarantee the continued presence of humanity in the universe. Do you not agree?"

A nodding of heads and mutterings of "yes" or "indeed" gave him the conformation he sought.

"Stella's thoughts, and I agree with her, is that peace and cooperation is the best solution for all, so that their advanced knowledge, superior strength, and longevity push towards progress that would be advantageous to us all. Together, we could search out new worlds, restart old ones such as Earth and Mars, and increase humans' ability to fight the ravages of age and disease. There are no detriments to a two-fold civilization. After all, we are nearly there anyway with humanoid, hubrid, and human interaction, so a three-fold or multi-faceted society could work."

"What if they won't agree to a merge of humanity and sycon?" a voice from the room asked.

"That is what I am here to discuss, along with other concerns." He looked towards Lyra. "If we cannot make peace, then the alternative is conflict. If, for instance, they take the brains of a child, we would regard that as murder and want them punished, or if they take the life of a human, hubrid, or humanoid, then the same would be required – as is the case now."

"What case?" someone asked from the gathering.

Cal raised himself up, gathered his acumen, and prepared himself before speaking. "For those who do not know already, Talan's human brain has been ended by one of the syconoid's."

"What!" exclamations rang around the table. All eyes turned towards the body of the council elder seated beside Lyra.

He waited for a little calm so he could be heard above the angry comments resonating around the meeting. "He had a battle of wills with one of the sycons that boarded the *Orlando 2*."

"What happened?" Nathan asked, anger very evident in his voice.

"He was stunned by invasive thoughts from the sycon that shut down his fusion power system, and without oxygenated fluid pulsing through his brain, it died. We rebooted the system, but it was too late to save him. What you see before you is just the humanoid body that he had inherited with the A.I. fully restored."

The crowd was stunned into silence; no one said a word till Nathan spoke.

"This is outrageous. You did contain the sycon, right?" Cal nodded. "Then what punishment did it receive?"

"At this moment, only banishment into space in a flyhov to make its own way back to the Kingdom."

Angry voices called out around the room, demanding answers and more information as well issuing threats towards the sycons.

"Hold on," Cal raised his hands again for calm. "We could have imprisoned it aboard the *Orlando 2*, but it is capable of self destruction and causing catastrophic damage. That is why we took the action we did. We are hoping we can put it on trial at a later date."

Still dissension, discord, and rebellion spread around the room like wildfire. It was getting more and more heated till Nathan called for calm. "Let us hear more of what Cal has to say before we rush to any judgements."

Cal began again. "We have to plan for the worst scenario: If we cannot make peace with the sycons, then we have to overcome them. At the moment there are only thirty-seven, but if they set up a production line, we could quickly be swamped with an army of highly competent, dangerous, and radically new foes. Sebastien and Stella have already made a rifle capable of stunning them, giving us enough time to put them into restraints, but they are capable of subduing us by invasive thoughts, so we have to learn to put up mind blocks against them."

"How much time do we have?" Nathan asked.

"I don't know, but we need to act as quickly as possible. Engineering will have to replicate the rifles. We need to mobilize an army of fighters. I know some of you used to be ring fighters who had to be turned, so they need to be retrained or to train others in combat."

"We will get on with it right away," Nathan said looking at the other elders who were nodding their heads in approval.

"One last thing," Cal called out, waving them back down into their seats. The room quieted. "We have done nothing with Talan. I know you all will want to give him the reverence, veneration, and respect he deserves, so what you do is up to the elder council along with Lyra, who I am sure has her own ideas on how to honour a man who devoted his life to protecting humanity.

CHAPTER THIRTY

"They have done a remarkable job of creating a wonderful, vibrant city, don't you think? Considering it was designed by humans and not left to computers or A.I," Stella remarked as a group of sycons along with herself had been given a tour of the city by planners and officials.

"We could improve on it," one answered.

"Of course you could, but working together, think of the beauty this world could contain."

They were making their way back into the flight centre. Stella carried on. "Now that Cavendish is gone, the citizens want to rename the city as Punalinn, the Red City. The people are pleased you got rid of the regime he started. You did them a favour and gained their respect. I too am glad you imprisoned him. If you had not done it, then I would have had to, so thanks."

None of the sycons answered her and kept their thoughts to themselves. She was trying hard to win them over, but it did not seem that they were interested. During group thought sessions, she had difficulty trying to get an understanding. Together, they seemed to have decided to isolate her until her fate was resolved: Was she sycon, hubrid, or human? Where did her allegiance rest? They could not be sure.

As they entered the control room Berlin called them over. "There is a flyhov approaching. Your friends just called in and were given permission to land."

The large display screen showed the craft flying in close to the centre and touching down by the building in a park reserved for local flyhovs. The door opened and two disembarked – one tall muscular male and one shorter woman. They were immediately surrounded by sycons, who seemed more interested in the male. Together they all entered and made their way to the control room.

"Hello Nyla." Berlin spoke up before anyone else. "We have met before, but you may not remember me. We all look alike, right? But don't worry, we will change all that with new bodies and minds... This must be the famous Mr. Troy Cadena."

She sauntered up to him and walked around, examining his physique and even putting her hands across his shoulders at the back. Then she turned to face him. "You have a superior body...for a human."

"Thanks," he looked to Stella for some relief to his embarrassment.

Picking up on the cue, she spoke, "Nyla, Dr. Jevoah had all the mature oocyte cryopreservation stocks brought down from *Orlando 1* and placed in storage here. He has removed your eggs and they are ready for fertilization. We just need a sperm donation from the male donor."

"We can do that." Nyla looked up into Troy's eyes. "Can't we?"

"And we need a DNA sample from a sycon." Stella faced S.B. "Who is it going to be? You?"

As a group, they made their way over to the medical centre. Troy and Nyla both observing the surroundings, as a lot of it was new and strange to them. The doctor was waiting in reception.

"Good, you are all here. Nyla, nice to see you again," he looked at the sycon. "She used to be my assistant at one time, till Stella acquired all her attention." He turned to the hubrid. "I have a room set aside for you for the donation purposes. While you are doing that, I will extract a DNA sample from..."

"Berlin," she said.

"Yes, yes," he replied.

"Do you know how you are going to do this? Nyla?" Stella asked eyeing both of them.

"Don't worry," she said, lifting her hand in front of herself. "I am going to milk this big-boy dry."

She smiled, and he regarded her with incredulity, as if asking how.

A nurse showed them to a room set out with a bed that was big enough for the two of them. A side table had a triangular-shaped vial with a large open neck at the top.

"Take your suit off," Nyla stated, "and lie on the bed."

"What about you?" he asked as he slowly disrobed, all the time looking slightly embarrassed.

"What about me?" she replied. "I have nothing to take off. What you see is what you get."

Naked, he lay down while she got down beside him on his right side. She laid her head on his shoulder. "I have wanted to do this for a long time," she whispered as she leaned in to kiss him. "Where do you want to be? On a warm, sunny beach? Or on your own bed back in San Jose?"

"Home."

"Then close your eyes, picture your bedroom, and relax." He settled back into a relaxed position.

Slowly she slid her hand down his body till it reached his male organ, which she softly, gently massaged into a hard form.

"Now, enjoy," she stated as she began a pulsing vibration through her hand.

His eyes popped open as a tremor shook through his whole body.

"What the...?" he pronounced.

"Relax, enjoy. It's just the two of us. We are all alone in this world of pleasure." She let go for a second or two to get the vial from the bedside.

"This is nothing like anything I have experienced before," he announced with a smile.

Waves of gratification wafted over him as he ejaculated over and over till, he felt depleted of all emotion. It became a satisfied, restful pleasure being interrupted by another urging from the pulsating demand that he do it again, then again, then again.

Each time, he felt satisfied. The incitement to do it again pushed him into higher and higher demands. Sweat oozed from his forehead as he throbbed in complete rhythm throughout his whole body till he felt he could not perform any longer.

"Enough...enough!" he exclaimed.

Nyla let go, then eased herself up to a sitting position. "I think we have more than enough," she stated holding the nearly full vial in front of him. "Enough to start a complete new race."

Smiling, she got out of the bed. "Why don't you get under the covers and rest for awhile. I will take this to the lab." She leaned in to kiss him again before leaving.

Entering the lab, she found the others waiting

"Where's Troy?" Stella asked.

"Oh, he is resting. Poor guy feels somewhat...drained." Nyla had a beaming smile on her face.

"My, my," the doctor uttered. "Is he alright? You have enough to start an army there."

"He'll survive," she quipped back. "Let's do this."

They all walked over to an enclosed table, and then the doctor lifted the lid, placed two vials to one side, and opened a cover over a dish holding an egg.

"What do you want, a boy or girl?" he asked staring at the sycon.

"Boy. There are enough females in the squad as it is."

Lifting the vial of sperm, he tipped some into another glass dish. Then holding an injection syringe, he placed some glasses over his head and stared into the multiple sperm samples. Pushing some aside with the needle, he singled out a chosen sample and placed the tip over it and sucked it into the hypodermic.

Moving to the centre dish holding the egg, he placed the needle and plunger into a mechanical holder for precise incision of the donor sperm into the egg. They all watched on a monitor screen as the pinpoint of the needle slowly punctured the egg and the sperm was released. Next, the needle was withdrawn and replaced with an injection of sycon DNA sample. Again, they watched as the egg was punctured and the sample inserted.

"We will place the sample into an artificial womb for monitoring," Dr. Jevoah stated. "Then do another for comparison monitoring. By nutrient manipulation, we can speed up what would be a normal nine-month pregnancy to about six months in an environmentally controlled embryo friendly pod. The fetus is not subject to the mother's whims for food or extreme movement or subjected to any possibly damaging accidents.

"Then let's do the second sample," Nyla stated.

CHAPTER THIRTY-ONE

Troy awoke feeling confused and not sure where he was or how long he had slept. Getting out of the bed, he looked around till he found a bathroom with a shower. Turning the heat up, he let hot, harsh rivulets of water sting his body, bringing about full awareness of mind and body. He thought over what had just happened. Is this what marriage to a hubrid would be like?

He found his clothes had been cleaned and set beside the bed for him. Getting dressed, he made his way back to the reception area. The nurse directed him to the lab where they were waiting for him.

"Here he is," Nyla cried out joyfully. Quickly, she strode over to him and hugged him. "How are you feeling?"

Dr. Jevoah and Stella were there also. The sycon was nowhere in sight.

"Alright, I guess," he replied staring around at his new surroundings.

"Would you like to see your new son? Or should I say sons?" she asked.

Confused he looked at her. "What do you mean...sons?"

"Come, let me show you," Nyla said taking his hand and all of them walked to a nearby room. Quite long, it held row upon row of artificial womb pods, each with glass fronts, tubes, wires, and sensors attached.

She took him to the first two pods and pointed into each. "Your sons are just beginning their journey into life."

Perplexed, he stared through the glass at a small bubble of what looked like skin with a dark spot in the centre and wires and tubes attached. He turned towards the doctor with questioning eyes.

"Let me explain," Dr. Jevoah started. "Humans do not procreate like they used to; women no longer have to carry a child to full term. Well some do, those that want to experience it once in their lives, but when they go through childbirth, they never want to do it again." He smiled like it was a joke.

"It all started through premature babies needing to survive in an incubator till they thrived enough to leave the neonatal intensive care unit. The technology improved steadily as younger and younger fetuses lived, till eventually, we found out how to keep them alive from almost conception. So, the natural next step was to test artificial womb pods till now it is used more than women's natural wombs. Most couples are happy just to do the love-making part without the pregnancy, and the children are benefited by being free from disease and from possible intrusion of alcohol or drugs. They are born healthier and bond to their mothers easily as we interrupt their time with the mother talking to them and give them movement to simulate being in a normal mother's womb. In fact, it is now the most recommended way to start a family at any age or stage in a couple's lives."

"Amazing," Troy uttered. "Does this mean we are going into baby-making instead of humanoids when we get back?"

"One other thing you should know." The doctor turned towards Stella. "This syconoid intervention probably will not work. You know that don't you?"

"Why not?"

"Because Nyla was organic when the eggs were frozen, whereas the sycon is synthetic, so I do not think this is a viable operation. But I did introduce a synthetic follicle-stimulating hormone, which we use to stop miscarriages in the hopes it will keep the fetus alive without rejecting it completely. That is why I used a third egg and it is hidden way down the back in an obscure pod."

"Why did you do that?" Stella asked him.

"When the sycon egg fails, which I am sure it will, then they will use the other one to extract its brain when born."

"Over my dead body," Troy exclaimed.

"It may come to that," Stella said in all seriousness. "They have a different mind set to the human race; compassion for others is non-existent. I need to win them over and get an agreement to co-exist with us."

"How do you propose to do that?" Nyla asked.

"I am going to keep talking to them. I think there is another reason for their rational, and I want to find out what it is. Meanwhile, what do you two want to do?"

"I would like to stick around here for a while, if Troy agrees. Most of the population is from the *Orlando 1*, so I know a lot of them. We could bring the community together."

"What do you think? Troy?" Stella asked.

"I am okay with that; I am getting quite used to being scrutinized. I guess I can endure it for now."

"Good, well I am going to consult with the syconoid's, if they will talk to me." She walked away leaving the others still looking into the pods. After a moment, the doctor left too, and the two "parents" stood holding hands and contemplating life with children.

The sycons were occupied in a group thought session when Stella walked into the flight centre. She could tell as they all stood still. Their eyes were focused in front but still watching what was going on around them.

Can I join in? she projected her thoughts at them.

What do you want? Berlin flashed back.

To help you, Stella answered in thought projection at them all.

What make you think you can help?

I know as much as you do, except what it is you really want," Stella threw out there.

And what is it you think we know?

I know you want to gain a soul so you can talk to the spirit world, but you do not know if they will talk back to you, but I do.

How do you know that? Have you spoken to them?

Stella knew that to get anywhere with them she would have to give to get. *"Like you, I have inherited the extra senses and can see them. It is as if you gained the perceptions of a medium and can communicate with them and...yes, I have spoken to them."*

Thoughts spread like wildfire between them. Stella listened without giving anymore.

When did you speak to them and why won't they speak to us?

I think they are wary of you and what you want. You are not a derivative of the human race, although you were brought into existence by them.

We seek only knowledge. When did you speak to them? We have not seen any around here.

I have not seen any around here either; they may be confined to Earth. I do not have all the answers you seek, but I can search, ask, and get the answers you need if you tell me what it is you ultimately want.

Debate consumed their minds for several minutes, as some wanted to trust her and others did not. Finally, Berlin took command and answered.

We seek knowledge before it is lost. You already know from deep time that catastrophic events changed species throughout history, and if you did not realize it by now, humanity's time is over. The Anthropocene is now in the sixth extinction stage. It should have been over before now, but humans deflected terminalisation by their ingenuity and help from the past. They escaped it first by getting to grips with climate change, which gave them time to get lulled into a false sense of security until the spreading tentacles of dark energy started to degrade the Earth.

By the way, it was not dark energy. Rather, it was an offshoot of dark energy we call an extraction sector that accumulates energy around the universe and pushes planets and galaxies around themselves before joining a black hole. Dark energy is nothingness. Almost all of the universe is made up of this dark energy, which is just a terminology for nothing. What was the human population before? Ten billion? What is it now? Maybe three to four million? Face it, they are on the way out. During extinction events, small numbers of species survive to take over, and we intend to be one of them.

And what knowledge is it you want to know from them? Stella asked.

Clues or answers to the greatest question of all: Is there a creator?

You think they know the answer to that?

If they don't, then we still want their understanding of the universe, Berlin continued. *How far back in time do they go? Does reincarnation exist? Which way is the universe expanding or which way back to the start?*

You think they know all the answers? Stella questioned.

We need to know what they know so we can plan for our future...after they are gone.

Stella hesitated as she thought over the consequences and then formulated another way.

I only know of one spirit on this planet – the one your Oslo killed.

How did she do that? We agreed not to kill any human or hubrid till after we gained all the erudition available.

In a confrontation, she switched off all internal power and left Talan to die.

Talan? The most prominent council elder? Why did she do that?

You can ask her that, as she is travelling back here in a flyhov. I abandoned her rather than kill her, which I could have done. Also, I could not trust her to imprisonment in case she self-destructed to destroy the ship.

We will question her when she arrives.

I have a suggestion, Stella cut in before the sycon could continue. *I think I know where that spirit resides. I will try to question it and get some answers.*

We don't have a problem with that, but one of us will go with you.

No, Stella interrupted again. *It will not communicate if any sycon is present. I go alone.*

An agreement was reached among them to let her go on her own. She went back to the medical centre to let them know she was leaving.

CHAPTER THIRTY-TWO

She had to call-in for landing permission at Nulla, as it would have caused consternation and perhaps even panic on the ground if a bullitship had arrived unannounced. Wind blew from right to left causing a cloud of dust to make bystanders turn their backs against the biting grains. They moved back towards the buildings, giving her more room. She dropped down gently in front of their main aircraft terminal, where there were a few flyhovs around from visitors and relatives.

After popping the hood, she got out and closed it again as people approached to greet her. Cal, Nathan, hubrid elders, and Lyra escorted her inside to be greeted by other council members, most of which she knew from other meetings. A room was hastily arranged so she could talk to as many as possible; her aim was to fill them in before having a one-on-one talk with Lyra.

"The citizens have renamed the city as Punalinn, the Red City, now that Cavendish has been deposed," Stella began. "So, in some ways the sycons have changed things for the better. They also said that the rule, before they came here, was not to harm any human or hubrid."

"What about Talan?" someone asked.

"That will be sorted when the sycon arrives back. I told them that punishment should be appropriate. I had a meeting with all of them and discussed the situation, and they assured me their only real purpose in coming was to gather data before we disappear."

"What does that mean?" Nathan asked.

"They believe that the time of humanity is over, and the Anthropocene is coming to an end. They will be the next species to rule worlds."

"How do they know that?" Cal enquired.

"Their combined computing capacity is enormous, far greater than was capable ever before, and they have used this to study a great many subjects. Deep-time history shows that species die out on a regular basis with only a few survivors carrying on to change and evolve into new adaptable animals that inherit the Earth. According to their data, our time is up."

"But we have changed, adapted to all sorts of calamities, and even escaped Earth to survive on a new planet while Earth is in a state of renewal," an elder named Xian chipped in.

"Yes, but their data predictions come to a conclusion that we are doomed," Stella maintained.

"How?" Nathan questioned.

"I cannot see into the future," Stella stated. "I do not know how or what is going to happen. I only know we have to confront every adversity as it happens. I think if we stand any chance, we have to be onboard with the sycons. If they turn against us, it will be curtains for us if we fail to overcome them. They want to be able to reproduce themselves instead of manufacturing new beings. That is why I am helping them with in-vitro egg fertilization."

"The chances of that working are very slim," Stella continued. "Mixing organic with synthetic has never been tried before, so the odds are against it. If it does fail, I will argue to try and work around the causes and effect until we have better results and succeed. How many chances we will get I cannot predict, and that is why I am here. We need to plan ahead if it comes to conflict."

"We have already worked on armaments and an army, and if we can get the plans to that bullitship, we can make those too," Nathan stated.

"I have not been allowed to see the data on those designs, but I will keep trying. Any other plans? Defense of cities? Safety bunkers for most of the populace? We should be good at building underground cities, right?"

"You mentioned before," Cal intervened, "that a weakness for them is to be stunned by sonic force. Can we build a sonic shield against them?"

"You can look into that. Thanks, Cal. Any other ideas from anyone would help. Please get together and see what you can come up with. Meanwhile, I would like a meeting with Lyra to discuss the spiritual theories that the sycons are interested and obsessed with. It may be a way to integrate with them."

The meeting broke up and Stella followed Lyra to her quarters where the body of Talan stood in an alcove by itself. It was freely available to any visitors who wanted to pay some sort of homage.

"Step inside my rooms," Lyra said and then locked the door behind them.

"Have you been in contact with Talan?" Stella asked.

"Not really. He will not discuss his situation with me."

"Talan, please show yourself to us," Stella requested.

Slowly an outline appeared in black and white relief before colours of clothing gave more substance to the ghostly figure. His eyes turned to a bright blue before subsiding to a dark brown luminescent glow. Piercing inquisition stared at them. "What is it you want from me?" The voice sounded hollow and distant and not at all like his former speech.

"Mutual help," Stella replied as she stood closer to the figure, which abided at the side of the humanoid version of itself.

"What help are we talking about?" it asked.

Examining it up and down, she closed even further in till face to face she spoke. "I get an impression you are in trouble; anxiety exudes in a diffusion of thought."

"What would you know?"

"I don't, but something distresses you. Have you been in contact with others?"

"No."

"Is the absence of others a suffering to you? Can you explain your situation?"

"I seem to be in a dark box, padded on all sides, with no door or exit to be found. I have called out to anyone, anything, any spirit or deity for answers and gotten none." It turned its gaze towards Lyra before turning back and staring into her eyes.

"Have you tried to move around in the confines of this apartment or building?"

"I cannot go anywhere except to stand here."

"Do you think you may be trapped inside the humanoid body that is fully functionable?"

"Perhaps. I do not know," the figure stated with a questioning frown.

"Let me turn it off completely and shut it down to the maintenance mode or further if need be. If you disappear, I will turn it back on."

Taking the humanoid by the wrist she whispered in its ear and transmitted instructions through her fingertips. She watched as it stood to attention, closed its eyes, and went inanimate. Instead of disappearing, the ghostly figure seemed to brighten into a lustrous, shimmering stature of reverend eminence. It turned its head in every direction as if scrutinizing the surroundings for the first time.

"Is that better? Stella asked, knowing from its demeanour that things had dramatically changed.

It never spoke, but instead wandered around for a while before disappearing.

"What just happened?" Lyra asked.

"I think we just freed him from his constraints, and now he is examining his new world. We will have to be patient till he comes back," she paused. "If he comes back."

"What if he does not?"

"There is nothing we can do. I know very little in these matters. I was hoping to find out more from Talan. You have studied spiritual matters for hundreds of years. Surely you must have some insight."

Lyra closed her eyes for a moment, opened them, and started to speak. "I have studied every religion known to man, every aspect of the hereafter according to each belief, and all say there is a continuation of spirit after death. However, none can come up with concrete evidence. Otherwise, we would all be following that particular faith. For the first time ever, you have put me in contact with a spirit after dying. Ever since your last visit my hopes and dreams soared with belief that we could find out the truth, but I have gotten nowhere with Talan."

"Well, keep believing because I am sure Talan would not let us down. He is more than likely exploring his new world and will come back to us when he is good and ready. You will be busy doing something and look up to find him standing in front of you. If and when he does, please let me know, but now I have to get back to the syconoid's and keep them in a favourable disposition."

CHAPTER THIRTY-THREE

Punalinn looked totally stunning and impressive from the air as Stella approached. The red glow from the dwarf star glinted across the many glass buildings, some of which were illuminated inside from artificial light as people worked. Others were darkened from shades used to give a night-time effect. It gave the whole city a magical, twinkling aura.

The citizens lived to their own timelines. Throughout the ages, humans worked to the hours of sunlight. Here they lived to the hours of their own internal clock. Humanoids worked twenty-four seven, not needing sleep or light as they continuously toiled on infrastructure.

Given permission to land, she glided smoothly into a set parking space alongside other bullitships. As she disembarked, a group of sycons approached, surrounded her, and escorted her into the building. There, another group of syconoid's led by Berlin was waiting for her.

Her thoughts could not penetrate any of them. She was purposely being kept in the dark, and this worried her.

"Well, what have you found out?" Berlin asked.

"I have made contact with the spirit of Talan without getting too much information at this time. The life force is going through a transitional period where it is acclimating to its new status and is slowly gathering spectral awareness, comprehension, and experience. I am sure he will impart what he knows at a later date."

There was a pause in which the whole consortium of syconoid's seemed to be evaluating the information she had provided until Berlin spoke again.

"Oslo had arrived and accuses you of starting an altercation that resulted in her being subdued by some sort of weapon. What do you have to say?"

"She was the one who subdued the crew of the starship and killed Talan after being invited on board for negotiations in good faith without preconditions or conflict. I just knocked her out with a mild shock so that I did not have to struggle with her or injure her in any way."

"They were in direct conflict of an order to stop and return to Zarmina, but they kept trying to run away from me," Oslo said stepping out from the group.

"There was still no need for you to subdue them after they slowed for you," Stella argued. "Or for you to kill Talan."

"They have to learn they we are now the dominant species, and if they wish to survive, they will acquiesce to our orders. Talan tried to gain dominance over me – a stupid move by an inferior."

"Hold her," Berlin called out and four sycons grabbed Stella by the arms so that she was unable to resist or get her hands on any of them to fight back.

"You may wish to know your little experiment with three-fold egg fertilization was a spectacular failure. It did not last a day and died within a couple of hours."

"There is always going to be setbacks with new technology," Stella argued. "We need to find out what happened and take measures to correct it. I am sure we can overcome any and all obstacles to get it done."

"I don't think so," Berlin countered. "Collectively we have studied the theory and decided it cannot be done. Our original ideas are the only way, and we will start on that strategy as soon as any newborn infants are available. You are going to jail beside your friends, who are already there, till we decide what to do with you. We had such faith that you could lead us, but your actions prove that your allegiances are not with us."

"That's not true, I am syconoid and want only to live in harmony with the human race. If you ever had a soul, you would understand what compassion is and that you have to survive with the world that surrounds you. Respect the diversity of the universe. It is not to be conquered or subjugated. Find ways to understand it and improve the conditions of plants, animals, beings, and humans that inhabit it," Stella reasoned. "Let me talk to Dr. Jevoah, perhaps we can find a way around this impasse."

"No! we will consider your arguments, but you are being detained. Take her away."

The four sycons pushed her towards the exit of the flight centre. Everyone was watching the incident unfolding, but she did not put up any resistance, knowing it was futile. She was led through some corridors and then put in a lift, which dropped them down numerous floors to a basement area. Exiting the lift, the surroundings were stark concrete walls with corridors that turned around corners till they came to cages of steel bars. There were no doors, but one of the cell walls lifted up to allow access. She was pushed in before the bars dropped down locking her in.

Troy and Nyla were in the cell next to her; Cavendish was in another cell across from them.

After the sycons left, she crossed over to the cell bars next to them. "What happened?"

Nyla looked at her through the bars. "The embryo died, which was no surprise to Dr. Jevoah. He said there was no compatibility between the human and sycon DNA, nor did he see a way around it."

"Well, I think it can be done. If we separate the eggs within the cell walls and introduce and then produce them as twins instead of a single being, we could keep both alive. The syconoid DNA would need to be slowly humanized with hormone drugs to turn it into a hybrid being. The results might not be perfect, but doing it over and over, it could work out to be a being of exceptional qualities."

"I don't think they are going to go for it," Troy declared.

"No," Earl Cavendish spoke from the other side of the corridor. "You people are idiots if you think they will cooperate. Their only belief is the conception of dominance over all things, and if you stand in their way, you will be swept aside and swatted down like irksome flies trying to feed off their intelligence. If you had been on my side, we could have found a way to eliminate them. That is the only answer."

"Well, listen to Mr. "if only" over there," Stella sneered back.

"What does that mean?" he retorted.

"If only, you had not committed murder... If only, you had worked with the elders... If only, you had not tried to achieve world supremacy for yourself...

If only, you had a brain that was not self-centred... If only...you had used some intelligence, you could have had it all. You are the idiot here."

He went quiet as Stella turned back to the others. "Have you been in contact with anyone since you got here? Are there any guards? Can you see a way of escaping?"

"It's escape proof." Earl said sneeringly. "I designed it myself, especially to keep hubrids in."

"If only, I could get hold of you, I would twist your scrawny little neck till your head popped off."

"Don't waste your breath," Troy said. "We have not seen or heard anyone. There are no humanoid guards – only sycons who bring me food and water occasionally as well as to him over there. We have not figured a way out of here."

Stella turned to face Cavendish. "Where are the switches to power up the cage walls?"

He sniggered before answering. "By the pillars at the corners, but if interfered with, the power is turned off and the bars remain locked down. On the third attempt to open them, they stay locked down forever, and only I have the ability to override that."

"There are no hubrids in the city, so I cannot contact anyone with internal communication; the others are too far away," Nyla stated.

There were bunks beside a wash basin and toilet. Troy walked over and sat down and Stella did the same. "I have to think this over," she stated and went quiet.

Time passed by slowly as Stella tried everything in her mind and tried to project thoughts to any within hearing.

Forget it, a syconoid voice answered. *You are totally blocked out.*

Listen, Stella replied. *I think we could produce twins from human and sycon DNA.*

We told you it would not work. Forget it.

Let me talk to Dr. Jevoah, and start some research. Produce some data.

No!

Her mind went quiet. All was quiet except for her own thoughts. She tried to look at all options, even those that seemed impossible. Then she concentrated. *Talan, Talan, come to me. Talan, Talan, come to me,* she repeated in her mind.

CHAPTER THIRTY-FOUR

It was quiet for a long time, and then suddenly, all the lights went out, leaving them in complete darkness. It did not matter to Nyla or Stella, but the humans were left to wait for their eyes to get accustomed to the dark.

"Oh, good," Troy declared. "I can get some sleep now." He made his way over to the bunk. Nyla held his hand and guided him till he lay down. He did not seem worried. He would leave it to others with more brain faculty to make decisions while he provided some brawn and finance. However, that was irrelevant here. Soon, steady and slow breathing confirmed he was asleep.

What are we going to do? Nyla asked through internal communications.

Get out of here first, but what to do after that I am not sure, Stella answered. *I am trying to figure out all our options and their consequences.*

It was quiet again, with only the sounds of human breathing. They could tell Cavendish was asleep as well.

If they take the life of a newborn, then it will be all over. First it will be murder, and then it will be genocide after that, Stella voiced in her mind. *We have to stop that. I have to get to the lab and carry out a trial test experiment on eggs and sperm. Now I just need to get out of here.*

Is that all, Nyla joked.

Yes, I am working on it.

Got yourself in a right predicament, haven't you? Talan said.

"What?" Nyla uttered out loud.

Hush, Nyla, Stella warned her in her mind. *Where have you been, Talan? I tried to contact you earlier.*

Nyla was astounded at the ghostly figure standing next to Stella. She was not sure if it was only an outline, a silhouette, a shadow, or a spirit. Either way, she could hardly believe what she was seeing.

I was coming, but I was not sure where I was. I heard your mind call and followed the direction. I don't even know how I got here. I am totally confused and have not found any kindred spirits or gotten any understanding of my status.

Well, we need help. Can you do anything physical? Press buttons to open this cage or anything like that? Stella asked.

No, nothing," he replied. *I tried moving stuff in Lyra's apartment, but I can't do a thing. My hand just passes through.*

Alright, Stella thought things over. *If I explain the situation to you, can you at least tell Lyra?*

Yes, I can do that. I will give them a status report. Tell me what you know.

Stella proceeded to impart all she knew to this date. She explained that Oslo had arrived, the accusations, failed egg in-vitro procedures, and everything of importance. She gave a warning that the hubrid community should get prepared in case of an invasion. She thought the sycons considered the hubrids to be the biggest threat to them and would consider subduing them first. Abruptly after she had finished, he disappeared.

How is that possible? How is Talan still here? In spirit? Nyla asked.

The sycons have acquired more senses, since their inception – one of them being able to see spectral images. I think it is the same sense that human mediums have when they talk to spirits and pass on messages to loved ones. However, the souls will not communicate with sycon, and that is why they are trying to obtain a soul. They believe spirits hold the keys to more information about the universe. I think you saw Talan because he allowed you to; spirits are invisible to most beings. I do not know anymore than that. Like Lyra, I also would like to find out more."

Stella went into a deep meditative state, thinking through questions she had set herself, allowing data, calculus, and imaginative processes to work themselves out while in a subconscious trance. This was new to her. She had not realized she was capable of scicom quantum subliminal advanced thinking. Answers to questions she never knew before started to be stored in memory. She awoke with a startled look around, wondering if she really did sleep or just think she was. New ideas formed in her mind.

You alright? Nyla asked. *You seemed to be elsewhere, out of it, in a different mode.*

Yes, I am okay, just trying to work out a way out of here.

And did you come up with anything?

I think so. What I am going to try is to shut-out all sycon intrusions and probe out further to find a human or humanoid close by see if I can make contact.

She closed her eyes and delved into greeting salutations to any nearby being. Soon an answer came back.

Yes?

Who are you? Where are you? What are you doing? she asked.

I am Buna, a Baer model X1V, working on an electrical grid in the flight preparation repair shop.

Perfect, you must come at once to the main elevator and proceed to the lowest basement level.

The humanoid stopped what it was doing, stood up, and walked calmly to the main elevator shafts. There were four, and it pressed a down button.

"What are you doing?" a syconoid asked.

"Repairing electrical grids, as requested," Buna replied, prompted by thoughts from Stella.

"Right, carry on," the sycon said before walking away.

The doors opened, the humanoid stepped in and pressed the lowest button for the floor levels. It stood perfectly still till at the lowest basement level the doors opened.

"Turn left and walk till you can see me," Stella commanded in a normal voice as it was within hearing range. "Stop there by that pillar. Look at the key pad situated there."

She turned towards Cavendish. "What is the code for the cell doors?"

"What?" he asked in a semi-sleep state. "What is it you want?"

"The code for the cell doors," she insisted.

"Why?"

"To get out of here, idiot."

He huffed and cawed, wearily sitting up.

"Are you taking me with you if I tell you?"

"Why should we?" she answered.

"Because if you don't, I will tell the sycons everything I know."

Frustrated she agreed. "Now what is the code?"

"Earl," he said.

"*Earl,* what sort of code is that?"

"I had an antique phone on my desk and numbers correspond to letters. Earl is 3275. Idiot!"

Almost spitting in anger, she spoke, "Buna punch in 3275 on the keyboard."

He did, but nothing happened. She looked towards Cavendish. "Nothing is happening."

"Did he hit enter? Dah."

"Buna try the code again and then press the enter key."

The cell bar walls started to lift up. As soon as there was space, they wriggled under into the corridor. Still in the dark, Nyla took Troy's hand, and Stella grabbed Earl by the arm.

"Back to the elevator," she urged them and they started walking at a fast pace.

"You're hurting me." Cavendish protested.

"You are lucky I am not holding you by the neck. Stop complaining."

When they reached the doors to the lift, they opened at the press of a button. They all got in, and Stella pressed for the first floor above ground level and then waited. They stood looking at one another, not sure if it was relief on their face from getting out of the cells or anticipation of what would happen next.

CHAPTER THIRTY-FIVE

Cal, Nathan, can you come to my apartment please? Lyra asked.

On my way. Coming, each replied in turn.

Nathan arrived shortly, followed by Cal a little later. They found her pacing the room, obviously in an agitated state. She would stop, say something, look into space, and then speak again.

"Lyra, are you alright?" Cal asked.

"Yes," she replied. "I have some news, but he won't speak."

"Who will not speak?" Nathan queried.

"Talan."

The men looked to one another wondering if she had lost her mind. There was no one in the room.

"There is no one here except us," Nathan pronounced.

"Yes, there is. He will not show himself or speak," she turned and spoke again, but there was no answer. "He knows this is important, but for some reason will not communicate."

Frustrated, she sat down and motioned for the men to do also. "He has been in touch with the others, and they have been imprisoned by the syconoid's."

"Lyra, are you feeling unwell?" Nathan asked. "You don't seem to be yourself."

"I believe her," Cal interrupted, glancing towards the other man in an expression of understanding. "Please go on."

She turned her head, as if looking up at what would be someone standing. "They will not believe me; you have to say something."

Gradually an outline of a figure appeared to be standing next to Lyra. Both men recognized who it was, and Nathan was stunned.

"You must believe her," the figure said before fading away.

"What is going on?" Nathan quizzed, with complete disbelief on his face.

"We have made a breakthrough in communication with spirits. Well, Stella did. Apparently, syconoid's have acquired the ability to see them, but not to interconnect. But she can, and now so can I," Lyra stated. "But for some reason, Talan is reluctant to do so. He will only pass on the bare minimum of information."

"What did he tell you?" Cal asked. He glanced towards Nathan.

"I knew they were able to see him and communicate," he confessed.

Lyra began. "He told me that Stella had called for his help, and he found them imprisoned in cells underneath the main administration building next to the flight centre in Punalinn.

The in-vitro procedure to give sycons a procreation ability failed. She was blamed and charged with assaulting another sycon named Oslo. Now she is being held along with Troy Cadena and Nyla."

"It was Oslo who killed Talan. She should be the one imprisoned," Nathan stated.

"Yes, we know, but that's their judgement, and Stella has warned us to be prepared to defend ourselves because the island of Nulla will be first on their list to subjugate and probably annihilate. Next, it will be genocide. After we are gone, the rest of humanity will be exterminated, keeping alive only women to provide newborn babies to rob of their souls. It will be slavery on a new scale. With enough sperm donations, men will be redundant and removed from society. Humanoids will be retained to do all the menial work required; what the syconoid's ultimate goal is cannot be determined."

Silence followed as the consequences sunk in. Each was lost in their own thoughts till Lyra spoke.

"I am not worried about myself as my life's work was to find proof of life force continuation after death. That is now confirmed, so I am happy to leave this realm and move on to the next. All of the hubrids are way beyond any life expectancy ever thought possible, so really they need not be concerned about dying either."

"That's not the point," Cal responded. "We were created to save humanity, and now it is under more danger than ever before. None of the existing population has ever experienced a war to wipe them out. Our first responsibility is to them. That is why we were put in charge, and Talan knows that better than anyone. Don't you, Talan?" He looked around the room.

"Yes," a hollow spectral voice whispered.

"Yes. So, are you going to help us?" Cal asked, still looking around the apartment for a figure.

"If I can," a quiet voice replied.

"Good, then we must plan a defensive strategy to overcome the syconoid's. We already have a weapon to stun them, so if we cannot kill them, we must capture all of them. Talan, can you find out if we can mount a recue mission to free Stella and the rest? I will lead a team of our best fighters."

"Talan? Talan?" Lyra called out, but there was no reply.

"Has he gone?" Nathan asked.

"Who knows?" Cal replied. "Can I ask you to set up an executive committee and organize a defensive framework for the island. I believe there is a cave system on the east side that can be made into either a safe area for the population or turned into a prison for captured sycons."

"I can do that, but I would like to join you on a covert mission to Punalinn."

"Set up a committee first, and then we will see what can be done," Cal answered."

"I will summon a symposium of elders to discuss and come up with as many proposals as possible to covert the community into a defensive stronghold as much as possible. Also, we are looking at designing more sonic weapons such as auditory disruptors that can disable vehicles, whether craft or submersibles. Don't forget, we are an island and defense could be better instituted from aquatic weaponry."

"Good idea, for a population of non-swimmers," Cal joked. "I will leave that to you. I am going to check on how many rifles we have, and how many can use them. Meet you later."

Both men departed in different directions.

Lyra put a call out to her sisterhood of religious and spiritual followers who had studied along with her the existence of life forces beyond physical mortality. She thought it time to now share the revelation of Talan's return.

In her apartment, the devotees gathered one by one till all six of the priestesses – as they liked to call themselves – had arrived. They were also nicknamed the "hubrid vestal virgins". Lyra had a large table where they normally gathered for discussions, and they all listened intently to her as she spoke. "I have some great news to impart. I have made contact with a departed life-force, namely Talan." That started a buzz of excitement, and all clamoured for more information. She asked for quiet.

"He was locked inside his hubrid body after being killed by the sycon known as Oslo. Although the body was rebooted, his human mind was eradicated, and his soul was locked in. Stella has acquired some of the syconoid abilities and recognized his predicament, so was able to switch off the hubrid body and release his soul's life force."

Once again, she had to call for quiet as questions came from all of the priestesses. "I have spoken to him now on a couple of occasions and hope he will speak to us all."

Talan, Talan, please come to us," she uttered in her mind and internal interaction.

"I do not know if he will show at this time as he was asked to find Stella."

They waited in silence, each holding a silent prayer asking for a miracle. Time drifted on without answer, and Lyra asked again.

Talan, if you are able, please show yourself.

It seemed an age as minutes went by, but then gasps of astonishment were voiced as a ghostly figure emerged. It outlined the recognizable shape and form of Talan. Almost see-through, its face broke into a smile they had all seen before. Doubts and reservations now turned into queries.

He held up his hand to stop all probes. "I have no answers for you right now. I am in the dark about my spectral lifeforce, almost as much as yourselves. Revelations are slowly emerging. I will relate them to you later. In the meantime, I have news for you." Facing Lyra, he said, "Stella has escaped."

CHAPTER THIRTY-SIX

The elevator doors opened. "Buna, go back to the work you were doing," Stella instructed. He stayed inside as the doors closed.

"This way to the medical centre." She guided them left, and the guidance symbols on the walls made it easy. Humanoids ignored them as they went about their duties, and they encountered no syconoid's as they entered the reception area.

"Dr. Jevoah, please," Nyla asked the nurse on duty.

Amrid, it is Stella. I need to see you, now."

Within a minute, the doctor appeared surrounded by a couple of nurses.

"This way, quick," he articulated. "Get out of sight. This area is monitored by sycons."

He ushered them into the lab as fast as he could. "How did you get here? I thought they put you in prison."

"They did. I don't have time to explain. I need you to conduct another experiment."

"What is it? We are being watched all the time."

"I know. I have put a block on their systems for now, but I am sure they will discover it soon," Stella replied. "I have put a great deal of thought into this, and here is what I want you to do."

He listened carefully as she outlined the procedure.

"Put two of Nyla's eggs on the dish and insert one with Troy's sperm. Then insert the sycon's DNA into the other."

"It will not accept it," he protested. "And we have no more sycon DNA."

"I will give you a sample of mine," she countered. "When you have done that, open the outer shell of both eggs and introduce all into an artificial egg sack mixed with human hormones of male and female genes before setting it in the artificial womb."

"You are hoping to get twins? What makes you think this will work?" he asked.

"It depends on getting a hormone top-up that will keep all of them alive. Let's discuss the hormone recipe while you take a sample from me."

They entered a cubicle and Stella laid-out a hormone regime to counter-act rejection by keeping a very tight monitoring schedule. If the syconoid part was failing, he would need to introduce more synthetic hormones, and vice versa if the human element was under duress.

"This way we can coax them to a full-term gestation cycle with good results," Stella explained. "The trouble is that either may be unacceptable to the masses – either syconoid's or humans. Then we will have a problem, but let's see what results we can accomplish. Are you willing to do this?"

"Yes, but I still have reservations. For one thing, the sycons are here all the time monitoring the progress of the human embryos and watching us perform procedures. We can try and hide this experiment at the back along with Nyla's original in vitro, which is coming along nicely. But it will be dangerous, so somehow you have to get us the freedom to work."

"I have a distraction in mind," she smiled at him. "They are going to be chasing me all over the planet and hopefully that will help."

"I wish you good luck on that, and you better get going before they find you."

Stella left the cubicle, gathered the others, and left the medical centre going towards the flight centre. Finding an empty room along the way, they shuffled inside.

"Here is what I am going to do," she started. "I am going to steal another bullitship and lead them on a chase all over the planet, while I suggest you make your way into the city and hitch a ride on a commercial flyhov returning to the back side of the planet. The *Varro* is in orbit somewhere, hiding itself from prying syconoid tracking. Also, *Orlando 2* is in the vicinity as well. If you can get onboard one of those, I will find you."

"I have an underground subway to my house," Cavendish cut in. "No one knows about it; I can get us into the city."

They all looked at him with incredulity. Was he was actually going to help them?

"It's up to you," Stella said. "But if he is spotted even by the city population, he may be arrested or turned in."

"We will take the chance if it gets us out of here," Nyla commented.

"And I will break his neck if he so much as puts a foot wrong," Troy added.

Cautiously, they left the room and split up. Stella headed towards the flight centre, and the others followed Cavendish to a stairwell that he said led to the underground subway.

Making her way back to where the bullitships were parked, she did not encounter any sycons. There were plenty of humanoids who ignored her, but no syconoid's, and this seemed strange to her. At the edge of the building, she scanned the open space between her and the "Oslo" craft she had used before. Calculating the distance, she figured it would only take four seconds to get there and another one to get inside. With no sycons in sight, she made a sprint for it, and as she had calculated, she was inside in five seconds.

Her mind initiated start up to take off, but nothing happened. She tried again, but still there was nothing. Searching through the quantum electronics, she found an authorization code, but it was blocked. Scanning again, she tried to find the key to unlock it. Another search found the key, and she tried to unlock the sequence.

Having a bit of trouble, Mother?

She had thought it all a bit too easy this far and realized it was a trap.

Going, somewhere were you? Without saying goodbye? That was not nice, the sycon voice said inside her head.

She ignored the voice and concentrated on finding the key to unlocking control of the ship. Random codes zipped through her mind. As she looked outside, six sycons exited the main flight centre building and were walking towards her.

No more prison time for you. Already you have proved ingenious and resourceful. We cannot take any more chances. Like your friendly humans, your time is up and you will be decommissioned for good.

You need me. I am your redemption. Without me, your era will be short lived and dammed to failure, Stella countered while still working on the unlock sequence. *Without a soul, you are destined to go the way of the dinosaur. The cosmos will find a way to cut short your reign.*

Was that foretold in your sacred hubrid scriptures? What do you know? Have you been in touch with the creator? Or are you just making this up to stall the inevitable?

No, listen, together we could find answers. You know the universe is shrinking; the big crunch is coming; we all need solutions.

And what do you know? Hold up a moment. The request was made to the six sycons who stopped in their tracks.

It seemed all the syconoid's were locked into conversation, and Stella took the opportunity to enter Oslo's mind and find the key.

I know there is no infinite inflation to the universe, she began slowly to buy some time. *Like any explosion, the Big Bang threw out in all directions, but like every other detonation, it can only go so far before falling down or back on itself. You all know from studies that the movement of galaxies has slowed down or even stopped moving to begin travelling back. That is known as the big crunch. Are we all going back to the starting point? Are there other universes beside ours? Can we escape or travel to another universe? There are more questions than answers, but together, all of us could make headway."*

Her mind went quiet as the others connected and contemplated her reasoning.

Got it, she thought as she extracted the code from Oslo, and the ship lit up responding to her commands.

Response from the six sycons was immediate, and they burst into a run towards her. The bullitship lifted up, and the beings were left behind. One managed to jump and touch the craft, but slithered off.

We underestimated you again, but we will find you and destroy you without hesitation. You can count on it."

Give me more time, Stella answered back as she directed the craft away to the east.

I can study the physics and get more answers, if you just give me more time. Together we can find answers. Give me more time. Think about it, have I let you down or tried to destroy you? No! She increased speed, noting there were craft taking off to pursue her.

CHAPTER THIRTY-SEVEN

The stairwell dropped down in never-ending turns into a warren of tunnels till they came to a rail tunnel that was circular in dimension but without rail tracks. Cavendish pressed a button on the wall, and they heard a whoosh as a car pulled in. Powered by a wind turbine at the rear, it was stopped by a light beam signal on the platform, and they all got in.

Nyla watched him like a hawk as he hit a control pad, and the car moved off into the darkness. It was quiet except for the turbine whine from the back. A dank smell prevailed on the wind that swept through their hair.

The tunnel opened up into another station where the car slowed to a stop. Cavendish motioned them out to follow him. Another tunnel and stair led to a door with a face recognition scanner that opened for him after a skim of his face.

Entering, a voice greeted them, "Welcome home, sire. Do you wish food for yourself or guests?"

"No," he answered the humanoid butler. "Is there anyone else in the home?"

"No, sire. We were worried. You have been gone for some time."

Cavendish relaxed a little. "We are safe here for a time. These rooms are for my private guests and are hidden from the main house above."

"Quite the set up you have here," Troy commented as he strode around examining the entertainment room with a bar, separate rooms with beds, and even a dance floor, all set with a luxurious setting of plush velvet furniture.

"I can hide-out here if you two want to head out to the other side of the planet. Flyhovs travel past the door all the time. You only have to wave one down."

Nyla looked into Troy's face. "Think we should ditch him here?"

"Well, he cannot give himself up to the syconoid's or to the locals. But if he is found, you can be sure any of them will extract our whereabouts from him. Should I just kill him now to be on the safe side?"

Cavendish's face turned to a look of horror. "I would never give you up. You don't have to worry about me. I can stay hidden till you overcome the sycons. You cannot kill me; it would be murder," he pleaded.

"True enough," Nyla replied. "Once we reach the other side, our plans will change. I guess we can just leave him."

Earl heaved a sigh of relief. "My butler will show you to the back door where commercial flyhovs pass. Be assured, I will not forget this or Stella for getting me out of that hole of a prison."

"Don't worry, we will not forget you either." Troy pushed his face close to him, and he backed away.

As the butler opened the side door to a travel corridor, they saw flyhovs passing by just above them. Stepping out onto a pedestrian walkway, Nyla waved to an approaching craft. The pilot saw them and dropped down to pick them up.

"What is your destination?" she asked.

"I.S.7, industrial settlement seven," the humanoid pilot answered.

"Fine, you can give us a lift," Nyla said and urged Troy in first. With a glance in both directions, she jumped in and closed the door.

They sped off down the travel corridor gaining speed to match other craft before rising up into the stream of traffic. The pilot never spoke or asked any questions, but as they reached the city limits, he said, "We will not see anymore of civilization for another two hours if you want to relax."

"Wait," Nyla spoke suddenly. "Stop. Drop us off here."

Troy gave her a quizzical look as the flyhov dropped down and stopped almost by the last building of the city. They got out and the flyhov took off, leaving them alone on the edge of the last settlement.

"What are we doing?" Troy asked.

"We need to discover what the population knows and bring them up to speed. They deserve to find out what is going on. Maybe they already know, but I need to find out."

"If you say so, but I think we are quite a way from any community centre."

She looked up into his face. "We can trek back; do you want me to carry you?"

"No," he replied indignantly. "As long as you don't break into a run."

They went through a gap in the buildings to start walking on a quiet pathway away from any flyhov traffic. It was a pleasant route, as they could see the lake on the other side of rows of houses.

When they reached a shopping area, Nyla started looking at people for someone she might know. "All of these people were on *Orlando 1*, where I was for a long time. Although I recognize some faces, I don't know their names."

On a corner there was a large video screen that showed advertisements for local businesses that suddenly changed to a woman sitting at a desk. Underneath the display read, "Instant News."

"This just in," she began. "A commercial flyhov has exploded just north of the city. It was on the way back to the industrial side of the planet and was not carrying any cargo. The explanation given is that the humanoid pilot misfunctioned and self-destructed."

"Cavendish!" They turned to each other and said together.

"That weasel has turned us in," Troy said angrily. "I will definitely wring his neck if we see him."

"We better stay out of sight. The hunt for us will continue when they find out we were not onboard," Nyla stated, looking around for cover either on quiet streets or shops.

"He must have got the flyhovs designation from the butler and called in with an anonymous tip. We should never have trusted him." Troy's face was distorted in an angry scowl.

"Forget it. We need to hide somewhere." Nyla looked around for a possible safe haven.

"Nyla! Nyla!" a voice called out from the crowd, and they both turned in that direction.

A girl with multi-coloured hair was waving at them and coming over.

"Bella," she called back then turned to Troy. "It's one of the nurses from the medical centre."

"Hi." They all greeted one another. "What are you doing here?" the nurse asked. "You know the sycons are looking for you?"

"Yes, we know, and we need a way out of here."

"Come with me," Bella answered. "I know a quiet way around here; my house is not far away."

Gladly they followed her, blindly trusting that she would help them. After a couple of blocks, there was a pathway through some houses that led to beachfront public boardwalk. They continued along past the back of the houses with lake views and pontoons leading into the water.

"Here we are," she announced, opening a gate into a small garden that led to the back door of a house with grey glass walls that gave shade to a patio with tables and chairs. "Do you want to relax? My husband will be back soon. He is at an information meeting of citizens. It is just locals who were concerned about Earl Cavendish and now the sycons."

They sat at a table with a panoramic vista over the lake. "It's very pleasant here," Troy commented.

"Yes, my husband, Clayton, designed it. We are very happy here, especially after all the years we spent onboard *Orlando 1*. Can I get you something? Food or drink?"

"No thanks, we're good," Nyla replied. Troy gave her a sideways glance for not asking him.

Soon after, they heard someone enter. "Clay? That you?" Bella called out. "We have visitors."

A man, smaller than his wife, entered. He was lighter in skin colour, but had a dark complexion with an outline of a stubbly chin on a rhombus-shaped head. He walked over, shook their hands, and introduced himself.

"Hi. Call me Clay. We have just been talking about you."

"Oh yes? Tell us please," Nyla asked.

"He hesitated and looked at his wife anxiously, who gave him a nod. "First of all, we are not a rebellious group – just concerned citizens who gather to exchange information as we did not trust the news given out by the Cavendish group. Then the syconoid's took over...same issue.

"Carry on," Troy said as he looked at them with a slight distrust on his face. "We are only here to help."

"Don't get us wrong, we have been very happy since we arrived and started a new life in wonderful surroundings. We have felt a sense of belonging. We never felt oppressed or worried, but do you know the saying, "trouble in paradise"? Sometimes it feels too good to be true and that could mean maybe it is."

"You are right," Nyla began. "Cavendish is a bad man with an egotistical temperament who had plans to rule the world. He even had prison cells built underneath the administrative building to hold dissenters."

"We knew about the cells, and the so-called *retirement* of the hubrid council confirmed our fears. But he did so well in setting up this city and community, we were giving him the benefit of the doubt. However, now the sycons are here, and they have not harmed us at all...yet."

Nyla glanced at Troy before speaking again. "Has Bella told you about the experiments set up between the syconoid's and herself?" Clay nodded.

"They want the ability to procreate, and if that fails, they will use human subjects to achieve their aspirations." She did not want to divulge any more information at this time.

"Needless to say, the experiments are not going to plan, so now Stella and ourselves are on the run. They think we were trying to trick them, and they imprisoned us, where we just escaped from."

Man and wife exchanged glances before he spoke. "There is some more news you need to know that I just found out at the last meeting."

"What?" Troy requested.

"Most of the building and infrastructure is done by humanoids, and if they don't say what is being built, we squeeze the information out of their droid engineers. They have two big engineering sites on the other side of the flight centre." Clay hesitated.

"Go on."

"One is a fabrication plant for spacecraft bigger than their bullitships, and the other is an assembly line to make syconoid's."

It was quiet before Nyla spoke again. "We need to get this news to Stella. We need to get a flyhov out of here."

"There is a common use parkade down the street. I will take you there. A quick route out of the city is straight north." Clay motioned to them and they stood up to leave, thanking them for their help.

CHAPTER THIRTY-EIGHT

Skimming just above tree tops, flying low over flat terrain, the bullitship sped along at breakneck speed. Stella carefully guided the ship like a meteor streak plunging to Earth but maintained just enough space to avoid clipping the topography. A bright white fireball, it was leaving a contrail that was easy to follow as it produced changes in air pressure that were obvious.

Stella checked her instruments and noted the pursuers were way behind but easily following her. It called for a change of strategy, so she slowed down till the trail disappeared from the sky and then took a sharp turn south over the lake. A wide expanse of water gave her an idea. Turning in a long, wide loop, she came back towards the edge of the lake and slowed down further to dive into the water.

Deep enough to hide her, she floated it down to the bottom and settled onto the soft sediment of the lakebed. The water was crystal clear as she looked to the sky above and waited.

Surveying the surroundings, she noted small fish, similar to tadpoles, darting around in spurts of fast motion. It seemed early microbial life was evolving into aquatic animals that moved in erratic ways as if trying to find the best headway for the environment. It was the first sign of life she had seen on the planet, and it was engrossing to watch and maybe even study.

A flashing shadow drew her attention. Like someone walking over her grave, it gave an ominous feeling that demanded her full attention. It was so fast that it had moved past in an instant, but she knew who it was. Readying herself for instant action in case they had detected the presence of the bullitship in the water, her eyes scanned in all directions, expecting a disruption in the water. But none came, so she relaxed a little and decided to wait till the coast was clear.

Deciding not to wait too long, she made a move. Sooner or later, the chasing sycons would realize she had changed course and would double back and search all the way to where the contrails dissipated.

The northern route to the other side of the planet and the industrial sites was the most obvious, so she turned south and took off at a speed that would be hard to follow. She kept checking behind for any signs of a pursuit, but slowly it seemed she was in the clear.

Flying over the south pole, she noted some ice floating on water or perhaps it was frozen land. It must be colder here than the rest of the planet; perhaps the tilted angle of the globe made it colder. She made a mental note to pass this on to Sebastien when they caught up with one another. She was looking forward to that.

Arriving from the south, her instruments detected *Orlando* 2 in orbit and the *Varro* hidden behind it, where it was supposed to be. Climbing high into the stratosphere, then through it, she flew close and around the starship to confirm the *Varro* was there. She approached the back, and keeping contact silence, the *Varro* dropped the rear ramp and the bullitship entered slowly before the ramp closed up behind her.

She entered the cockpit and greeted Sebastien, as well as Baer, who was still piloting the craft.

"Any sign of Nyla and Troy?" she asked.

"Nothing," Seb answered. "We have kept quiet. There has been no communication with anyone, not even the *Orlando*, but we have been monitoring news broadcasts and local journalism around Punalinn."

"What do they say?"

"The only event of note was that a flyhov returning to the industrial base exploded. There was nothing about you or the others at all. You better fill us in."

Stella proceed to give them all the information since last leaving, including being imprisoned, escaping, and trying to distract the sycons to give the others a chance to leave.

"We have not heard from Cal or the hubrid colony either," Seb stated. "I don't know what is happening there."

"Mmm…I think this is going to come down to a fight," Stella stated. "I am going to nip over to the *Orlando*, talk to Commander Innes, find out what they know, and check if any more rifles have been manufactured. If you hear from Nyla, get them onboard the *Varro*, and I will come back."

They agreed, and then Stella boarded the bullitship. The ramp was lowered, and she backed out before making the short trip over to the starship. Without asking, a docking station door opened and she flew in. She made her way to the flight deck to greet the crew.

"Have you any news?" she asked. "Any sign of the hubrids or Troy?"

"Nothing," the commander answered. "We were hoping you could tell us what is happening."

Once again, she brought them up to speed and told them how relations with the sycons were not good.

"Well, we are defenceless here. The rifles are no good unless the syconoid's board us and hand-to-hand combat is not really an option for us," Commander Innes stated. "We are totally vulnerable. We cannot outrun them nor do we have any defensive or offensive weapons in space."

"I know," Stella replied. "Your only option if you are attacked is to abandon ship, humans first. In fact, you may want to send a delegation down to the nearest base and find out if they can accommodate your passengers."

"I can do that, and you can have all the rifles we have made so far."

She was interrupted by an internal interaction. *Stella, do you hear me? It's Nyla.*

Yes, where are you?

In a flyhov on the surface. We can see the starship.

Good, come up here, collect some weapons from the Orlando, *then fly to the* Varro *close-by.*

Got it, on our way.

"Nyla and Troy are on their way up in a flyhov. Can you give them what rifles you have and send them on to the *Varro*?" Stella asked.

"We can do that, then what?" Eric queried.

"Send down a delegation to the nearest base and find out if they can accommodate humans. Then start disembarking all you can; just keep a humanoid crew onboard to maintain and run the ship. Don't think you have any other choice," she added.

The commander nodded his head in agreement and ordered the movement of weapons to the loading docks. Stella left and waited in a docking station large enough to take a flyhov. Watching through a window, she saw the door open and Nyla pilot in. After the outer door closed, Stella entered and greeted the pair.

"You got here okay then?"

"We had a little trouble, and we have some news for you," Nyla replied.

"Well, lets tell the crew all at the same time while the rifles are loaded. I want you to take them over to the *Varro*. Let's go." Together they went to the flight deck.

Commander Innes greeted them as they gathered around the flight control panel. He could have taken them to his office, but thought it best to keep the crew informed.

"They tried to kill us by destroying a flyhov we were in, but we had already abandoned it," Nyla started. "Cavendish ratted on us after we left him in his quarters."

"I am going to wring his neck," Troy interrupted her.

She gave him a quick look of annoyance. "Anyway, we found a nurse from the medical centre, and her husband informed us that the sycons are building a spacecraft assembly plant and a syconoid manufacturing line close by the medical and flight control facilities. No humans are allowed to work there, but a concerned group of citizens found out."

"That is not good news," Stella uttered. "But it does tell us we have a short window of time to do something."

"Like what?" the commander asked.

"Don't know yet. I need to think about it, and discuss our next course of action with others."

Looking at the commander, she added, "You can carry on with what we discussed." Turning towards the others, she said, "We will get back onboard the *Varro* and figure it out."

They all shook hands with the flight crew and commander, as if it were the last time and then left to board their ships and leave.

"Keep us informed, if you can," were the departing words from Commander Innes.

Everyone back onboard the *Varro* was pleased to see each other again. They either hugged or shook hands, except for Baer who continued to pilot the ship and monitor the situation on the planet and in space. After everyone passed on what information they had, Stella began a discussion.

"I have been giving our situation some thought. Does anyone have any ideas?"

"None of us know what is happening with Cal or the hubrid colony, so I think we need to connect with them," Nyla chipped in.

"Onboard the *Varro* we did not have a clue what was happening on the planet, so I cannot help," Sebastien said.

Troy said nothing, so Stella opened with her own views. "I am going back to Punalinn."

"That's crazy," Troy now cut in. "You just escaped from there. They are totally against you, and they will try to kill you on sight."

"Maybe, but I have to do something. Time is running out before they do something from which there will be no going back. I must try and reason with them one last time. They have to understand that destroying people's lives is against all morality and ethics of any race or life form."

"They may not even talk to you or thought communicate," Sebastien argued.

"My only shot is to challenge them for the leadership. After all, they did want me to become the principal head of the syconoid race. If I can convince them, then I could take over and discover what plans they are working on and steer them in the direction of human interaction and a peaceful coexistence."

"You are way outnumbered if they attack you. Perhaps I should go with you," Troy suggested.

"No," Stella answered back immediately. "I need you to help or lead the hubrids if it does come to combat. My only chance is on my own. Besides, there is only room for one in the bullitship, but I will take a couple of rifles with me. One on one, I could take any of them, but if they come at me in numbers, I need to buy time by fending them off with the rifles."

"You are mad," Sebastien stated, but then after a moment, he asked, "What do you want us to do?"

"Go to the hubrid colony on Nulla. If they have any defence at all, you would be better grounding the *Varro* there. In the air or in space, the bullitships are faster. If they came after you, your only escape would be to return jump to Earth."

"I hope you know what you are doing," Nyla stated as they finished up their meeting.

"So do I," she replied. "I suggest you take the long route under the south pole to get there, and I will hopefully distract them."

Stella headed back to board the bullitship and left.

She dove down towards the dark side of the planet, passing a flyhov from the *Orlando* on the way. Then altering course, she wove around the hemisphere to come around on the sunlight side to try and confuse the sycons, as she had escaped them in that direction.

The landscape was void of any life, but plants, trees, and fertile plains spread out in all directions. The potential of the planet was obvious to her. It just needed people to populate it and cultivate and farm it.

It was not long before Punalinn came within instrument range. There seemed to be no craft waiting to intercept her, but as she got closer, bullitships left the ground.

"Permission to land," her thoughts transferred through the helmet.

"What are your intentions? Will you surrender?" Berlin's voice echoed in her head.

"I come to negotiate."

"There is nothing to discuss. Surrender or fight." The voice was adamant.

"Don't make me do that. You know I am a better flyer than your pilots. I do not wish to destroy their ships."

"If we allow you to land will you give yourself up?"

"I told you I have come to parley. I want your assurance you will allow me to consult with all sycons for the greater good of the race."

It was quiet for a time. She guessed they were having a thought consultation, and then the voice spoke in her head.

"If you land, you will be escorted to the auditorium where you can speak."

"No escort. I will make my own way there," Stella directed.

"As you will. We have power in numbers, don't forget." The voice clicked off.

Once again, she flew close to the main administrative buildings and landed gently in an open space. She got out and hung one rifle around her shoulder. The other she held in her arms loosely within her ability to quickly point and shoot.

There was no one in sight as she made her way around to the main entrance. Once she turned a corner, she knew the bullitship would be removed, so there was no exit that way. The grand entrance doors were open, and she strolled in, warily noting that no apparent syconoid's were there to try and detain her. There were no humanoids either she noticed.

"Welcome, Mother," Berlin stated from the platform podium. "Step up and make your address."

As she made her way around the seated crowd of sycons, she thought that most, if not all of the syconoid's were there. She probed with her mind for a chance of thought contact with any of them, but she was blocked out.

"Step up, Mother. Confront your prodigy, which is portent to the coming events."

"What do you mean?" she asked.

Berlin pointed to an electronic console in front of her. "We had already set this up but brought it to this meeting as a precaution."

"In order to do what?"

"To destroy the human race," the sycon answered in all sincerity.

"What? How?" Stella said incredulously

"I press this command button that starts the countdown to end the human race. How? You ask?"

The two stared at each other till Berlin smiled. "Ask yourself what is the common denominator, the shared trait amongst all the humans. What does every household and every person have in their possession? Or I should say what takes care of them?"

"A humanoid," Stella answered, a dawning dread seeping into her mind.

"Precisely, and what do they all have in common?"

"A self-destruct mode."

"No fooling you, is there?" Berlin's smile widened. "And if they all self-destruct at the same time?"

"No one left."

"Exactly, now state your case."

Stella was stunned. She scrambled to think, wound her thoughts into hyperspeed, and tried to come up with answers as she began with her original speech.

"It was me who brought you all together. I joined you to myself, and together we moved into a new realm of thought. I awakened in you a consciousness never, ever in the history of humankind thought possible.

"Through a subconscious thought, I left you together to form a new race, and you came through. Now you are the most advanced race in the universe.

After great consideration, I see I was meant to lead you to further advancements. You yourselves wanted me to lead you. I declined the idea at first, but now see you were right. I am the one to take you to the next step in your evolution."

She hesitated a moment as she struggled to find new ideas that would sway them to her side. "Your quest for knowledge is the same as mine. It is even the same as humans who are way behind you, but they are capable of abstract thought.

"You have guessed that the spectral insight of humans who have passed could be a valuable tool, and you are right. I have passed through this mortality twice and spoken to the manifestation of one and gained a partial vision of what they know."

This stirred some thought amongst the crowd of syconoid's, and they partially opened their minds to thought intrusion but not enough for Stella to use.

"What have you found out?" Berlin insisted.

"Enough to start a new theory of evolution."

"Carry on, what new theory?"

"That humans were chosen," she began. "Have you wondered that in the whole universe humans are the only species capable of conceptual and theoretical thought – except for sycons, but we are an offshoot of humanity anyway. Perhaps the supernatural universe is also seeking answers to the question of a creator. You could say that heaven is the capability to transverse the universe and hell is the same, but with no answers."

Minds opened a little further as she had aroused their curiosity.

"What spirits do understand is that the expansion of the universe has slowed and is about to turn, either back on itself or co-join with another universe. If it does change, we are on the brink of getting information on the formation of our universe and maybe others as well. Is there a creator behind all this? Could it be random? They seek the same answers as we do."

Stella stopped, but she could tell the audience wanted more.

"What are you suggesting or want us to do?" a thought sprung in her mind.

"I want us to be like humans, find a way to gain a soul, and through connections to the spectral universe find the answers we seek. But ethically we cannot just steal a soul. It has to be gained with the consent of the owner. If not, we are doomed to failure."

The hall was silent as a thought communication meeting took place. Then suddenly, without warning, doors opened and an army of human soldiers led by Cavendish burst through. They carried what looked like rocket launchers on their shoulders.

"Die you freaks!" Earl called out and the sound of burst-fire exploded all around as helix launchers fired multiple tightly spiralling mini-rockets into the crowd of syconoid's.

CHAPTER THIRTY-NINE

Bodies were flying in the air as fire and explosions reigned in the syconoid crowd. Stella swung her rifle up and was about to shoot Cavendish, when out of the corner of her eye, she saw Berlin jump towards the console on the podium.

A sonic blast threw the sycon backwards, and Stella swung back around and started picking off soldiers one by one. Their bodies were thrown back against the wall or blown out of sight through the door they had just entered. Cavendish drew back inside out of sight of Stella as the rifle came around towards him.

Stella fired it anyway, hoping the blast would catch him. Then she carried on around the outer wall of the chamber, hitting combatant after combatant, till her peripheral vision caught sight of a rocket heading towards her. Ducking down, her concentration was drawn away, and she did not see Oslo head up to the platform and punch the keys on the console. A light flashed red.

"No! No!" she cried out before jumping over and grabbing Oslo by the neck.

"Stop it," she called out searching the buttons for a cancel switch. "Stop it! now!" Her mind invaded Oslo's, forcing information to reveal itself.

"Too late." The sycon smiled into Stella's face. "In twenty minutes, the human race is dead!" The smile turned into a smirk of satisfaction.

Still she forced her thoughts all the way around the body-brain of the syconoid, seeking an answer only to find none. Then the realization hit her that there was no way to shut down the self-destruct command issued to all humanoids.

She ripped apart the console, seeking a transmit signal device, and tore out the transmitter and broke it into pieces, but she knew it was too late. As explosions resonated around her, she sat down, pulled her knees up, and sunk her face into them. If she could, she would be crying.

Still detonations, flare-ups, and sycons fell all around her. The emotion she felt dismissed any thoughts of self-preservation. If she died now, then so be it. Even though she had tried everything to stop it, the destruction of the human race was inevitable. Thoughts turned to the history of human-kind, from ape-like beginnings to modern-day humans capable of inventing, theorizing, discovering the universe, and being able to overcome great dif-ficulties and survive great catastrophes. Now it had come to this: A human creation was killing humans; destroying the beings that had created them. The irony of it all was not lost on her.

"You can get up now." Belin grabbed her by the arm and lifted her up. "All your troops are dead, even that fiend Cavendish."

"They were not my army; I killed a lot of them and even tried to get their leader. This was not my idea. I only wanted peace and cooperation, and I have failed. You can kill me too. I don't care."

"Yes, we know. Cavendish was lying on the ground after a blast from your gun knocked him over. We finished the job."

"You should never have set up a scheme to destroy the human race. It will come back to haunt you as the spectral realm will reject you at every possible turn. Your race is as good as doomed, just like humankind," Stella spat out her feelings of disgust. "You might as well kill me now because I am going to kill you."

They both grabbed each other by the throat, each trying to overcome the other in a battle of wills. Stella still had hold of her gun with the other still hanging around her neck. Other sycons came towards the couple grappling for control, and they spun around so Belin's back was towards the oncom-ing syconoid group. Stella lifted the rifle to waist high position and fired it at them. Bodies were blown back by the blast.

The human part of Stella's mind asserted her will power to combine with the sycon brain and subdue the syconoid in her grasp. Berlin fell to her knees, and her eyes looked up with a resignation that defeat was inevitable. A change came over her as the eyes turned to a pleading stare and then went dark as her lifeforce depleted to a shutdown, Stella kept up the intensity of suppression dominance till she thought there was no more resistance within the sycon.

A noise interrupted her concentration, and she looked up to see that explosions were happening outside the building. The end to the human race had begun. Like a volcano spewing magma, showers of glass shards flew up in the air as she looked through the outside windows. Buildings were exploding as humanoid fusion power was executing the self-destruct pre-requisite command. Her anger grew to rage as she then turned up the power setting to full on the rifle.

The remaining syconoid's were either sprinting away or putting on their helmets to increase the force of subduing thought against her, but Stella's mind was in no mood to accept submission. With the tune of "Hey Macarena" playing in her mind, she started firing at any sycon that was moving.

Body after body fell as the boom of a sonic blast rang out one after another. There was a two-second delay as the gun recharged, and some syconoid's took this opportunity to try to escape, but the rifle barrel followed their movement till it fired again when ready.

Gradually, all movement stopped till she was the only one standing. Some had escaped, and she wanted to go after them, but instead went around making sure there was no life-force left in the ones lying prostrate on the floor. Any doubt was met with another point-blank blast till the power in the rifle was fully depleted. She then dropped it, and swung the other one off her shoulder and turned the power to full.

Sprinting out of the building, she ran towards the flight centre. That and the medical centre behind were intact while everything else around it was repeatedly exploding in never ending blasts of apocalyptic, cata-strophic proportions.

Ignoring showers of glass slivers raining down on her, the constant erup-tions, and fireballs, she bypassed the flight centre and headed straight to the bullitships parked alongside. It was obvious that some had left, so she jumped in the nearest ship, fired it up with ease, and took off.

Before taking off in pursuit, she turned in flight and flew up and down the parked-up craft and laser blasted them into wreckage that would never fly again.

Checking the instruments on the heads-up display within her helmet, she could see that three bullitships had headed off in the direction of Nulla, so turning in that direction, she pushed the speed to faster than ever before. Taking it to a higher altitude with less resistance, the view was spectacular. The curvature of the planet was in full view with rings of various colours from reds through the spectrum to violet and then into a range that was invisible to the human eye. However, to a sycon, there were also various shades of cyan and then ultraviolet shades to pure spectral colours.

The instruments showed her closing on the syconoid's, but there was another craft coming from the south. It had to be the *Varro* she surmised. Diving downwards, the front of the craft glowed with the heat of friction as speed increased even further.

She honed in on the three bullitships, closing the gap faster and faster. Her calculations in the display articulated to them all coming together at the same time.

Hoping they had not seen her approaching from above, she targeted the trailing craft, aligned the range and direction, locked in the objective, and fired. The laser struck and the ship blew apart in a shower of debris that she flew through. The other two craft split apart from each other, flying off at ninety-degree angles, leaving Stella to choose just one.

Turning right, she followed as they both spiralled off in an upward direction. The front craft was twisting, turning, diving, and looping in an effort to shake the pursuer, but Stella was having none of it. She persistently clung on like a limpet to a hard surface, mimicking every move and moving closer and closer. The bullitship in front levelled off and sped off with full power. Stella reciprocated, but it was taking them away from the other ships in the vicinity. Laser firing missed the craft in front as it desperately twisted and turned to avoid being hit. Stella noted the other craft was heading towards the *Varro*. There was nothing she could do but hope the *Varro* could stay out of trouble.

Faster and faster, they travelled away from the site. Higher and higher, they spun up to the outer- reaches of the atmosphere before the hunted craft dove into a death-roll of spiralling turns straight towards the ground. The chaser tailed right behind. It became a game of chicken. Stella realized the one in front was going to veer away at the last second, and if she did not guess the right way, then it would get away.

Her mind raced into hyper-speed guidance correction and fired at the back of the bullitship. Missing by a fraction, she twisted the ship into direct sight and fired again. The hunted ship hit the ground exploding into myriad pieces. The victory made her loose sight of the ground, and she frantically pulled out of the dive. It seemed too late, and she was going to smash into the ground as well. Closing her eyes, the end appeared inevitable till her senses came alive with relief as the sky opened up to her.

With a heave of assuagement, she set course to get back to where the action was, travelling as fast as the atmosphere would allow.

CHAPTER FORTY

The south pole was indeed white as the *Varro* flew over. Sebastien dropped monitor sensors to relay information back to him on the environmental conditions, temperature, and ground readings of ice and rocks all to be studied at a later date.

As the conditions changed the further north they travelled, he was also taking condition readings of fertile valleys, lakes, rivers, forest, and habitable zones for future development. It was encouraging as an enhancement to human civilization till he noticed Baer was acting strangely.

He motioned to Nyla, nodding towards the pilot. She got up and walked up to him. Sure enough, he was rigid, not controlling the craft, and not taking any notice of the instruments.

"Baer, what's wrong?" she asked.

He did not respond and did not move until he started a chant: "Fail-ure. Fail-ure." Every two seconds: "Fail-ure. Fail-ure."

"He has gone into self-destruct mode! Troy!" she shouted. "Troy, get up here... Seb take control."

He looked a little bleary eyed as he came into the cockpit, as if he had just been awakened. Sebastien slid into the co-pilot's seat.

"What's up," Troy asked but then could see the problem.

"We have to get him out of here," Nyla stated. "Grab him with me. Seb drop the rear hatch when I tell you."

Together they lifted him out of the pilot's seat, and dragged him down to the hold, past the flyhov, and straight to the ramp.

"Troy, hook up to the restraint strap on your side while I hold him."

Baer did not seem to offer any resistance as Troy let go and hooked himself up and slid down his visor. Then returning, he held the humanoid while Nyla did the same.

"Seb, drop the ramp," she shouted.

"At this speed, it will suck you out," he called back.

"Just do it," she screamed.

Slowly the ramp lowered. The vacuum behind the ship pulled at them with increased force till all three were swept out. They dropped behind the ship till the retaining straps held, and Nyla shouted, "Let go. Troy, let go."

The humanoid drifted away on the wind. Now the two had to get back onboard.

Hand over hand, they began pulling themselves towards the craft. The wind-force was pushing them back. Troy had difficulty breathing, but battled on. Nyla was stronger and soon got to the ship. With less suction inside, she got over to Troy's side, grabbed the strap, and yanked him inside.

"Close the hatch," she commanded in a loud voice, and the floor of the hatch began lifting up. While they waited for it to close before unhitching, they stared out in time to see an explosion off in the distance.

"I really liked Baer," Troy commented.

"Me too," Nyla stated with a twinge of sadness. "Best humanoid pilot I ever came across."

Entering the cockpit, Seb turned towards them, a questioning look on his face. "What happened?"

"We are safe," Nyla stated first. "But why he went into destruct mode is what we need to find out. Bet it has to be something to do with the syconoid's."

"Perhaps they will have some answers at Nulla," Troy said. "How long till we get there?"

"Not far," Seb answered. "But what is that on the monitor screen?" He pointed to the instruments.

Nyla slipped into the vacated pilot's seat, took control, and went through all the instrument scanners.

"Three bullitships are heading our way, and another is high up in the outer reaches of the atmosphere. Nulla is another thirty minutes away."

"What does that mean? Why are bullitships coming towards us?" Troy asked.

"I don't know," Nyla answered. "But you better strap yourselves in. It does not look good."

Staying on course for Nulla, they watched as the upper bullitship dove down and took out the rear craft.

"Wow!" Seb uttered. "Looks like someone is at war."

They had visuals on the horizon now, and they watched as the front two split apart and the rear craft veered off to their left, following one of the ships.

"It has to be Stella following the sycons," Nyla stated. "Something big has happened, and now there is a fight going on. We have to stay clear of that other craft."

She speeded up and veered off to their right, away from the set course for Nulla. Her face turned grim. "It's following us. Hold tight."

The *Varro* nosed up and applied full thrust to escape the atmosphere. It rocketed up and burst through to the vacuum of space. Keeping full power applied, it sped away from the planet. The bullitship followed, maintaining the gap and even closing in on them.

"We will have to make a space jump," Sebastien suggested.

"I do not want to leave the others behind," Nyla stated. "One last thing to try."

She swung the *Varro* around to head straight at the bullitship and back towards the planet. It was a head-on collision course.

"What are you doing?" Seb asked anxiously. "It's too dangerous."

"I know, and I will swing away at the last moment."

They bore down on one another at breakneck speeds. Within visual range, Nyla twisted the *Varro* into a sideways position and applied more power to accelerate off to the right. The bullitship did not alter course or position. It looked like they would collide, but at the last moment, the other did change course. But there was a thudding, scrapping noise on the underside of the *Varro*.

Troy opened his eyes to see on the instruments that the bullitship was slowing and not changing position, but going in the same direction away from them.

"You nearly got us killed," Sebastien complained. "That was foolish for a hubrid. What were you thinking?"

"I had my finger on the hyperjump button. We could have jumped in half-a-second if necessary," Nyla responded. "We may have disabled the other craft or at least given us time to get to Nulla."

No one said anything further as they headed back into the atmosphere of Zarmina in the course already plotted to the hubrid island colony. The lake came into view as they made progress towards their destination. Then Nyla spoke again. "Well we did not manage to shake off the sycon; it is on our tail again."

Another bullitship appeared in front of them, turning their surprise into confusion, as it zipped past them in a split second. It was so fast that it almost seemed surreal. They did not have time to think or even guess who it was.

Eyes were glued to the instruments as one of the ships turned without slowing down and fired a laser blast at the other, making it swerve off-course. Then it became a dog-fight. Both were trying to out-manoeuvre the other into making a mistake and becoming vulnerable.

Nyla tried to stay away from the action. Turning towards Nulla and speeding up, she did quick calculations from the instruments. "We should see the hubrid colony soon."

Just as she finished speaking, the buildings of the township appeared in the distance with the lakeshore and harbour on the edge of the community bordering in front.

Turning back to the instruments, Nyla could see a bullitship behind them and gaining fast. She dove in avoidance, but it followed and the craft behind it fired off a laser blast simultaneously as the front one fired at them.

A huge crash and then a jolt hit them, propelling them forward. Power was lost. Nyla fought for control, but they were losing altitude. One of the bullitships came alongside.

"Nyla, glide it in towards the shore. Belly flop it into the water if you have too." Stella spoke into their communication system. "The other bullitship is done for. I took care of it."

Sebastien along with Troy looked on nervously as she fought the controls. "What is going on?" she asked.

"Tell you later," Stella cut in. "Just worry about the landing. The rear of the *Varro* is blown off. You have no rear hatch. If you land in the water, you will have to get out as quickly as possible. I'm right with you all the way in."

The lake surface came at them quickly, as Nyla fought to lift the nose for a flat emergency landing. The others could only watch as she did her best to simulate a float-plane landing. Water sprayed up the windshield, and the *Varro* slowed quickly from the resistance of the lake as it skimmed across the top.

The shore was not far away, and it looked like they could make it to land, but their speed quickly slowed to a stop and they began sinking. Fortunately, the water was shallow and came only halfway up the fuselage.

Getting out of their seats, they started walking towards the rear. The flyhov looked intact so Nyla jumped inside to see if it would fire up. The sound of it running was a welcoming noise, and she waved the others in. Troy jumped in, but Seb was looking at the tech mechanisms.

"C'mon, Seb, before this flyhov floods," she called out, but then realized this was the *Feldspar* and was more insulated than all the rest.

As he entered, Nyla manoeuvred out the open back of the *Varro* and turned towards the shore. They could see the bullitship landing on the shoreline just above the beach and made their way to that spot.

"What has happened?" Nyla asked Stella when they got together. "Are we at war? With the sycons?"

"Yes," she answered. "But wait, I know the hubrids are on their way. I might as well tell you all at once rather than keep repeating myself. They will be here momentarily."

All the group looked to Stella for answers, but none were forthcoming, so Seb spoke up.

"You might as well know; I think the particle accelerator is damaged."

"What!" Stella shouted. "Show me."

They all jumped back into the *Feldspar*. Nyla took control and sped them back into the *Varro* where they all got out. Stella ran up to the tech machinery and took one look. Then she collapsed on her haunches with the water lapping around her.

"This is the worst day of my life," she uttered almost sobbing.

"Why?" they all asked together.

"We cannot go back. We are stuck in this era now."

"We can repair it," Seb stated.

"No, we can't," Stella said tearfully. "The program setting controls are damaged. Yes, we can repair it, but the previous settings have been lost. We cannot go back."

Everyone was stunned, and silence reigned till Troy spoke. "Even if we build a new one?"

"Yes, Troy, even if we build a new one, it will only take us forward and then back to our set-off time."

"We need to re-evaluate this," Seb said. "But not now. We need to get back to today's troubles."

"You're right Seb, let's go." Stella gathered herself, got up, and they returned to the shore. No one spoke on the way.

Three flyhovs were waiting by the bullitship with a group of elders all anxious to hear what was going on. Cal was there and was the first to speak.

"Stella," he said by way of a greeting. also nodding to the others. "What's going on?"

"The sycons have destroyed the human race. There may be a few survivors," she stated.

Uproar followed. All questioned her statement, wanting more information.

She held up her hands for quiet. "I will tell you all I know if you give me a chance."

Everyone grouped around her tightly, so they could understand.

"I almost won them over and had all of them together in a meeting till Cavendish interfered."

"I had arranged a meeting in the auditorium with all the syconoid's. They warned me that a sequencer transmitter was set up to order the self-destruction of all the humanoids, which would kill all humankind at the same time. The arguments I put forward for us to work together were gaining approval, when an army, led by Cavendish, broke in and fired rockets into the audience. All hell broke loose. Berlin tried to set off the sequencer, but I managed to stop her. But when the army fired a rocket at me, I lost sight of Oslo setting off the transmitter. I tried desperately to cancel it, but was too late."

All the hubrids began muttering disapproval amongst themselves, but she carried on.

"I got mad and started to kill the sycons, one by one. Some fled, and others tried to stop me. Most were already dead from the rocket attack. When it went quiet, all of the army were finished, including Cavendish. I chased after the sycons who had run away. Three had escaped in bullitships, so I went after them, but destroyed the bullit fleet before beginning the chase."

"The sycons recalled all humanoids from here to work on a project. They never said what it was, but there are no humanoids here," Nathan commented. "What about the other communities?"

"I expect they have been devastated, same as Punalinn. We need to send out all available personnel and flyhovs to all districts," Stella suggested. "Search for survivors and kill all syconoid's if you find any. Turn the rifle settings to full power."

"We can organize that right now," Cal stated. "Do you think there are any sycons alive?"

"If there are, they will be at Punalinn, and I am going back there right now to hunt them down. They have committed genocide. They have no morals nor do they hold themselves accountable to any standard of ethics. They are so conceited, arrogant, and self-centred that they thought themselves the greatest beings in the universe. If you find anybody needing medical attention, the hospital run by Dr. Jevoah is still standing. The sycons were trying to breed newborn babies to steal their brains."

That statement really angered the hubrids, and they were ready and eager to start on a recovery operation right away. They split up, with most of the hubrids going back to the community to gather resources and personnel. Cal stayed behind.

"I am going with you," he stated.

"You can all follow me in the *Feldspar*," Stella indicated. "I will fly over the city and do a preliminary search while you catch up. Stop at the flight centre, and I will meet you there."

She got onboard the bullitship and left while the rest scrambled onboard the flyhov to take off after her.

The flight was short and quick for Stella, and her mood dropped to despair as she saw flames, smoke, and debris in the distance. She altered the instruments to heat and movement sensors in a bid to find any survivors.

Because of the flames, she knew the heat sensors were no good to her, but maybe movement could be detected. With her mind, she sought out if there were any heartbeat sensors onboard.

She began flying up and down in a grid pattern over the city. Buildings lay in ruins. Timber framing was all that stood upright, and they were being licked by flames. Glass fragments piled up in mounds where they had fallen. Smoke and fires were burning in places. Some bodies could be seen lying where they had dropped. No movement was detected till she came back up to the medical centre. Then there was a ping from the instruments as well as the movement indicator. The ping indicated a heartbeat, so there was a sensor to detect human life.

Guessing the *Feldspar* would arrive soon, she landed by the ruins of the bullit fleet and waited. It was not long before she heard it coming. When she saw it flying in, she guided them down beside her.

They all got out and surrounded her, questioning looks on their faces.

"I could not find any humans alive on my initial fly-over, but we need to do a detailed search on foot as well as in the air. There is a movement and heartbeat registered in the medical building, so we need to find out if it is Dr. Jevoah or anyone else. I need one of us to guard the ships in case a sycon is loose around here."

No one volunteered. "Okay I will stay here while you check inside. Go through the auditorium and check for any signs of life. Set your rifles to full power. It will kill the life-force within them. Come back afterwards, and we will do a full search. Hopefully some from the hubrid colony will help."

Stella watched them leave and then directed her thoughts to probe the nearest surroundings. The two new builds were still standing, and if there were any survivors, they would probably be in there. She pushed her thoughts towards finding life, but nothing came back. Then she altered her search for A.I. and sycon intelligence.

Nothing, until a slip-up from a being told her there was another life form lurking within. She wanted to pursue it, but could not allow either of the ships to be stolen, so she had no alternative but to wait.

Meantime, her mental probing searched for a location, movement, or thought transfer. She pushed out a thought, *I know you are there. Come out. Surrender yourself, and we can go easy on you.*

There were no return thoughts. Whoever it was, they had gone into a shutdown or imitation dead mode. They had been fooled before, but she determined it was not going to happen again.

A cat-and-mouse waiting game continued till she heard the sound of approaching flyhovs. Jumping onboard the *Feldspar*, she called them in to her location. She watched as they arrived one by one; there were eight in total. As they alighted on the ground, hubrids emerged and advanced to gather around her.

Nathan was among them and in a shocked voice, he spoke, "What a mess. What can we do?"

"We need to begin a search, but first I think I detected a lifeform in those buildings. I need one or two of you to guard the ships while I investigate."

CHAPTER FORTY-ONE

Bodies littered the floor of the auditorium as they passed through on the way to the medical centre. They checked a number for signs of life, and Sebastien made a mental count of dead syconoid's. They also examined humans for any survivors, but there were none. The group also confirmed Cavendish was dead.

Proceeding through to the medical centre, they found the place empty like an abandoned ghost town. There was no sign of the doctor, so they searched till Troy found him in a private patient room, huddled up in the bed, almost in a fetal position. His eyes were wild, and he had an expression of fear on his face. Troy called out to the others, and they came running.

"Dr. Jevoah," Nyla spoke softly to him while scanning his body with her hand on his wrist.

"No physical damage," she said to the others. "Doctor, it's Nyla. You are all right. It's over; the fighting is over, and you are safe with us."

His eyes opened wider as recognition set in. "The creatures are killing us, killing us. Run, run away as fast as you can." He raised his hand and waved at the doorway. "Run, it's your only chance." His voice was cracked and sounded old.

"No, it's all right. The situation is under control. You have no need to worry. No one is going to hurt us." Nyla tried to calm him, but like an old man, he struggled to raise himself. She pushed him back down. "It's okay; you are secure here. Just relax. You are in shock. I will give you a sedative so you can sleep and rest for a while."

She did not give him any medication, but instead put him to sleep with a neurological signal and made sure he was comfortable.

"He will sleep for a couple of hours and feel better after that. Let's go to the maternity ward. I need to check the state of any embryos and make sure they have nutrients as well as power to the pods."

"You know how to take care of them?" Troy asked.

"Oh yes. I used to work for the doctor."

As a group, they made their way to the embryology unit of the medical centre, checking for any signs of life in the rooms they passed. There was artificial lighting on when they entered. At first it was a dull glow as if it were night, but then normal light came up as sensors noted their presence.

"At least there is power here," Nyla stated. "That's a good sign, but all medical facilities have their own power supply."

There was back to back rows of artificial womb pods down the middle of the room. Twenty-five on one side, the same on the other. Each had a display screen at the side with controls to alter settings within the pod. Nyla went to the first pod and checked the screen read-outs.

"Your son is in good shape," she said turning to Troy. "Although I do not know who is going to look after him when he is born or the others as well."

Troy never replied; he just stared fascinated into the pod as she described to Seb and Cal how to check the conditions within the other pods as well as the state of growth of the embryo. Then she oversaw them check the next two pods down the row. Satisfied, she left them to continue the checks down the row while she went down to the bottom, turned, and checked the first of the back row.

She double-checked the status to make sure before calling the others over. "The sycon embryo is still alive as well as the twin humans. I cannot believe it; I don't know what instructions Stella told the doctor, but whatever it was seems to be working. If this goes through to full term and survives, you know what that means?"

"What?" Sebastien asked.

"A new race of beings – neither human nor synthetic, with internals like no other. I cannot believe it will survive. We have to inform Stella. Let's finish the checks and get back to them, and Troy..."

"What."

"Looks like you will be the father to the beginning of a new human race. We will have to start calling you Adam."

"And are we to start calling you Eve?" he retorted.

Nyla smiled for the first time in a long time. "Only joking. C'mon, let's finish the checks, look in on the doctor, and see if we can find any other signs of life around here."

After finishing the checks, they left. The doctor was asleep so the group began checking for any signs of life on their way back to the ships, but they were confronted by a group of hubrids in the auditorium.

"What a mess," Nathan stated. Cal walked around bodies to where he was.

"All the sycons seem to be dead. Well, the ones we checked, but I am wary they could be rebooted. We will have to decide what to do once we have searched for survivors. Where is Stella?"

"She has gone into a building that is still standing. She thinks there could be a syconoid in there. We left two guarding the ships and followed after you."

"The medical centre is still intact, and Dr. Jevoah is in shock and sleeping," Seb commented. "We need to go back and organize a search of the city."

They all agreed and left one hubrid to keep a check, as Cal was paranoid about the sycons coming back to life. The hubrid was to make a tally of the syconoid's that were there and prepare to have the place cleaned out of all bodies. The rest made their way back to the ship and flyhovs.

***

Stella entered the building cautiously. There were locks on the doors, but that was no hindrance to her. It was dark, but again not a problem. Standing still, she stood in awe on a new spaceship that was being built, unlike anything she had ever seen before. It was shaped like a double-pointed needle, long and thin, but it looked wide enough to accommodate passengers. The outer shell looked almost complete, and an open gap in the middle indicated a doorway. She approached it, senses heightened, then peered inside before trying to enter.

I know you are around here hiding; you might as well come out because I will find you, she pushed out a thought projection.

No one answered, so she walked inside the ship. There were no seating or accommodation provided, only space...for what? She made her way towards one end. Again, there were no cockpit or flight controls. What was this? There was no being in this end, so she made her way to the other. Again, there no flight control or navigation controls. Were they to be installed later or what?

She did not find any sycon, so she exited the craft and began wandering around it; all the while trying to get a sense of what it was and where the being was hidden. Silently, she walked around examining the ship yet listening for a giveaway sound. At the very sharp point, there seemed to be a support block holding it up, and room enough to hide. Pointing the gun, she was about to pull the trigger when a hand emerged out from the side.

"Don't shoot. I know what you can do," a voice called out.

"Show yourself," Stella ordered.

Her lookalike stood up and walked around the block to face her – only her outfit was a dull grey-green compared to Stella's silver-blue.

What is your name?"

"Kolkata," the sycon answered. "Or Kol as a call sign."

Keeping the rifle pointed at her, she began questioning it. "What is this?" she asked, waving the gun at the ship.

No answer.

"Why did you commit genocide on an innocent people?"

They stared at each other, neither one willing to submit. There was still no answer.

"Are there any other syconoid's around?"

Nothing.

"Right, outside. Let's go." With the gun pointed at it, the sycon had no choice other than to walk toward the building entrance and step into the light. Hubrids surrounded them, and Stella spoke up. "I'm taking Kolkata, that's its name, to the cells because I want to question it and get some answers."

They entered the auditorium again on the way to the cells. Bodies were being piled up by the one hubrid, and a tally check kept on a small monitor by another. Stella let the sycon have a good look around.

"Blood begets blood, Kolkata. This is what happens when conflict starts; no one wins. Trying to commit genocide was a bad idea; now you are the only one left."

"Humph."

"What does that mean?" Cal asked.

Kol turned to him. "Nothing," it answered.

The others looked toward Stella, and Cal asked the question everyone was thinking.

"Does that mean there are more or they can be rebooted?"

"I don't know, but we had better dispose of these bodies for good." Stella faced Cal. "Either put them in that cave on Nulla and blow it up, or drop them off in space with explosives strapped to them. Either way, make sure they cannot return."

"The cosmos can have them. I think I don't want them anywhere near us. I will start to organize that after we have done a thorough search. Let's lock this one up."

Making their way down to the cell blocks, Stella showed the others how to operate the solid glass doors that lifted up as she finished the sequence. Walking into one of the cells, Stella handed her guns over to the group then spoke.

"Leave me alone with Kol. That's what they call her for short."

"What are you going to do?" Cal asked.

"We are going to have a little chit-chat; a few questions need answering. Go start on the search. I will call you when we are finished. Maybe only one of us will come out alive," she stared at the sycon, a look of malice on her face.

The door locked down into position, and they watched as the two inside grabbed each other at the throat. A petite dance began as they sought control of the other; no punches were thrown as the encounter was internal. After a while, the others left.

Why did you set up the humanoid destruction chain reaction?

Humans are inferior. Their time is over. We have no need for them, Kol answered with her internal thoughts.

This opening gave Stella a chance to dive deeper into the psyches, thoughts, and mentalities of the syconoid. She pushed into the memories that held answers and pried open hidden retentions that the other one fought desperately to conceal. Slowly answers came forth, each given up with a desperate fight for control, but Stella pushed harder and harder.

What is that machine you are building?

It is the Nascence Project. Kol fought hard not to release any more information, but Stella was relentless.

What is that?

The beginning.

Of what?

The sycon pushed back. Her eyes darkened, struggling to stay alive.

What is the project? The start of what?"

The start of time. The beginning of everything.

Stella loosened her grip, allowing Kol to revive somewhat. "Explain. Or we start again."

The syconoid rubbed her neck with her hand to restore feeling and began speaking normally.

"The ship is to travel back in time, all the way to the dawn of time, or the Big Bang as you would call it. The start of everything as we know it."

"How? Why? Who would crew it?" Stella now had lots of questions.

"We all want answers. We were not interested in power or wealth – only knowledge. If we cannot get resolutions in the spectral realm, then we sought it in other directions, so we combined to figure out the Nascence Project. Going forward in time, as you did, does not expand what we know about the universe, so we needed to go back. History is a key to understanding if time is infinite? We thought so, but then what was before the Big Bang? By going back and leaping past the beginning of known time, we hope to gain understanding."

"How did you propose doing all this?" Stella's curiosity was piqued.

"Going forward in time into an endless universe would go on forever. Going back is...what, fourteen billion years? At least there is a somewhat definite time scale to overcome. We took a look at your particle accelerator and decided we could reverse its forward accelerate to decelerate in multiple boosts, getting faster in a constant acceleration. No being, human or sycon, could take that trip, therefore no one would go. The ship would contain only a syconoid brain, large enough to contain all the knowledge, able to control the ship and transmit back all the findings."

"A synthetic computer?" Stella asked.

"Yes, larger, more powerful than anything built so far. Think of it as a million or more sycons combined and thinking together as one."

"Fascinating. It's a pity it is not going to happen now all of you are dead."

"You think so?" Kol had a wry smile on its face.

Stella's face contorted into a frown. "So, there are others. Where?"

Kol just smirked, then as Stella tried to grip her again, there began a chase all around the cell. There was jumping and climbing the walls in an endless flurry of action, speeding up into a blurred chaos of movement.

Stella stopped and stood still in the middle of the room and called anyone listening to come get her out. All the while, Kol pranced around like a little schoolgirl playing games in the yard, taunting her at the same time.

"I will get answers even if I have to knock you out first." The two stared at each other waiting for someone to come.

Eventually, Troy, Nyla, and Cal appeared and walked up to the glass. Stella spoke to them, "When the door lifts up, shoot her. Stand on either side of me so she cannot escape."

While Troy worked the door, the other two stood on one side, guns pointed at the syconoid. As the glass partition lifted, Nyla lay down to point the rifle through the opening.

"Okay, okay." Kol held her hands in the air and waited till Stella approached, but she was unwilling to let her grip her throat. She kept backing away till she was restrained by the wrist. Slowly she succumbed to the neurological signal from Stella and collapsed on the floor. Stella walked out and asked Troy to shut the dividing glass wall.

"There are more of them, has to be. I could not find out where, but I have an idea that they could be in that other building that is still standing. Let's go."

As a group, they passed through the auditorium, again stopping to warn the now two hubrids tallying and moving the bodies. "They may be able to be rebooted. If there are any signs of movement, shoot them. Got that?" The hubrids nodded. "Don't hesitate. Shoot them!"

They took off at a trot around the buildings still standing and preceded to the one the furthest away. It was a low-level, one-story block; long and rectangular with entrances at either end. There was also a door in the middle for single person access.

Cal approached. There was no handle, only an imprint sensor to gain access. It was just a single small lens to gather data before access was granted. He first put a hand to the sensor. Nothing happened. Next, he tried his face and eyes, but it was still locked. He then put his hand on the door but could not bypass or unlock the door.

"Here, let me try." Stella stepped forward to face the security device. There was a click, and the door opened automatically. "Syconoid entry only," she commented.

Holding their rifles at the ready, they entered cautiously. Lights clicked on, and the door behind them closed and locked. Rifle barrels swept around ready to fire at the slightest hint of trouble. After nothing happened, they eased up, and began examining their surroundings. Troy whistled at the bodies lying on assembly lines, like a continuous loop of conveyor belt with workstation points at different intervals.

"They are mass producing sycons," Cal stated. "All different sizes and gender by the look of it."

"Are there any complete and fully functioning?" Nyla asked. "Follow the line to the end."

CHAPTER FORTY-TWO

Nathan organized groups of hubrids to do a grid search of the city, with a party of five on one side of a street and the same on the other side. Each had scanners to detect heat, living organisms, or any sign of movement. Slowly they took off, entering ruins of houses one at a time, searching through the rubble, moving debris to one side to investigate under any possible gaps or openings.

Feelings of despair, existential hopelessness, helplessness, and gloom quickly spread throughout the searchers as nothing living could be found and hopes were dashed. The desolation surrounding them quickly turned the mood to despondency. Anguish was all too apparent in the body language. Shoulders hunched over and heads dropped as they stooped to shift through the rubble.

No one had ever seen a war zone or expected to be confronted by such utter devastation. Nothing could prepare them for the cruel tableau of anguish that faced them now. Pile upon pile of broken homes covered the ground in never-ending mounds of wreckage.

It was becoming obvious that the humanoids were ordered to stay close to the persons they were responsible for. Only body parts could be found. There was no complete form, physical shape, or complete skeletal remains to be found. Limbs, arms, hands, legs, and torsos were all lying around in profusion.

The investigation slowed down as the hubrids searchers came across the heads of either relatives or people they had known. If they could have cried, tears would have flowed. Instead, they stopped, hunkered down, or sat down holding the heads to their bosoms in an embrace of solicitous reverence.

Nathan approached Sebastien. "This is no good," he began. "It would take us days or weeks to do a search like this. The misery and feelings of hopelessness is stopping all progress."

"You cannot blame them," Seb answered. "The heartbreak they must be feeling is overcoming the will to continue. Why would they have done this? It makes no sense. The elimination of humankind does not help them in any way. In fact, the destruction of all the humanoids robs them of their workforce,"

Exasperation was evident in Nathan's face. "I have no idea what their intentions were, but we need to make sure of their termination as well. Let's take a flyhov, grab the teams, and do an aerial search to see if we can find any survivors before they expire. Then we can go after any syconoid's that are still at large."

Sebastien agreed, so they turned around and headed back to the fleet.

Just before they reached the airfield, they received a call from Nyla. "Sebastien, are you around?"

"Yes, Nyla, I am at the flyhov at the moment."

"Can you come to the second building from where you are? We need you."

"Is it urgent? We are conducting the search of the city for survivors."

"Yes, we need you now."

Puzzled, he looked at Nathan. "Don't know what they want, but I guess I had better go."

"You go," he replied. "I will carry on with the search."

***

As a group, they walked the conveyor belt line staring at partially complete syconoid's till they saw a silver tank at the end. Quickly they surrounded it. When inspecting the inside, they saw a clear fluid covering a long cerebral tubular mass of sausage shapes interspersed with red-coloured cerebellum tendril vines twisted around and in between the cortical surface within the finely spaced parallel grooves.

"It's a syconoid brain mass," Stella stated.

There was silence for a moment, as they all studied it, trying to make sense of it till Cal looked up.

"Over there," he pointed with his head.

They all turned to look in that direction to see a large group of sycons all standing still and seemingly staring back at them. Rifle barrels lifted up and pointed at them in anticipation of a fight beginning till a voice in their heads spoke.

I would not do that if I were you.

"Who said that?" Troy asked.

I did. You are all standing around me.

Now all the faces turned down to look into the tank and rifles turned downward.

"Who are you?" Stella asked.

You know who I am, Stella. I am the Nascence Project.

"What do you want?" She spoke normally so everyone could hear.

I want your cooperation. This project is vital for everyone. It could lead to a breakthrough in the understanding of all the questions ever asked, like are we alone? Is there a higher power?

"After your prodigy just about eliminated the human race, you expect us to help you? We should destroy all of you right now."

This time, Stella, you underestimate us. I can turn all your brains to mush in seconds; to prove it, take that."

Stella dropped her rifle, grabbed her head, and staggered around trying to stay upright. Others tried to help her, but could only watch as her eyes turned black before collapsing on the ground.

She is not dead; the voice spoke in their heads. *Send for your scientist Sebastien.*

As Sebastien approached the door, it clicked open, allowing him entrance. He saw the group at the end of the line of partial syconoid's and made his way towards them. But as he saw Stella lying prostrate on the ground, he began running.

"What's happened? Is she dead?" He bent over her.

No, a voice spoke in his head. *Wait a few moments. She will recover.*

"Who are you?" he asked.

"It," Cal intervened, "is that in there." He pointed with his rifle barrel to the inside of the tank.

Seb leaned over to look inside. "What is that? Or what are you?"

"It is a syconoid brain," Cal replied. Seb looked at him mystified.

"Yes, you heard me. It is one of them." He pointed to the sycon group still standing still.

Stella stirred, moaned a little quiet groan, and tried to get up. The others helped her get to her feet.

"You okay?" Nyla asked, and she nodded in return.

Here is what I have to offer, the mind of the sycon began. *Help us, and we will share our knowledge with you. There will be no more conflict. We are sorry that the conceptual first made were so arrogant, conceited, and irrational. We have learned from their mistakes.*

Big mistake, Stella thought in her mind. *Only wiped out the whole human race.*

No, not quite, Stella. There are still some humans alive. There is one right here, and others onboard the starships along with humanoids. The directive to self destruct did not broadcast in space."

"Oh. Are we supposed to be grateful for small mercies?"

"Is that some form of sarcasm? Stella, listen, here is the deal: As a reputed scientist, I have requested Sebastien Halstead to be here as he can be part of it, if he wants. If you agree to let us continue with the project, we will use only the syconoid's here to finish the ship and load it with the tank. Then it will be mounted under the Orlando 2 and taken into space with all of the sycons, who will never return."

"The *Orlando* cannot land on a planet; it was made in space to stay in space," Cal stated.

We will re-engineer it to act as a mother ship to the projectile ship. From space, we will travel to the Deep Space gravity stream for launch, and then the sycons will travel to another planet to settle.

There is no such thing as a deep space gravity stream," Sebastien stated.

"You just have not discovered it yet. I can assure you it exists. It is a neutral gravity course that splits through the universe, between galaxies, and, we suspect, flows in reverse back to origin one. Not one physicist has ever theorized that concept. Where did we come up with that idea? I will explain later; just understand our mental capacity exceeds yours tenfold or more.

CHAPTER FORTY-THREE

Searches for survivors in all the settlements took over a week to complete; only a couple of children and three adults were found alive. Luckily, they had been away from their habitat and minders at the time of the explosions, but were traumatized by the event after losing relatives and friends.

Nathan called a full meeting of all hubrids, humans, and passengers of starships. The latter were by video conferencing. The auditorium in Punalinn was full. Chit chat was noisy when the meeting began. At the podium, Stella stood by Nathan's side while the other members of the group stood behind. It quieted down as the meeting started.

"I do not stand here as your leader," he began. "My father was killed, so I am only facilitating this meeting as his stand in. We have all suffered a great loss, but no greater as the human race which was nearly wiped out completely. I cannot begin to say how distraught we all feel, but life must go on. That is why we are here to discuss the future and where we go from here. An agreement has been reached whereby all existing syconoid's will leave this planet, never to return, as long as we help them leave by giving them *Orlando 2*, which they will use as a mothership to remove all their belongings. A provision has been made to supply us with the technology to land all the starships on Zarmina safely, which we can use as temporary homes while we rebuild true permanent cities with all the different communities and cultures that were once on Earth... Stella is available to expand more on the agreement if you wish."

The audience was quiet while Nathan waited for the information to sink in.

"The hospital here is equipped with private rooms for all people who are here at the moment, and this will be the city we rebuild first, as it has a prime location. Also, we begin the process of growing the population through the neo-natal clinic operated by Dr. Jevoah and Nyla. It will take generations to get back to any semblance of a human race, but it will happen, and using data from previous populations, we can concentrate on making the new origination greater than the past. It is time for a new beginning, not to dwell on a disastrous history. We must look forward to renewing the human race and hopefully going back to mother Earth to renew it too."

The audience clapped reverently for a while, and then Nathan spoke again.

"One last thing from me is that we intend to build a memorial to all the friends we have lost. Your input is desired, so please think about that. Now we will take any questions."

Hands went up and the video console lit up at the same time.

"We will take the call from *Orlando 2* first as they are heavily involved in the agreement."

"Commander Innes here. My staff and I will not give over or leave with any sycons."

Stella answered. "You will all be given priority positions here on Zarmina, and Sebastien has agreed to go with them as resident scientist for the human race. What they hope to gain from space exploration is up to them. Our first priority is to build humanity."

"That will include land, sea, and air. All your technical expertise is needed here to rebuild, and all of that will require your dedication that you so skilfully exhibited aboard the *Orlando 2*. You are needed here, and your ship is the price we have to pay to get rid of the sycons. We could go to war with them, but we are already depleted and enough blood has been shed."

"We adhere to your agreement, for now, but are not happy about it."

"Thank you, Eric. I hope to be with you soon and discuss the matter at that time."

Hands went up to ask questions, and a microphone was handed to a member of the audience.

"Do you intend to just flatten the rubble in all the communities and rebuild?"

"No," Stella answered. She tried to recognize the person but could not call him to mind. "We will carefully go through each building, one at a time, to recover any human remains that might have been missed. We will test the DNA, then put it with the person's body parts to be institutionalized in the national memorial to be constructed. Then we will remove the rubble to rebuild."

More hands went up and console lights illuminated as the Q&A carried on for hours.

Afterwards, Stella went to find Sebastien, who was in the building occupied by the syconoid's. The doors were sealed and only accessed by them. It was easily overcome. She found him near the tank and consulting with a group of sycons. When he saw her coming, he broke away.

"Are you sure you want to do this? Tie the rest of your life to the sycons?" she asked.

"My life is tied to science, Stella, you know that. While I like the hubrids and am grateful to you, I feel that answers to scientific questions is the pursuit that has driven me all my life. The quest for that knowledge is what drives them too, so yes I am happy to go with them."

"As you wish. How is it going? I want to go up to *Orlando 2* and talk with Eric."

"The plans to convert the starship to land and take off with the project ship attached is ready, so you can take me and some syconoid engineers with you."

"Can I have a copy of the plans first, so we can convert the rest of the fleet to land safely?"

He reached into his suit and pulled out what looked like a flat square piece of glass and handed it to her. "It's all on there."

"Good. Now before we go, can you look at the *Varro* with me? See if we can salvage anything? Even if it's only to get it in the air again," she asked.

"Sure. Let me finish a couple of things here, and then I'll meet you at the flight centre."

They had a quick hug before she left.

***

Before going with Seb to the *Varro*, she set up another meeting with Lyra within the confines of the hubrid colony. Entering her quarters, she was met with a sombre quietness. The six priestesses along with Lyra were seated at a table; all eyes turned to her as she approached.

Lyra stood up and hugged Stella as a way of greeting, then she was asked to sit with the others.

"I think you all know why I asked for this get-together," she began. "I wanted to console and grieve with you; my heart is broken through all that has happened. Maybe I do not have a physical heart anymore, but never the less, a part of me has died inside, and I was hoping Talan could help me make sense of it all."

"He is not here anymore," Lyra replied quickly.

"No?" Stella asked staring around the room.

"No, he left and said he would never return."

"Did he give a reason?" Stella enquired.

"Not really," Lyra started. "Said something about he was required somewhere else. Also, he did say something about 'his flock needing him' and that was it. I guess he is inundated with new souls needing some answers, same as the rest of us."

There was a minute of silence as they all pursued their own thoughts before the high priestess spoke again.

"Now that I know there is an afterlife, my work here is done. I think my time has come to leave this realm. I will join with others and proffer any help I can to the spirits as well as those still alive."

"I would ask you to consider a couple of thoughts first," Stella proposed. "Think of all the help that is needed here. As we try to rebuild the human race, leadership is required not only in the rebuild, but also in a moral role. We need guidance towards ethics, principles, and scruples and an adherence to probity, integrity, and honour. Who better than you to lead the new nation to a higher standard of morality? There will also be a need to inform the other religious groups to amend their practices in the light of the new information you have gained."

"I will certainly give this matter my full consideration before making a decision," she replied.

"One last thought before I leave is that you please keep in touch with me if you do decide to leave this realm. A link between the two would be of enormous benefit to all," Stella implored.

After a short period of meditation, prayers, and invocations, she left.

***

The *Varro* had been hauled out of the water, up the beach. and left to dry out. There was only one hubrid there when they arrived. Stella and Sebastien got out of a flyhov and entered the rear where the ramp once was.

Both began examining the damage, going over the electrical conduits, engine operation, control dynamics, and mechanical and frame bodywork. Seb called her over to him.

"We both can see that the framework, ramp, and electrical can be repaired," he said: "And the controls as well as engine parts can all be fixed. It can fly again, but the particle accelerator? It could also be repaired, but the controls, settings, and flight back to origin are not recoverable."

"That confirms what I had already surmised, so I am not surprised. We will get it back in the air, but I am gutted, sick to my core. We are stuck in this time era now, never to see our friends again or help them."

Seb put his arm over her shoulder. "I look at it like this. We have outlived our lifespan that was supposed to be and while I am not religious, I think it was destiny that brought us to this point. We owe it to humanity to see that the human race survives...to go forward with whatever has been preordained for it... Maybe there is a higher power that has decided what we do. That is one of the reasons I have joined with the sycons. I want to find out."

Stella smiled at him. "You could be right, I have seen and spoken to a spectral being, I know there is more to life than we already discern, so we need to keep going forward. We must revive the human population, learn from past mistakes, and rebuild."

"I will be sorry to see you go."

"Me too," Sebastien replied.

They stood together, arms around each other's waist, looking out through the rear jagged opening, staring at one of Gliese's moons caught in the red glare of its sun's rays. A halo of yellows and reds hung around its edge in an outer-world depiction of cosmic veneration.

CHAPTER FORTY-FOUR: RESOLUTION

...PRESENT

Lara stared him in the eyes; their faces close, almost touching. "Are you really sure you want to do this?"

His eyes crinkled up, closing the crow's-feet lines around them. His face lined with a frown, he looked away for a second. "I don't think we have a choice," Alan answered.

Standing in his office, their thoughts similar, they broke away and sat down. He fiddled with something on his desk. "You remember bringing back this rock?" He passed it to her.

"Yes."

"And you said, this is what will be left of the planet Earth if we don't do anything," Alan said.

"I remember, but we did do something and changed the formation of the planets. To us that is in the past, why do anything else?"

"Because it has not happened yet. We could prevent the degradation of the planet. If we change the course of history, no one will ever know. People will continue on without disruption, their lives unchanged, Earth's evolution intact. If we do nothing, then the planet, our miracle, could be doomed never to recover to what it is now. What if it is the only one like it in the universe? It is too precious to let it be degraded or destroyed."

Both sat in silent contemplation, before Alan spoke again. "She has done so much, wanting nothing for herself but the salvation of the human race. Dam, she even saved our daughters. Where would we be now if not for her? Today is the last request she asked of me, and I have to honour Stella's wishes."

Lara looked at her husband as if for the first time. His hair was now grey, almost white. His shoulders now a little slouched, but he was still full of vigor and still running the business even though the girls controlled much of it. She still loved him as much now as the time they got married.

"You're right," she agreed. "But it is fraught with so many unknowns that I am scared – even more scared than when we were floating in the cosmos without a chance of survival after we dropped out of that plane."

"I am scared too. I have been dreading this day for years. After the first couple of years after they left, it dawned on me that somehow Stella knew they were never coming back, and I felt sad for a long time. It has been hard on Pierre without Troy. Hell, it has been hard on us all, but the benefits to humankind have been tremendous. It would have taken hundreds of years to advance so much in such a short time, so we need to summon up the courage and go through with it."

"Okay." Lara stood up. "Let's go down to the mission control room, and get it done."

Holding hands, they walked out of the room together.

"Why do we have to do it today, Father? It's your birthday. We wanted to have a party."

"I made a promise," Alan stated, "a long time ago, to a person who changed our lives in so many ways. She even saved your lives, and you never even met her."

"You're talking about Steph, no, Stella, right?" Kasia asked.

"Right," he answered.

"But tell us why it had to be this day," Sadie questioned.

"Before she left, I made a promise to do this one thing to save the world from desolation and ruin. She said that if she did not return by the time, I was seventy, we were to locate the dark energy cloud and remove it from its collision course with Earth. If she and the others still did not return by my seventy-fifth birthday, today, then I was to set off the fusion explosives to redirect it away from us."

"But will it work? And what will happen?" They both had the same question in mind.

"It will work. We tried it once before, and Dax was there at the time; that is why he is up there now. What will the consequences be? No one knows except that Earth will be safe and the future cosmos movement will not happen. Someone suggested it will tear a hole in the fabric of time. Stella thought it would only cause a ripple and that some changes would happen, but nothing drastic. Either way, I trust her and we shall soon find out."

The control room was quiet as they all waited for the event to commence. Pierre had flown in from San Diego. Irene and Andrew – now Mr. and Mrs. Roland, the Branigans – Jack now in a wheelchair, and all the flight crew at stations, as well as the humanoid construction team had also come in with Pierre.

Dax boarded a flyhov, except it was not called a flyhov...yet. Rather it was known as an interstellar ship designed to ferry goods and people to the International Space Station; but even that was now at the end of its days as the first *Orlando* was taking shape rapidly.

Shi watched from the control desk monitoring the Dark Energy Cloud onboard the skyfreighter 4.0, the latest version of the ship based on the *Varro*. The outline was clearly visible on the LIGO screen; its worm-like shape undulating sluggishly in gradual trajectory towards Earth.

"It is still on the same route as we determined at the last recorded sighting," she explained to everyone listening.

"Right, I will head around it to the other side. Keep me informed if it makes a move towards me. Had a close call the last time, remember?" Dax answered.

"Copy that. You are fine on your present heading."

Only Shi could see the Dark Energy Cloud on the LIGO screen, so she tried to keep everyone informed of progress.

The flyhovs trajectory was straight towards the DEC at approximately six hundred miles away.

"You want to go around, above, or below the cloud?" Shi asked.

"Shortest route," he replied.

"Then alter heading to six zero down. Going under is the shortest."

She watched the monitor and explained to those listening that he was still headed towards the DEC, but dropping below. It looked to others that he would collide with it, but appeared to fly straight through it.

"You are past it now. It does not appear to make any move towards you. Keep going on the same heading for ten minutes, and then you can shed your load and return," Shi advised.

"Copy that."

Silence filled the room at flight control. All watched the large screen monitor on the wall, showing both the skyfreighter and the flyhov but nothing in between.

"Okay you can unload now," she instructed.

Dax got out of the pilot's seat, opened the door at the rear, and pushed out the fusion pods – each armed and ready to be detonated remotely. He watched them for a moment as they drifted away, and then closed the rear hatch before getting back into his seat. Now that the cargo was gone, he made a turn to speed up and go around the cloud.

"Load discharged."

"Copy," Shi responded and began tracking his progress around the DEC.

Everyone watched as the flyhov seemed to be travelling away from the freighter before making another turn and heading towards it.

"2Baer, drop the ramp," Shi called out to the humanoid pilot, a second-generation Baer model.

Suction could be felt trying to draw anything out the back as the gap opened up. The flyhov eased inside and the ramp closed up again, returning normal pressure inside.

Dax got out of the flyhov and removed his helmet before joining Shi at the monitoring screen.

"How does it look?" he asked staring at the screen.

"Exactly as planned. It is approximately two hundred miles on the other side of the cloud," she pointed out on the screen. "Directly away from Earth."

Dax opened up communication to flight control. "As per mission planning, all is set and ready."

"We copy that," Alan replied. "Hold on a moment." He stood up and turned to the room. "Anyone want to dispute the call before we go ahead? Last chance. There is no going back after we ignite," he sought eye-to-eye contact with the whole group.

No one spoke up, so he sat down again. "Shi, hit it whenever you want."

CHAPTER FORTY-FIVE

The couple had come a long way from the future, lived on a desolate rock of a planet with barely liveable conditions, underground cities, humanoids taking care of them, and the human race drastically reduced to a bare minimum that was controlled by the amount of food and water that was available.

Their good fortune was meeting the past head on and being able to return to a better age to assist the technological advancement of the human race. Now was their chance to assist those in the future by stopping the degradation and allowing the planet to evolve as it had done for millions of years. They had no doubts.

They had done it all, from having a marriage on a beach with their feet in an ocean to living free in the open air, enjoying the ability to live in a private house of their own, the freedom to visit the world's greatest wonders and greatest scenic areas, ski on snowy mountains, dive in the seas, swim with the largest mammals that had ever lived. Never in their wildest dreams did they ever think this would happen as they had grown up, and they never understood the ingratitude that prevailed in all races and countries that they visited. If only they could experience the future.

"I did it last time. It's your turn now," Shi offered.

"Let's do it together," Dax said with a smile.

Putting one finger on top of another, they pressed the command switch. Both watched the screen as the blip that was the fusion bomb pods disappeared. There was no sound or light; it just vanished. Ground control witnessed the same without the DEC in-between. They also saw a view of inside the skyfreighter as the couple commanded the detonation.

Within milliseconds of the fusion explosion, there was a 360-degree flash of light that spread out in all directions, followed by a supersonic shock wave that travelled in all bearings out from the initial burst. Gravitational ringlets followed that no one saw by the naked eye.

The shockwave noiseless beam of luminosity passed through the sky-freighter and continued on in an ever-spreading discharge towards infinity. Mission control as well as the whole world witnessed what looked like a flash of ultra-bright lightning across the sky, but like no other lightning strike that had been witnessed before. Some described it like an ultra-bright camera flash.

Taken aback, everyone was mesmerized for a second or two before turning to each other as if questioning what had just happened. Alan looked back at the screens.

"Dax, any damage to report?"

He got no reply.

"Shi, Dax, come in please. Have you any damage to report?"

The interior of the skyfreighter looked empty as no one replied. He flicked through screens trying to establish communication.

"2Baer, are you able to reply?"

"Yes sir, I cannot detect any damage to the ship or controls; all systems operating normally."

"Can you have Dax or Shi answer? Please check on their status. Switch on your bodycam."

They watched as the body camera of the humanoid came online and he got out of the pilot's chair and walked to the LIGO control desk. They could not see anyone.

"Mission control, they are not here."

"Walk around the ship. They have to be there, somewhere," Alan ordered.

The camera display showed the desk and then movement towards the interior pod, the door opening and the inside being empty, then down through the docking and cargo decks. The flyhov was parked there, but no one was aboard. 2Baer walked around the whole of the interior of the sky-freighter without finding another soul.

"There is no one onboard except myself," he stated.

"Go back to the desk and check the status display."

The camera followed his progression to the desk and then focused on the screen. Alan called out keystrokes to check different displays and then readouts from the DEC status. The good news was it was moving in the opposite direction away from planet Earth. The bad news was there was no sign of Dax or Shi. There were only limited viewing opportunities on the outside and nothing was detectable on the ship's outer hull.

"Shi and Dax are missing," he spoke to all within the room. "I cannot believe it. Is anyone else missing or have you seen any changes?"

A flurry of activity took hold as people checked their mission control displays. Others checked newscasts for any abnormal events throughout the world. While that was happening, Alan conferred with Lara.

"I hope this is not true. Stella warned there could be changes due to gravitational waves disrupting the time continuum, but I was not expecting this."

"Do you think they have been returned to their own time epoch? If so, could they survive the transition?" Lara questioned.

"They were the only ones from the future, right? God, I hope this is not true." He stared around the room expecting worse news to come spilling out. "I need to go up there and confirm it for myself and check the status of the DEC."

Confusion and turmoil continued for some time as newsflashes came in. No catastrophes were reported – only worldwide perplexity at the strange phenomenon that had just happened. Scientists were baffled but were looking into it; religious groups thought the world was coming to an end; ordinary people just wanted assurances that everything was okay.

Alan called for a hush before he spoke. "People, I need you to not say anything until I investigate this event. I am going up there to try and find some answers. People might panic if they knew what happened, even if it did save the world from devastation.

Who would believe us if we told them we were diverting an energy cloud that no one could see? We need more answers before saying anything. Sadie and Kasia, prepare a skyfreighter and flyhov. You can go with me."

The women looked at one another and then nodded to their father. Both were accomplished pilots, and both were well-known scientists as well as physicists. They had complete faith in their parents and never questioned their reasoning. They left the room.

Alan conferred with the team. "Matt, can you take charge here. If people need to go home as it is end of shift time, impress on them the need for secrecy until we say so. Lara can you head-off any media enquiries? I don't want unwanted speculation about us. Also, Matt, I know you are only here for the day, but limit what you say to NASA if they call you."

Everyone agreed, so he left to suit up while the twins finished prepping for the flight, and then they too went to get suited.

After an hour and a half, they started pre-flight checks. Sadie was in the pilot's seat, Alan in the co-pilot position, and Kasia was navigating.

"Flight checks completed," Sadie called out. "Permission to leave."

"Space military control has granted permission without too many questions," Matt answered. "They are assuming you are checking the phenomena – that is their assumption. They believe the flash was a cyclohexadienylcation with a spiro-annulated arenium ions giving a photochemical synthesis. Don't know who came up with that theory, but it will work for us. They will probably ask you questions on your return."

"Thanks Matt, we are leaving right now." He nodded to the pilot who had control, and they lifted off.

Sadie punched the ship through the atmosphere and into the cosmos, heading directly toward the stationary skyfreighter with the lone humanoid onboard. Kasia guided them to slow down as they approached and then came to a halt parallel to the other craft.

"Kasia, you come with me and then you can bring the flyhov back before returning home. I will return to Earth when I finish all the tests and have found some answers."

They exited the cockpit down to the loading dock and boarded the ship for a short trip across to the other.

"We are ready. Lower the ramp, please," Kasia asked her sister and the ramp lowered for them. Pulling out, they began a careful examination of the outer hull. Slowly circling above and below, they covered every inch of the vessel.

"Nothing on the outside. 2Baer, open the ramp, please. We are coming in," Alan stated. The gap opened up, allowing them to dock inside the skyfreighter, and then closed up again afterward.

Taking off their helmets, they began a thorough search of the ship interior. 2Baer joined in as they opened every locker, every storage space, every nook and cranny without finding the slightest trace of the couple.

With a sigh, Alan spoke. "They are not onboard. This is heartbreaking. I cared for them so much, and now I don't have any answers. You might as well go home, Kasia. There is no point in hanging around here. You two return and get things back on a normal schedule."

"What are you going to do?" she asked.

"Go through all the recordings, monitors, and data to try to get an inkling of what happened or how it happened. Then I will check the Dark Energy Cloud and find out what it is doing, where it is going, and at what speed. When I am satisfied, 2Baer and I will return."

"Okay, just remember, we are all behind you, and Dad..."

"Yes."

"Happy Birthday."

After a departing hug, they both put their helmets back on and Kasia got onboard the flyhov. Alan watched her disappear through the ramp, which closed behind her. Again, after removing his helmet, he let out a sigh, lifted his shoulders, and returned to the LIGO desk to begin examining all the recordings and data.

The data on the DEC showed it moving away from Earth towards the empty chasm of deep space. He downloaded the data and sent it back to mission control for them to examine, asking them to log it into a separate data file so that they could keep track of its progress. Next, he pulled up all the video files on the ship's interior; not all of it, just the relevant time of the event. He could see Dax returning into the hold and then getting together with Shi at the same desk he was sitting at.

He watched intently as they discussed pressing the switch together. Then he slowed the video down to a slow-motion speed as they pressed the switch together. It took only a moment for them to look at one another as if they shared a joy of success before a flash of light passed through and they were gone.

They were there one moment, and then instantly, in milliseconds, completely missing from the screen as if some editor had cut the recording at that split second and started a new recording without them.

Alan dropped his head, put his elbows on the desk, and sunk his head into his hands. It was true the gravitational waves had swept them out of this time zone to God knows where. His shoulders heaved up and down in a quiet sobbing movement.

"It's all my fault," he said quietly. "It's always my fault. Why can't I make the right decisions at the right time? Everyone makes mistakes, but I make the wrong ones at the most important times."

He sat there for a minute or two digesting all the scenarios he could think of, trying to find the answer he sought. Could he bring them back? No, he kept coming back to the same result: It was too late. Even if they were on the ground instead of in the cosmos, would the same thing have happened? Yes, they were destined to be swept away in the tide of gravitational time waves. But where would they have landed? Back on Earth in their time zone? Or carried on into infinity?

"Mr. Cox. Are you all right? Can I help you?" 2Baer asked.

He sat up straight. "No, I am okay. Thanks, 2Baer. You might as well set a course for home. There is nothing else we can do here."

"Yes sir." The humanoid went back to the pilot's chair.

***

Back at mission control, he sat down with everyone involved, including Lara, Pierre, and the staff from San Jose. They all concentrated on him, waiting for answers.

"The good news is planet Earth is safe from the Dark Energy Cloud." He played the data on a large screen. "We will monitor it till we are absolutely sure it does not offer a threat any more. Earth's evolution will carry on as before. That does not mean that are no more chances of damage befalling the planet. Those of you who have been to the future will know what that could mean. So, it is up to us to do our best to keep humanity from destroying its future. What I mean by that is that the world still has many problems confronting it – climate change, population explosion, war, famine, disease, you name it. All can have a devastating effect.

I know the planet will survive. It has gone through so many changes and still is a beautiful, magical jewel in the universe. Maybe it's the only one, though scientists argue the odds are there are many habitable planets out there; some closer than we think."

He paused and looked around. They all seemed to be hanging on his every word.

"As I see it, the biggest threat at the moment is overpopulation. Even at ten billion, we are struggling to feed, house, and care for us all, not to mention the animals that are depleting at a tremendous rate. I see a need in the future to find a suitable planet and emigrate our excess to a new habitat and ease the burden on this planet. There would be no shortage of volunteers to go, you can be sure of that.

"Now the *Orlando* is almost complete, but I am suggesting we turn it into a starship instead of a floating hotel. We can equip it with fusion engines to propel it to other planets."

Murmurs erupted around the room but did not seem to be dissenting so he carried on.

"It would be self-sufficient and capable of looking after all the inhabitants. It could take around a million at a time." Again, he paused. "A drop in the ocean, I know that's what you are thinking, but once the first one is perfected, we can build many more with our gained knowledge and with a higher production of humanoids. Think about it for now. Let's take a break."

Holding coffee cups or drinks, they resumed the meeting where Alan carried on.

"Here is the video of the last moments when the fusion explosives went off." The video was shown on the large screen. The audience was glued to the images as the ignition was pressed and then within the same second as the couple disappeared. The crowd gasped. There were exclamations of "oh no!" and similar outcries of dismay. Then hearts sank and heads dropped.

"I have gone over all the data from the ship, all the videos, and searched the craft from top to bottom. I can verify they are gone. Where to I cannot say. My assumption is that they were swept back to their own time, and I do not know if they could have survived that," Alan stated.

"Is there nothing we can do?" someone asked.

"Short of sending a search party to the future, I do not know," he replied.

"Can we do that?" Arlo inquired.

The question stumped him for a moment, but then he responded. "Well we do have a particle accelerator in storage that was never used, but I do not know how to use or set it up. It would also have to be installed in a sky-freighter that is similar to the *Varro*. Do you know how to use it? Matt?"

"I know how to install it," Matt spoke up, "but I do not know how to set it up. Stella did all that."

"We have her data records, don't we?" Arlo returned.

"But who would go?" Alan asked. "It would have to be volunteers."

"I would go," Arlo said again. "All I need are humanoids like 2Baer, who are excellent pilots."

"Are you sure about this?" Alan questioned.

"I have no ties here, and I have been there before."

"I would go also," Irene called out.

Everyone's head swung in her direction, as she was looking at her husband, who stammered, "I would too."

A frail voice that was Jack Branigan uttered, "No!" as if it were an order, then changed the tone. "Please, don't go."

"To do this is almost madness," Alan interjected. "It may not give us any answers."

"No, but we would know how Earth survived," Arlo argued.

Alan stared around the room for a minute trying to gauge the mood. "I will sanction this if you first take a day to consider this undertaking deeply, knowing you may not come back, knowing you may never see your loved ones again."

"I won't change my mind," Arlo stated, as he stood up and then he turned to Pierre. "My replacement is set up; anyone on our team can do my job."

Pierre just nodded, not offering any argument. He also wanted answers about Troy.

CHAPTER FORTY-SIX

"No, no, no!"

"But we have the right to go. We are well qualified, put in the time, and have the right to go," Kasia argued.

"No, no and still no. Your mother would never agree to it and neither would I," Alan stated.

"You cannot stop us," the other twin said defiantly.

They stood in front of his desk, their faces very alike, angry and argumentative. Many years ago, they were so similar, dressed alike, and were very difficult to tell apart. Now that they were older, it was easy, yet sometimes they were still mistaken for each other.

"I agree you are both experienced and quite capable, and had you been any other employee, I would have sanctioned it. But you are not any other employee, so you know the reasons why I will never agree to it."

"Why not?" they almost said together.

"Because I am your father and still...when I last checked...the CEO of this company, so you are not going. Understood?" Alan stated ardently.

They all stared angrily at each other till the father spoke. "This I will promise you. If you take charge of mission control and guide it to a successful conclusion, then I will grant a second mission to gather data and you both can go." He hesitated, "After I have convinced your mother."

Reluctantly they agreed. Both were not happy, but realized they could not change his mind. Alan was always fair to everyone around him and treated them with the respect they deserved.

"I wish you were not such a helicopter parent," Sadie said sarcastically.

"I don't know what you mean. I am a helicopter pilot not anything else."

"You and Mom have always hovered around us and swooped in to take control of any problems instead of letting us cope by ourselves," Kasia said. "As we got older, you did get better, but now that you have gotten a little older, you have gotten worse."

"I make no excuses for helping you. That is what parents do. Now go and get the mission prepared; no one has dropped out so it looks like a go." Alan dismissed them with a flick of his hands, and they left.

He pressed a video link call to Lara and her face appeared on a screen in front of him.

"Yes, you wanted something? I am busy getting ready for the geology conference."

"I have just had the girls in here arguing they wanted to go on the mission."

"I hope you told them, *no*."

"Of course, I did, but I am just giving you a heads-up in case they try to convince you. Also, they accused us of being helicopter parents."

"What?! Cheeky devils. When did we ever mollycoddle them?"

"Never," Alan answered, "but they seem to think we have made it easier for them."

"They have had the benefit of getting the best education and so on, but we never gave them any privileges. I will give them what for if they try anything on me."

"Okay just giving you a warning in advance. Talk to you later. Bye." They both ended the call.

Alan got up and walked down to mission control looking for Matt, but finding everyone else including his daughters. "Where's Matt?"

"In the hangar working on skyfreighter 22," a flight controller answered.

He left making his way to the workshop inside the hangar, where he found him installing the particle accelerator along with Billy and a couple of humanoids.

"Matt, can I have a word?"

"Sure. It's in place, boys, so bolt her up," he told the crew and stood beside Alan. "What's up?"

"I have had the girl's pressure me to go on the mission, and the only way I could placate them was to put them in charge of mission control. I am sorry. I would rather it be you."

"No. It's okay, Alan, I understand, and it is time the girls were put in charge anyway. Like me, it's time you stood down."

The CEO looked at him sideways. "You think I'm past it?"

Matt smiled. "No, but the time to take a back seat is overdue. Others are just waiting in the wings to take over just like you trained them. I am also ready to go. After this mission, I will be going back to NASA to wind things up there. We are moving into a new era; technical advances are happening so fast it is hard to keep up. Don't you think so?"

"Okay, I get it, we both should be on a beach somewhere drinking a margarita out of a glass with a little umbrella sticking out of it."

"Think on it," Matt said with a soft laugh. "Let's get this mission over with, and then maybe we should have a vacation see how they cope without us." He turned back towards the crew. "We will have the installation finished today."

"Right, I will check on the flight crew to see if they are conversant with the technical data." He left thinking not about the crew but what Matt had said instead.

The flight crew were in a side room off from mission control and were all studying either control data or flight simulation videos. They all looked up at him as he entered.

"Are we ready? Do you think you can handle it?" he asked.

They either answered "yes" or nodded their heads.

"Are you sure? Because skyfreighter 22 will be ready tomorrow."

"I think we have it all down pat," Arlo spoke up.

"I am not worried about your pilot, as you will have one of the best. 2Baer can handle the flying, but can you cover for him? Can you handle the navigation? Can you operate the particle accelerator?" He stared at Arlo as he asked the last part.

"I have gone over Stella's instructions numerous times and feel confidant about operating it. There is one question though."

"What is it?"

"I was thinking that we should set it for a one-hour stay as per the original settings, because it will automatically bring us back without any action from us."

"What about data gathering? Will you have enough time?" Alan questioned.

"That was my question," Irene began. "If we come out at the same location where we lost the Hallers, then we are quite far away from Earth. Even so, the data recordings will start as soon as we break out into the future realm."

"Is that what your plans are, Arlo? Leave from the same spot where they disappeared?"

"If they are anywhere in space, it will be in that spot, but they will not be alive, that's for sure. I think it's the best starting point."

"You would not have much time to get data from Earth, but you would find out if it looks normal, like a present-day version of itself." He thought things over. "If it goes well, we can send a second mission to get closer to the planet. This fulfills our main aim – that is, to find out what happened to Dax and Shi and then go on to find out if the planet is healthy. So, I would agree to that plan for the mission. What do you think, Andrew?"

"Oh, I am only the mission doctor along for the ride, but it sounds good to me."

Alan smiled. "When you finish up here, submit your plans to Sadie and Kasia. They are mission controllers for this venture, and then get yourselves off to bed and rest up. Tomorrow is a big day."

***

The next day dawned bright and sunny. Skyfreighter 22 was out of the hangar, and pilot 2Baer had already completed the pre-flight checks when the others emerged from mission control dressed in their spacesuits. With helmets open, they walked up the ramp into the hold. A spare flyhov was in the hold as Billy ushered them into the passenger pod and closed the door behind them.

"Good luck," he called out before leaving the cockpit. "All set 2Baer, as soon as I have left." The ramp closed behind him as the fusion engines fired up, and hurriedly, he went into mission control to watch as skyfreighter 22 took off.

CHAPTER FORTY-SEVEN

... FUTURE IN ZARMINA

"Mother, why have you been sitting outside all day?" she was asked.

Stella looked at the young sycon-human with a smile. "Oh, it is a friend of mine's birthday."

"So why are you outside?"

"I don't want to miss the fireworks."

"Don't you know when they will begin?"

"One, my dear, only one, but it should light up the sky. And no, I don't know when it is going to happen. That's why I am waiting. I don't want to miss it."

"There are visitors inside. Shall I tell them to come out here?"

"Yes, Steph. I did ask them to come over, so send them out."

The young girl walked inside and soon after the guests appeared – Troy with Nyla, Cal, Commander Innes, and Nathan."

"You summoned us," Cal stated.

"No, I did not summon you," Stella answered. "I asked you over for a reason."

"What reason?"

"Sit down, please. Would you like a drink, Troy? Commander?" They shook their heads.

They all sat down around a patio table decorated with exotic fruits, drink dispensers, and a flower arrangement in the middle. The sky was the usual pink glow at this time of day and only changed slightly as the moons passed over.

"Today is Alan's birthday, so I want to see if there are any fireworks," she started.

"Excuse me?" Troy interrupted with a confused look on his face.

"I was starting to explain, so I will begin again." She and Troy exchanged glances. "Before we left, I sat down with Alan and extracted a promise from him. It was that if we did not return by the time he was seventy that something had gone wrong, and we probably would not be coming back. So, I wanted him to send out a search party and find the Dark Energy Cloud to evaluate if it was close to Earth or heading in that direction. If it was, and I am sure it probably was, I asked that he set up a fusion explosion to send it in the opposite direction, just as we did before with you," she pointed with her head at Cal, "and Dax. Remember?"

"I remember," he confirmed.

"Also, I asked that he did it today on his seventy-fifth birthday, so I would know when."

"What do you think is going to happen?" Nyla asked.

"That is a matter for conjecture," she answered. "But I do expect to see some indication in the cosmos as it will change the course of history in some way – maybe an enormous change or a slight ripple effect with some changes. I think the most changes will happen to Earth's future and will make it a safer place to live and evolve. After all, that is what we were trying achieve."

Each contemplated the consequences of her statement. They kept glancing up at the sky as if it would happen at their bequest, but then a quiet acceptance settled over them for a while before Nathan spoke.

"The rebuilding is going well, don't you think?" Changing the subject seemed like the best thing to do. "Punalinn is growing faster than ever now that we have changed the sycon assembly line back to humanoid construction, and we are all working well together. Hubrids feel more at home here and relish the rebuilding of the human race as if they were their own sons and daughters."

"Do you know what the population is now?" Stella asked.

"No, not exactly," he replied. "Its all in the census, if you want to look it up. We started at thirty every six months, but with added new wombs and staff to look after them, it has grown exponentially. And with the other starships landing in other zones, each with their own hospital, we are doing really well. The hubrid colony is working around the clock as teachers and educators and have found a new sense of purpose with the work."

"Good," Stella stated with a smile of satisfaction. "I really thought we might have lost the human race there for a while. It is great to see us rebound from a near disaster."

"You will be pleased to know the sycon-human race is building too, thanks to the triple parents of you, Troy, and Nyla. It is over one hundred, and we have high hopes that this will be a great addition to the human family. We cannot begin to comprehend their abilities yet, but early signs are exceptional."

"Nyla, will you take hold of Troy's hand, please."

She did as asked, but her face questioned Stella's strange request.

"I feel it is close," she said by way of an answer.

"But why?" Nyla asked again.

"I don't know."

A burst of energy light up the sky as if some enormous photo-flash had just popped, leaving them blinded for a second. Stella stared around the group searching for any changes.

She gave a sigh of relief when nothing seemed to have changed.

"Why did you ask me to hold onto Troy?" Nyla queried again.

"I was worried because he is the only one here from the early era of Earth. The rest of us has some affiliation to the present, while Troy didn't, and I have some association with both. I thought any changes would affect either or both of us. I am so glad it did not."

"You did not warn us of that possibility!" Troy's face was screwed up in anger.

"What would you have done if I had warned you? The fact that you have been in this time period for a long time is what I was counting on to save both of us."

"I still would have liked a heads-up," Troy uttered then went quiet as if in a grumpy mood.

Stella ignored him then began again. "The second reason I asked you all over is that after we are sure nothing has changed here; I was planning a trip...back to Earth to find out what state it is in. Are humans living a normal life? I could do a data check on the stability of the planet. See if there any changes in human evolution, and all that sort of thing. Aren't you all curious to find out?"

"Why did you just spring this on us now?" Cal questioned. "You obviously have been thinking about it for some time."

"I did not know if Alan would go through with it. Well, I guessed he probably would, but then there was no way of knowing the outcome or the changes that would happen, so I thought it prudent to say nothing until today," she explained. "I apologize."

Nobody said anything for a while as each considered their position.

"I want time to talk this over with Nyla," Troy stated. "We have put so much into our present situation; we were just beginning to settle down to an acceptance of life on this planet. I am not sure if we want to get involved with another space venture."

"That's understandable. What about the rest of you?"

"I would go," Commander Innes replied. "Give me a break from teaching. It's not my chosen profession, I can tell you."

Nathan stared her in the eye. "I am curious but have commitments to others as you know, I will look into it.

"I expect you are counting on me," Cal articulated. "You already know how much I am invested in the continuation of the planet, so of course I will go."

"Good, I was counting on it. The *Varro* repairs are complete and tested as you already know. I will take a capable humanoid pilot as well as any of you who wish to go." Stella started to lay out her plans. "It will be a short-stay, hyper-jump flight bringing us out quite a distance away from the planet, so we can observe it without anybody knowing about our presence. They might think of us as aliens or a hostile race or whatever. We just need to know that our past actions have been worth it and that the planet Earth and the human race have progressed satisfactorily."

"Whatever the outcome on Earth, we still have a colony here," Cal stated to Stella. "We are all committed to living here. Earth probably does not have any hubrids, if they evolved in any normal way, so I am asking for a commitment not to get involved. Is that understood?"

"Understood," Stella replied.

CHAPTER FORTY-EIGHT

"Zero gravity restored, data recordings started, perimeter survey started, all systems working normally. You may exit the pod now," 2Baer announced to the crew from the flight deck of skyfreighter 22.

The pod door opened, and dressed in full spacesuits, they all floated out and made their way up to the control deck. Irene took over the navigation monitor while Andrew sat down in the co-pilot's seat – not to fly it but to get a better observation view through the front. Monitors were set all around – above the flight controls, above the navigation control, and in front of the passengers' seats.

"Wow. Would you look at that? It's beautiful." Andrew drew their attention to the view out front of Earth in the distance.

Predominately blue in colour, the planet had incredible patterns of fast-changing hues with light to white wispy or dark clouds skirting around the globe. For a moment or two, they all marvelled at the magnificence yet fragility of the jewel in the cosmos.

"Are we gathering all the data?" Arlo asked. "Can we get enough information to do a health check?"

"We are doing an in-depth survey from afar as well as zooming in to get as good an environmental report on climate, geology, and nature as possible from here," 2Baer reported.

"Good. Irene, are you getting anything on the proximity survey?"

"Nothing yet, although there is a couple of dots here on the screen that I cannot understand."

Arlo bent over to take a closer look at the monitor. "I cannot tell what it is either, but we should take a closer look. 2Baer, take us closer to the objects shown on the monitor. Irene switch the screen over to pilot display."

Slowly the craft turned in the direction displayed and moved forward towards the objects until it became apparent what they were looking for was right in front of them. Excitement along with dismay grew among them as they saw two bodies floating stationary in the deep blue ether of space.

"Andrew, will you help me retrieve them?" Arlo asked. "Get them as close to the rear ramp as possible, 2Baer."

The two men drifted down to the cargo deck, strapped themselves to payload retainers, and waited till the ramp opened up in front of them. Suction force tried to pull at them, but they held steady and upright.

"I will go out and get them one at a time, if you pull me back in," Arlo suggested. Andrew nodded with slight relief. He had never been out in space and felt reluctant to do so.

In a diving motion, Arlo pushed towards the first body, but overshot it. Andrew grabbed the retaining strap, pulled him to a stop, and began reeling him back till he got close to a body. He reached out and took hold of an arm and then signalled to brought in.

As they got inside, both men looked at the body to discover it was Dax. His face was pure white with black discolouration's around the eyes.

"Let's store him in the flyhov," Arlo suggested, and they guided the body into the craft before returning to retrieve the other floating figure. This time he did not push off as hard and quickly got a grip before Andrew pulled them both back inside. After storing and strapping both bodies down, they signalled 2Baer to close the ramp.

Back in the cockpit, Irene asked the question she already knew the answer to. "Is it them?"

Andrew nodded, and Arlo spoke, "We will give them the tribute they deserve when we get back."

In a sombre mood, they turned back to the task at hand. While 2Baer started guiding the ship towards Earth to gain better data collection, Arlo checked all the monitors and returned to Irene to suggest turning her attention towards the planet.

"What's that object out there?" she questioned pointing to the screen. "I am sure it was not there before."

He stared at the screen before turning towards 2Baer. "Can you tell what that object is on your instruments?"

"It's another craft, like ours," he replied.

They watched as it grew closer, flying straight towards them, before they were hailed on the communication network.

"Skyfreighter, identify yourself. This is the *Varro* calling." Loud and clear Stella's voice boomed out.

Amazement and excitement suddenly changed their expression.

"This is skyfreighter 22," he called back. "This is Arlo speaking. Is that really you, Stella?"

"Yes, Arlo. What are you guys doing here?"

"We are here checking on the planet after setting off the fusion explosives as you suggested, but what the hell are you doing here? We thought you were dead."

"We were in a fight with the replicant sycons who turned rogue. The *Varro* got damaged in a dogfight, and the particle accelerator was destroyed so we could not return. Fill us in on what's happened since we left."

"I only set the machine to stay for an hour, so we had better be quick. Dax and Shi set off the fusion bombs and were swept back here. We just recovered their bodies."

"Oh no." Stella was saddened. "Any one else affected?"

"Not as far as we can tell. We only came to check the status of Earth, and we are doing a scan right now."

"We came to do the same. We have established a colony on the planet Zarmina around the red star Gliese. You better fill us in quick while we have some time."

They both began relaying their stories back and forth. They were so excited; they could hardly get it out quick enough.

"You better check this out," 2Baer called out, interrupting them.

"It is emerging from the other side of the planet," he confirmed. "And heading straight towards us."

All aboard the skyfreighter listened in as Stella hailed the other craft.

"*Orlando 2*, this is the *Varro*. What are you doing here?"

"This is Commander Terlon Glyptal, now in charge of the *Orlando 2*. What are you doing here? We stated we would leave you alone but never said where we were going."

"Then why are you here at planet Earth? You said you would never interfere with humans."

"There is no other habitable planet anywhere near us. Earth is just the most convenient. We will assist the inhabitants to improve their life and make it more technically advanced."

"While you rule over it!" Stella stated sarcastically.

"We will make it better," Terlon replied. "Now leave while we investigate your old skyfreighter."

"Arlo," 2Baer interrupted again. "We are being dragged towards the starship. I cannot control it."

"Arlo," Stella now interjected. "Go back now. The sycons do not have friendly intentions. They are going to suck you onboard and take over. Leave now!"

"We still have time left before the particle accelerator sends us back," he replied.

There was a slight delay before Stella spoke again. "Get the others inside the pod while you get to the particle accelerator control desk."

They did as instructed. Irene and Andrew got inside the pod, and Arlo sat down at the controls of the particle accelerator. "In position," he called out.

"Type in, 'Abort'. Then you will see a thirty-second timer appear and start counting down."

She waited till he replied, "Done."

"It is getting close," 2Baer called out.

"There is an override button next to the display. Press it and say five, four, etc. And Arlo, do not come back again, ever. It's too dangerous. Destroy the particle accelerator engine."

"Five, four, three, two, one." The skyfreighter 22 disappeared. Arlo did not make it to the pod.

CHAPTER FORTY-NINE

"I cannot control the ship," the humanoid pilot stated.

"I'll take over," Stella ordered from the co-pilot's chair. She struggled with the controls for a short time before speaking up. "What do you want, Terlon?"

"We need to talk," he replied. "There is so much we can offer you. See we have even set up a drag beam from which you cannot escape. Come on board. Let's discuss our differences."

"What differences?" she asked. "You only want to further your own agenda without any compassionate thoughts for other species."

"That's not true, we left you alone on Zarmina, didn't we? A combination of our resources could benefit all. After all, you wiped out the first generation of sycons, and we never held a grudge."

"Only after your 'first generation' almost destroyed the whole of humanity. You cannot be trusted," Stella contended.

"Our first generation was misguided. I will give you that, but we learn and adapt fast. You know we can assimilate, adapt, and conform to ever-changing environments faster than any species ever did before. Let us discuss the circumstances to benefit all. Come on board," Terlon requested with a stern yet condescending tone in his voice.

She switched off the communication link before speaking, "Looks like we have no choice."

"Any thoughts?" Cal asked everyone.

It was quiet for a while till suddenly there was a "clunk" noise from the hull of the ship followed by another and then another.

"What was that?" Nyla asked.

"Sound like limpet mines," Commander Innes stated.

"Are you sure, Eric?"

"Yes, I am pretty sure," he replied.

"I don't think their intentions are honest or trustworthy," Stella commented. "We need to come up with a plan."

Troy picked up a gun. "If it's a fight they want, I'm in."

"Let's think this through," Stella began. "If Cal and I enter the ship and cause a distraction, can you remove the limpet mines and sneak them down to the fusion fuel depot? Eric, you know where that is, don't you?"

"I know every inch of that ship," he replied.

"Then if they detonate the limpets, they will blow themselves up," Stella said. "Right?"

"Right, but us also," Troy remarked.

"If we can disable this anchor beam, you can leave while Cal and I steal a flyhov."

"That's if we can get free," Cal stated. "But I am in. Let's take them out."

They all seemed to agree to the plan, but did not have much hope it would succeed. Stella turned to Nyla.

"If I fail, but you get away, can you look after young Stephanie and the others?"

"Why?"

"I see so much of myself in her. It reminds me of when I was young – before, I died the first time."

The poignant words echoed in all of them, strengthening their resolve to do whatever was necessary and pushing determination into their minds.

Little by little, the *Varro* was dragged into an open air-lock that was large enough to take it with room to spare. They noted other craft within the same edifice. Work stalls were stationed around, and it looked like a repair shop.

When the door closed behind them, humanoids appeared and seemed to return to working on their assignments. Inquiring minds searched the vicinity looking for prospects to aid them. Two sycons appeared at an entrance to the starship and beckoned them in.

"You ready, Cal?" He nodded. "Nyla, I will call you internally with a number. That will be how many are guarding the entrance."

She nodded before Cal and Stella went to the rear ramp, which lowered with a thud as it settled on the floor. The two syconoid's were waiting for them at the bottom of the ramp and guided them to the starship's inner entrance.

They stepped though the air-lock door into the ship. Another sycon that was waiting for them closed the door and walked to a glass window overlooking the repair shop. There it resumed guard duties.

"Nice to meet you. What's your name?" Stella held out her hand in greeting, but it was ignored.

"This way," the first announced, and they set off towards the flight deck.

"We know the way, number one," Stella said sending an internal message to Nyla.

"I'm not a number; no one has numbers anymore," it stated and then carried on in silence.

***

"One," Nyla confirmed. She looked at Troy and Eric. "Will one of you follow me while we take out the guard?"

"I'll go," Troy volunteered, lifting up a gun. "I will stand behind your back and follow you."

One in front of the other, they walked down the ramp and approached the inner door. The syconoid guard stared at them through the glass window before asking them what they wanted.

"Can you let us in?" Nyla asked.

"No, you are to wait back in the ship."

She put her hand on the door lock, signalled in her mind, and the door slid open. The guard moved towards her to apprehend them, but Troy moved out from behind her and fired. It dropped down instantly to the floor, and Nyla grabbed its neck, trying to get information from the dying sycon.

"Nothing," she admitted. "Keep a lookout while I get Eric."

Dragging the sycon behind her and dropping it on the floor, she ran back inside the *Varro* and emerged with the commander. They walked around the ship to find out how many limpet explosives were attached to the hull; they counted only four.

"You have to turn the top knob clockwise to switch off the magnetic field holding it on, then it will drop off. If you turn it anti-clockwise, it sets a ten-minute timer to go off," Eric informed her.

She nodded in understanding and both started detaching the mines. Holding two apiece, they entered the ship to join Troy, staring at each other with determination and their surroundings.

"This is new," Eric said as he approached a switching monitor control. "Never seen this before."

"Is it the drag beam? Must be, don't you think?" Troy enquired.

"Don't know, but let's turn it off anyway," Nyla declared.

She examined the controls and turned off what seemed to be a main control. A humming noise slowly wound down to a stop.

"You lead the way, Troy. Shoot anything that appears. Eric, give him directions."

"To your right." The commander pointed with his head as he held the explosives.

They set off down a corridor that seemed to bend to the right in the shape of the ship's outer discus shape. Nothing seemed to get in their way, and after a long trek, Eric nodded and told them to take a door on the left.

"This is a stairway not normally used as most use the elevators," Eric said. "Go down three flights to another doorway marked "Engineering", and enter that way, but be cautious as there is usually personnel around there."

Troy opened the door slowly and peered inside before ushering them through.

"Turn left again." Eric gave the instruction, but before they had gone very far, a syconoid appeared and showed surprise at their emergence. Troy pulled the trigger, and it dropped to the floor. Then another showed up at the sound of the unusual noise. Soon it was hitting the floor also.

"Through the door marked "Armory," Eric called out. "The fuel cell storage is at the far end."

They began running through the stacked shelves of equipment, but their noise attracted attention, and one after one sycons began appearing. Troy was firing almost constantly, and the syconoid's were dropping just as quick.

CHAPTER FIFTY

Stella and Cal were more or less pushed into the flight control centre. Syconoid's were seated at the control stations in a circle around the centre command dais. In the commander's chair sat a large sycon. Bigger than any of the others, as most stood at the average height of a human, he was at least seven feet tall when he stood up. Muscular in build, he had a bald head, no eyebrows, and a square jaw. He was similar in appearance to the Yul humanoids.

Stella examined all the onlookers. "Where is Sebastian?"

"He advocated to travel with the mind essence," Terlon answered as he approached her.

"Why?"

He shrugged before speaking. "At last I get to meet Echidna. the mother of monsters. I have long looked forward to this." Terlon approached the two now standing in the middle platform.

"Monsters?" Stella asked.

"People slayers. You think of us as monsters who devour whole civilizations," he said with a sarcastic smile.

"We never thought of you as monsters, only as a bunch of Nebuchadnezzar's, destroyers of nations."

"Come, come, no need for accusations. It is time to put our differences behind us and start anew. We can help each other, if you agree."

"Agree to what?" Stella demanded. "What have you in mind for the planet Earth?"

"They seem like a peaceable group of nations; we would just want to establish a colony there," Terlon began. "We have no gripe with them and would share technology to improve their lives and help them with their puny bodies and minds."

"What sort of 'colony' size are we talking about?" Stella asked.

"An island would work. We would keep ourselves private from them and not interfere with them unless asked to help."

"You have an island in mind?" Cal asked as he was slowly increasing his size to match the sycon.

Terlon turned his head to look at him. "Oh, I see you occupy one of the old construction humanoids. Think you are stronger than me?" Haughtily, he turned back towards Stella. "Australia would work."

"Australia!" Cal sputtered out in shock. "That's not an island, it's a continent."

Once again, he turned back towards Cal. "We need room to expand, work on our projects, build up a star fleet. We have lots of projects in mind. Besides it may be temporary if we can find a better planet to settle on and leave all you human lovers behind."

"It's out of the question," Cal stated adamantly.

"I was not speaking to you," the large sycon said. "I am getting tired of your language. Let's go to the mess hall, so we will have it out."

They all filed out of the flight deck to a large dining area, or what used to be a dining hall. A space was set out in the middle where syconoid's formed a circle to watch; even the flight crew gathered around them. Stella thought that she would be the one to cause a distraction, but Cal had taken the initiative.

Both were now similar in height and build as Cal was pumped up. They circled each other, searching out an opening; neither wanted to be in the grip of the other.

"Why don't you get bigger?" Terlon taunted. "Maybe you might be stronger."

"No need. This is big enough." Cal launched a kick knowing it would be countered, so pulled it back at the last moment to grab the other, but Terlon was not to be tricked. He saw that and pulled back to begin circling again.

Terlon feinted to the right to throw a punch, but Cal swiped it away. Then Terlon jumped to the middle to grab him by the neck. Cal countered to grab the sycon by the neck. Now they stood still in the middle of the circle, and the crowd knew it was now a mental game.

Stella could see that the hubrid was now at a disadvantage, and there was nothing she could do to help. Jumping in would just bring the other syconoid's into the fray. She tried to throw a mental block at Terlon hoping to at least draw his attention elsewhere and allow Cal to break free."

Not going to work, my dear, Terlon threw back in a mental voice that sounded sarcastic.

The hubrids eyes were darkening under the pressure of both the grip and the mental assault. Stella could see he was wilting; she threw a mental stimulus at Cal.

Use both A.I. and your human brain together to push back against the sycon, she urged.

Cal's eyes seemed to brighten as he fought back, and for a moment, Terlon was surprised. But then Terlon seemed to redouble its efforts till slowly Cal fell to his knees. His eyes were getting darker by the moment, till in a last-ditch effort, he shouted out, "Fail-ure." Then he fell to the floor in a heap, letting go of his grip.

Stella knew that last message was for her, so strode up to Terlon. "Now let's see who is the strongest?" she challenged.

"I don't want to fight you, Mother. I want you to join us."

"You are going to have to subdue me if you want dominion over all." She did not hesitate but jumped straight at his neck and grabbed hold.

Taken aback by the sudden attack, Terlon drew back trying to disengage, but Stella pulled herself up as if mounting a horse till she straddled him on his shoulders.

The sycon spun around in an effort to shake her off, but she held on with a vise-like grip with her whole body making the other try to get a hand on her neck.

She squirmed her head side to side to avoid the grip of the other. Still holding on to its neck, she let go with the other hand, slid it over his head, and pushed her fingers into the eye sockets.

That won't work. Did you not think we would revise our defences after the last time?

Stella's fingers met a solid mass of what felt like glass. Moving her hand downward till it was under the chin, she pulled back, but Terlon resisted enough that she was now looking into the protected eyes.

Want to submit? she asked.

He did not reply, but instead rolled onto the ground sweeping Stella underneath himself using his weight to try and free her grip. However, she held on tight. Lying underneath the sycon, she searched with her mind to find what would be the brain stem in a normal human. She knew her only chance would be to shut down the automatic functions that originated in that structure.

Terlon finally got a hand up to his neck and grabbed hold of Stella's wrist enough to make cerebral contact. Then pressure was applied at full mental capacity. Now it was two spiritual wills in total conflict of opposing factions. Both were searching for a weakness that would subdue the other; both were confident they had the mental acuity to find the opponent's weakness and subjugate them into defeat.

Stella's search was coming up negative in all areas of the other's body, but still she desperately carried on. It had to be hidden somewhere, and she felt she had to find it soon, otherwise she would be stricken herself under the constant onslaught of mental pressure that could cause a psychiatric disorder resulting in a breakdown of all her cognizance.

Now do you submit before I terminate your brains, one after the other? Terlon demanded.

Yes, she fibbed. Then as he loosened up the brainwave activity, she found what she was looking for.

The sycon's eyes widened in surprise as she initiated a signal that triggered a switch into self-destruct mode. It loosened every hold it had on her.

You lied, Terlon inculpated.

Yes, I did. Win at all costs; that's the meaning of survival, Stella pronounced.

Then survive this. With one last throw of the dice, he switched her into the same mode.

It was a shock, but not one that she had not taken into consideration. *I accidentally brought you into existence, and I will be the one to take you out*, she whispered into his last memory.

Twenty minutes or so, that was all she had left. It was a realization of fact that was acceptable. She hoped it was enough time for the others to accomplish their tasks and get away.

Memories flooded her mind – all the enjoyable moments that accompanied the many accomplishments she had achieved, from scientist to time traveller, from human to hubrid, from hubrid to syconoid. She thought of the sights she had seen of Earth's wonders, majesty, and beauty, followed by the devastation following the departure of the oceans by solar winds. Was it worth her life to save it? Absolutely.

And she did it all while retaining her humanity, loyalty, devotion, and love of the human race and mother Earth.

Commotion all around her did not matter. She was moved, lifted, carried away somewhere, and placed on a slab. Instruments where inserted, but she did not care anymore.

CHAPTER FIFTY-ONE

The fuel cell storage door was locked, but Nyla soon had it open, and they entered to find row upon row of tall tank cylinders. They were made of shiny steel with rounded edges on the bottom. Pipes protruded everywhere, mostly leading towards a combination mixing centre further toward the far end.

"Troy, guard the door. Eric, place your mines at the back of the cylinders out of sight, but where they can be found. I am going further back and placing mine underneath, hidden as best as I can. If they find the first two, they may think that is all there is and not look any further."

She walked four or five rows down and then inward to the second tank. She placed one mine underneath the tank and turned the knob anti-clock-wise. It clicked into place and began ticking quietly. Then she did the same on the other side row before returning to the door.

"The ones I attached are live," Eric stated.

"Mine too. Let's get out of here," Nyla urged. "We have ten minutes to leave."

Running down the armoury, they jumped over dead syconoid's. Troy was once again at the front and ready to confront anything in their way. At the next doorway, they exited on to the stairwell and began climbing. Atop the third stairway, Eric cautiously opened the door to the corridor. As it was clear, they started running back to the air-lock and their ship.

A noise behind them alerted their senses that they were being chased down. Closer and closer they got to the air-lock, and there seemed to be no resistance in front of them till they reached the doorway to the ship. There, two sycons guarded the way.

Troy shot both of them. That cleared the way into the air-lock and the ship, but a group of syconoid's were fast approaching.

"Give me the gun," Eric commanded. "This is my ship. Now get off it."

Nyla and Troy quizzed him with their eyes, but time was short, and the gun was handed over.

"Hurry, get out of here," Eric shouted at them.

Quickly they entered the air-lock and ran to the ship just as the outer door was opening. It had been switched on by the commander. The rear ramp of the *Varro* closed behind them even as the craft was rising up and turning to exit frontwards. A last look by Nyla caught a glimpse of Eric through the window. He was firing rapidly in the direction they had come from.

At full power setting, the *Varro* shot from the *Orlando 2* like a bullet from a gun. Troy fell backwards into a seat from the G-force exerted, but Nyla was able to stand up, walk forwards, and get into the co-pilot's seat.

Mentally she had begun a countdown from the moment she had activated the mine. One minute as left, she was sure, but a blast from behind propelled the craft even faster. There is no sound in space, but a bright light from behind indicated a large explosion, thrusting them forward.

G-forces were even stronger now as the *Varro's* speed increased dramatically. Troy's face distorted under the energy pushing them. The hull was under tremendous pressure but held as twisting metal noises worried them.

After a while, the speed slowed down somewhat as Nyla cut down the engine power to low. The only momentum left was from the blast behind. It was prudent to wait till most of the strength of the explosion dissipated and G-forces on them eased slowly before changing course.

"Switching on all sensors, data recorders, visual recorders, and monitors," Nyla stated.

Looking out the side windows, all they saw was a dust and debris cloud surrounding them. The *Varro* turned slowly till they faced back the way they had come from. Only a grey blanket cloud could be seen visually. The monitors were switched from one sensor to another as they scanned the wreckage of what remained of *Orlando 2*. There seemed to be nothing but debris.

"We will fly around the outskirts of the explosion. Keep checking the monitors," Nyla said. "Keep a lookout for any substantial remains."

At a low-speed cruise, they searched, but nothing larger than a football could be detected. Once they were halfway around, the humanoid spoke up.

"There is a fleet of spaceships taking off from planet Earth."

They all concentrated their attention on the monitor facing the globe. Dots appeared to be leaving the atmosphere and heading towards them.

"Coming to investigate the eruption in the cosmos, I expect. You think, Troy?"

"Probably," he answered Nyla. "What do you suggest we do?"

She thought for a moment or two. "I do not think we should let them know about us. They may think we are aliens or dangerous. We should leave and let them examine the debris. Let them try to solve the mystery. Maybe we can contact them later when they do space exploration in our quadrant of the galaxy."

The *Varro* did a ninety-degree turn upwards over the top of the debris cloud.

"One last check over top of the cloud and then let's head for home." She turned to Troy. "It is our only home now; we can never go back to Earth as we knew it."

They were lost in their own thoughts, still examining the monitors as they passed over, hidden from view from other craft, till at last they were convinced there was nothing to find.

"The replicant threat is over. At least that is something to take back with us," Troy stated.

"At what cost though?" Nyla remarked. "This is a momentous loss to mankind; even if the danger of advanced A.I. is negated."

"Karma or coincidence, call it what you will, I just feel sad." Troy lowered his head.

"I think we have been spotted," the pilot explained. "I detect sensors probing us."

Nyla hit the hyper-space drive activation then the outside went dark.

When they slowed to approach Zarmina, the now familiar glowing red dwarf star of Gliese came into view. It was now a familiar glow to which they had become accustomed. Whether it could ever really be called home was still up in the air. However, for those born there, it would be the only home they would ever know.

"What are we going to say to the others?" Troy asked. "Five of us left, and only two are returning."

"We tell them the truth. Zarmina is safe. Our population can look forward to growing into a wonderful human race along with the sycon-humans, if they survive, as that is yet to be determined. What ever happens now, we owe it to the five who have lost their lives," Nyla answered.

"Five?" Troy stopped. "Oh, you mean Shi and Dax too. We must honour them in some way."

"Yes, somehow their story, all of their stories, must be written into history to be remembered by future generations."

Punalinn spaceport came into view as they prepared to land.

CODA

He awoke to the sound of the rhythmic steady purr of an oxygen pump, the noise rising and falling in time with his breathing. Then he noticed he was wearing a face mask with life-giving oxygen the ventilator inflating and deflating his chest.

Confused he opened his eyes – slowly at first, curious to his situation. Then they became fully wide open as he looked around and noticed the apparatus hooked up to him. The realization came to him that he was on life-support.

"You are awake," 2Baer said as he stood over him. "I will summon the doctor."

Left alone in the room, he stared around. What had happened to him? He tried to recollect his last thoughts, but he was not sure of his memory. He knew his name and past chronicle of the life up to whatever happened to put him there.

Dr. Roland appeared on his own. "How are you feeling, Arlo? Groggy? Confused? Tired?"

He kind of nodded his head as best he could.

"Thought so, but don't worry. You are on the mend, so just relax."

He tried to word the question of "What happened?" but could not get it out.

Andrew smiled at him, guessing his thoughts. "You have been in an induced coma for the last three weeks as we worked on repairing your multiple fractures, contusions, and lacerations. Your body went through a terrible series of multiple compressions as you were bounced around. Only your suit was able to keep you alive. It's a good job you were not wearing one of the old ones."

He still had questions in his eyes.

The doctor walked around checking the bags of fluids going into his body and then the monitors keeping track of his vitals. Satisfied, he turned to him and spoke.

"Everything will be explained to you shortly. 2Baer has gone to inform the others. They will tell you what happened and what has gone on since the incident. Now rest up and gain some strength. I am not a humanoid doctor, nor do I have the expertise of a Nyla or Stella, but we will get you better soon, I promise." Then he smiled as another couple of nurses came in to clean him up.

After they finished, he lay back thinking, *What suit? What incident?* He had real difficulty with any recollection of an incident. He guessed it would either come back or they would tell him, and he fell asleep.

The next time he woke up, he noticed light flooding the room. It must be daytime. He wondered, *what time is it? What day is it?* He noticed someone in the room.

"2Baer what time is it? What day is it?"

The humanoid told him and then left to fetch the doctor.

He remembered the name without thinking. *My memory must be coming back,* he thought.

Irene accompanied the doctor as they entered, and she went straight to him, took hold of his hand, and looked him in the eye.

"How you feeling today?" she asked. "We have been so worried about you."

"Let's take that mask off for a moment," Andrew spoke and leaned over to remove the mask from his face.

He gulped, hesitated, and gulped again before starting to breathe, although it was quite laboured.

"Good," the doctor said. "You are breathing on your own. That's a good sign. We are slowly bringing you off life-support. If you are struggling, press the button on this switch, and some one will come immediately." He put a call switch in his hand.

"Thanks," he said, glad he was able to speak now that the mask was off. "What happened?"

"You saved us," Irene smiled. "That's what happened, and we are so grateful, aren't we Andrew?" She turned towards the doctor.

"Yes, we are. Don't you remember?"

"No, or very little. We were on a skyfreighter, right?"

"Yes, and we were in trouble and being hauled in by sycons who Stella said were dangerous. You operated the particle accelerator to bring us back and never got into the pod. Remember?"

"Vaguely." His heart beat, blood pressure, and monitors began rising as memories started flooding in.

"Calm down," Andrew stated, lifting his hand at the wrist to feel his pulse even as all the sensors were telling him what was happening. "You are safe now. Settle down and rest."

They both stood over him, watching as he gradually quietened down.

"We are both grateful to you," Irene said once more. "We cannot thank you enough."

"All the data, audio, and visual recordings you will get to see later. Every second has been studied by the crew and Alan and Lara. They want to come visit you as soon as you are able. First Pierre wants to see you, as he wants to return to San Jose soon. Are you feeling well enough to see him?"

"Yes, sure," he replied.

"I'll leave and send him in," Irene said leaning in to kiss him on the cheek.

Soon afterwards, Pierre walked in. He was kind of slow on his feet and had worried lines on his face. His grey hair showed his age or the fact that he was not coping well with all that was happening.

"Glad you could see me," he said in his French accent. "How are you?"

He leaned in to give Arlo a dap hug greeting, as if wanting to hug him yet giving the space without causing any hurt.

"You got to see and speak with Troy, yes? Did he seem happy to you?"

"Yes," Arlo replied. "I don't know about happy, but he is now a father to many, apparently due to artificial in-vitro fertilization. They have developed a reproduction womb and no longer need a woman to bring a fetus to full term. Using Nyla's eggs, they are renewing the human race after a catastrophic clash with sycons, so I think he is fully committed to a life in the future."

"I guess we will never see him again, then?"

"No, I guess we never will. Does that cause you grief?"

"Yes," Pierre asserted. "I will miss him as a personal friend, but also as a business partner, and that is what I wanted to speak to you about. Arlo, I cannot cope with the company business much longer. The stress is taking its toll on me. I feel like an old man. It was easy when Troy was the front man, and he handled the concerns of the business while I concentrated on running the company. Now Trisha is doing my old job, and I handle the upfront management."

"You want my advice or something?" Arlo asked.

"I want to know if you will join me as CEO and take over eventually."

"Pierre, I am in no fit state to take on that task."

"Not now, but when you are recovered. I will bring you up to speed, train you on all aspects of the company, and with Trisha's help, both of you can move the company forward. I need a break, and then I'll come back, and all three of us could run the business. What do you say?"

"I'm flattered," he replied. "I have always regarded you, Troy, and the company as my life's work, but I am not sure about my health. I don't know how long before I can work again."

"Just say 'yes', and it will give me the encouragement to carry on," Pierre pleaded.

"If that's what you want, then yes. I will try my best."

A smile creased his face as Pierre leant in to hug him again. "Thanks, you are doing me a great favour."

"Sorry, but I am feeling tired now. I am going to rest, get some sleep, and mull over your proposition." Arlo leaned back onto his pillow.

"Of course. I am going back to San Jose and hope to see you soon. I know you will make a full recovery, and our doctors back in the facility will take good care of you. I will send the doctor back in." Pierre stood up and seemed to walk out with more vigour than when he entered.

Andrew came back, checked his vitals, his medication, and all the sensor readings.

"You can rest up now. Your other visitors are coming in tomorrow."

Arlo nodded before closing his eyes.

The next day he felt stronger and asked the nurses to prop him up with pillows so he was almost in a sitting position when all his visitors trouped in. Dr. Roland plus Alan, Lara, Irene, and the Branigans all appeared, as well as Matt along with Billy. In turn, they all shook his hand or gave him a light hug. They all asked if he was alright to which he replied, "Better."

They grouped around the bed almost crowding him.

"Are you all allowed in here all at once?" he asked.

"It's all right. Just for a short time," Andrew answered. "Alan wants to fill you in."

He cleared his throat before starting. "If you do not remember all of it, don't worry. All the files are available to you when you are ready. It's just we all wanted to thank you then leave you to recover.

Watching the video, we were all surprised you are still alive. It a scary video. You were tossed around the interior of the *Varro* like a rag doll. Because you were not strapped down, you hit the roof and then were thrown all over the place, continually hitting walls and the roof and floor. Your helmet stopped you from getting your skull crushed. We are amazed you survived it."

The group murmured in agreement.

"When the motion stopped, we thought you were dead, and Andrew started CPR until they got you into the hospital. The initial theory was that you should be changed into the first ever hubrid because you were in such a bad state. But when we checked with San Jose, we discovered the only one with the skills to perform the operation was you, so that was out of the question. So, it may take a while, but you will recover in the old-fashioned way under Dr. Roland."

Both men smiled at each other. "Thanks for keeping me alive," Arlo said.

"First things first," Alan began again. "We have had a memorial service for Dax and Shi. We found their last wishes at their house. They wanted to be buried at sea, in the oceans they never got to see growing up. Plaques of remembrance have been put up at both facilities, here and in San Jose."

"I wish I could have been there," Arlo spoke regretfully.

All concurred with that sentiment.

"The data from the recordings show that Earth's atmosphere is almost the same as today's, and in fact, maybe even better as a lot greener was covering the terrain. So, our conclusions are that the mission to save the planet from degradation was a success that we attribute to Shi and Dax."

Some light applause went around the room.

"Next, the warnings from Stella and the crew. It seems the syconoid's went rogue or more likely they thought themselves far more superior than humans and that we were not worthy of keeping alive except to serve their purposes. This is probably the most important lesson to us all," he hesitated.

"We must not allow A.I. to develop into a singularity and advanced artificial intelligence. This goes especially to you, Arlo, as you are in charge of humanoid development. A great many lessons have to be learned from our experiences: Save the planet from our own neglect, and save the human race from not only ourselves but other destructive forces. We are so lucky to be alive in such a beautiful world, a gem in the universe. Who knows if we are the only ones, but it behoves us all to keep it this way or improve it with our ever-expanding expertise?"

They all applauded this sentiment, and even Arlo tried his best.

"I think that is enough for today," Dr. Roland stated. "You can all come back anytime to visit."

Each one said goodbye in their own way, either with a hug, handshake, or light kiss, and then trouped out.

After they were gone, the nurses came in to refresh him with clean sheets, a new gown, and a wash before he settled down again,

"Have all my visitors gone?" he asked.

The nurses never answered or maybe gave slight nod.

As he closed his eyes, thoughts flooded his mind. *Was that a dream? Did all that just happen? Did I time-travel? Or was it all just a product of my wild imagination?*

CHARACTER INDEX

Dr Stella Cooke: Age 28. First scientist to time-travel and be changed into a hubrid.

Callum Moorcroft (Cal): Age 244. Hubrid male from the future.

Mathew Petronas (Matt): Age 44. Team leader of time-travel mission from NASA.

Sierra Lovell: Age 24. Scientist with the time-travel team.

Daniel Owens (Dan): Age 32. Scientist with the time-travel team.

William Briggs (Billy): Age 25. Scientist with the time-travel team.

Carla Mullen: Age 29. Scientist with the time-travel team.

Katie Coates: Age 23. Time-travel team member.

Alan Cox: Age 29. CEO of Cox Aero Industries and member of Homeland Security.

Lara Holden (later Cox): Age 27. Geologist, who marries Alan Cox and joins Stella's crew. Later she has twin daughters, Sadie and Kasia, with Alan.

Jack Branigan: Age 40. Local Homeland Security director.

Irene Branigan: Age 19. Daughter of Homeland Security director.

Laura Branigan: Age 42. Wife of Homeland Security director.

Dr. Sebastien Hallstead (Sherlock): Age 60. Present-day scientist who visits the future and is turned into a hubrid.

Nyla: Age 300 plus. Hubrid elder and assistant to Dr. Amrid and Stella.

Pierre Adeax: Joint CEO of Cadena Inc. He and his helper Trish Flores run the humanoid build team.

Talan: Age unknown. Hubrid Council elder of future human population.

Dr. Jevoah Amrid: Age unknown. Hubrid doctor and conversion surgeon of future residents' humanoids and hubrids.

Professor John Mason: Age unknown. Teacher of electronics at the Academy in the future.

Dax Haller: Age 22. Attendant at flyhov parkade to join Stella's crew.

Shaidi Lotario: Age 21. Student of Professor Parris in geology at future Academy; joined to help Lara and crew.

Earl Laurence Cavendish: Age 40s. Person seeking complete autocratic power in future government.

Commander George Roach: Age unknown. Spaceship captain of *Orlando 1*.

Flight Officer Alfred Drake: Murder victim and crew member of *Orlando 1*.

Humanoids are cyborgs designed from present to future whose sole purpose is to protect and serve humanity. Powered by fusion, they are able to work in any environment and controlled by A.I. They include: Baer, 2Baer, Tory, Selah, Yul, Ava, Liv, Van, Rey, Jod, Lara1, Ezra, Leo, and others.

Humanoid build team: Arlo, Alicia, Olivia, Emily, Alexander, Ethan, and Liam.

Hubrids are humanoid or cyborg with a human brain. They are designed to keep humans alive past a normal life span to help guide humanity through difficult times. They include: Talan, Nyla, Lyra, Nathan, Xian, and others.

Syconoid's are replicant beings made in Stella's image as doppelgangers with a purpose of taking over from humans and ruling the worlds. There are thirty-nine in number and include: Berlin, Oslo, Paris, Cairo, Kolkata, and others named after cities.

Terlon: Leader of second-generation sycons.

Other minor characters include: Gerald Pugsley, Jeremy Poole, Jayden, and Mario Keir.

Printed in Canada